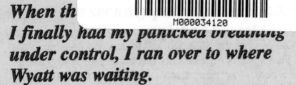

When th ***I finally had my panicked breathing under control, I ran over to where Wyatt was waiting.***

"That was a rush!" I said. I'd missed this adrenaline kick, the way it spiked the blood.

But Wyatt grabbed me by both arms. "That was the most idiotic thing I've ever seen." The look in his eyes bore the stark remnant of fear. "You could have been killed."

Then he leaned toward me and captured my mouth fiercely. At the hot insistence of his kiss, a shudder ran through me.

No. Attraction wasn't supposed to happen. Not between *us*.

How easy it would be to allow this to go further, to keep the adrenaline rushing. *Too* easy. I pushed myself away. "Sofia..." I breathed.

That magic word—the name of the woman whose heart had given me a second chance at life—had him withdrawing. He needed someone, but it wasn't me.

Dear Reader,

As I was writing this book, New Hampshire was phasing out the Old Man of the Mountain toll tokens and phasing in the E-Z Pass system. So when my mechanic source suggested I use a penny to clog up a seat belt, I thought of letting the Old Man live just a little bit longer through the pages of this book. Sometimes a story comes whole and stays that way. Others don't behave and love to stray. This one took me into many foreign situations, so I'd like to thank everyone who helped me with the technical stuff. Any mistakes are certain to be misunderstandings on my part.

Sincerely,

Sylvie Kurtz

Sylvie Kurtz

DETOUR

Silhouette®
BOMBSHELL™

Published by Silhouette Books

America's Publisher of Contemporary Romance

SILHOUETTE BOOKS

ISBN-13: 978-0-373-51418-2
ISBN-10:   0-373-51418-2

DETOUR

www.SilhouetteBombshell.com

Printed in U.S.A.

SYLVIE KURTZ

Flying an eight-hour solo cross-country in a Piper Arrow with only the airplane's crackling radio and a large bag of M&M's for company, Sylvie Kurtz realized a pilot's life wasn't for her. The stories zooming in and out of her mind proved more entertaining than the flight itself. Not a quitter, she finished her pilot's course and earned her commercial license and instrument rating.

Since then, she has traded in her wings for a keyboard, where she lets her imagination soar to create fictional adventures that explore the power of love and the thrill of suspense. When not writing, she enjoys the outdoors with her husband and two children, quilt-making, photography and reading whatever catches her interest.

You can write to Sylvie at P.O. Box 702, Milford, NH 03055. And visit her Web site at www.sylviekurtz.com.

A writer's gifts come from those who came before her
I thank
My grandmothers—
for the gift of adventure and the gift of laughter
My grandfathers—
for the gift of poetry and the gift of silence
My parents—
for the gift of independence and
the gift of freedom to follow dreams

Chapter 1

Thursday, January 13

Thirteen had always been a lucky number for me. And today it didn't let me down. I spotted my elusive target the second I walked into the old warehouse housing the Black Bridge Gym in Nashua's downtown hospital district. There, Finnegan Murdock, aka The Hammer, taught a Wrestling Federation–style class at night.

Finn stood in the middle of the ring, grunting as he simulated pounding his opponent's face to a bloody pulp. The slap of his foot against the mat made a wet *thwack* mimicking the sound of fist-on-flesh that echoed in the cavernous room. I aimed the hidden camera in my parka lapel square at him.

"Push off," Finn instructed the apprentice wrestler at his side, then hefted the man's body over his head. He spun the apprentice around and launched into a series of instructions on the art of mock anger and crowd rousing at the eleven brawny male wrestler-wannabes peering up at him from the ring's edge.

The place stank of testosterone-soaked sweat. Red punching bags hung from black ceiling beams on black chains. Chrome weight machines lined two walls. And a mirrored wall reflected the black-roped boxing ring built on a red platform.

Finn, all 285 pounds of him, stood as erect as a Colossus in his skimpy black Spandex leggings and silver tear-away muscle shirt, sweat gleaming off his bulging pecs and delts under the stark fluorescent lights. The sharp angles of his bald head, beady steel-gray eyes and hooked nose probably accounted for his stage name. So did the hammerhead-shark tattoo on his steroid-enhanced chest.

As he twirled his student over his head, he caught sight of me in the shadows of the ring. Uh-oh. Not good.

"Who the hell are you?" His gravelly voice rocked through the air.

Tapping my chest innocently with a hand, I stood up. I took in thirteen pairs of slitted eyes staring at me and realized I was way outnumbered. Mind spinning through options, I said, "Me? I'm Jennifer Jones."

"Who let you in here? How'd you get past the guard?" He glowered as he dropped the man he was holding to the mat and stepped to the ropes. He shook a finger at me. "Wait a minute, I know you. You're the broad who wanted help changing a flat tire yesterday afternoon."

I gulped, then pasted on my best bubblehead smile and batted my eyelashes at him. "What can I say? I'm a fan. Can I have your autograph?"

Suspicion dawned in his beady eyes. "Someone get her!"

I didn't hang around to argue. I booked out of the joint, knowing he'd come after me and, this time, the bloody pulp face wouldn't be faked. He couldn't afford to let me show the images I'd caught on tape to his insurance company.

Sierra Martindale, private investigator, was once again on the run and loving it.

Finnegan Murdock was a part-time wrestling instructor and a full-time mechanic for an oil-change company in Hudson on the other side of the Merrimack River. Nothing wrong with multitasking. I was rather good at it myself. The problem was that Finn was supposed to be in so much pain from his on-the-job shoulder injury that he couldn't possibly heft the poundage required by his work.

My job was to get him on tape to prove insurance fraud. A bone my brother, Van, a lawyer, had thrown my way, knowing things were a little tight for me at the moment what with my boyfriend, Leonardo's, betrayal last Thanksgiving. That made Finn's and my goals mutually exclusive. Someone was going to lose, and it wasn't going to be me.

So here I was, lean and fast, hauling ass through the back black door of the corrugated metal building into the slap of frigid January night air, where my hot breath steamed like exhaust. The offices of Martindale & Martindale were about six blocks away on Pearl Street and, on these cold days, I couldn't trust my van, Betsy, to start, so I'd walked. With the spur of adrenaline giving me wings, I was getting a lead on the muscle-bound thug pounding the pavement after me, not to mention the posse of would-be wrestlers charging after him.

Unfortunately, they shot out the front door, forcing me away from my family's law office. I ran down Harbor Avenue, hoping to get back on course on East Hollis Street. I hadn't counted on my pursuers splitting into two packs and cutting me off. I ended up racing down Hudson Street, boots slipping on snow, down the ramp near the train tracks and onto Temple Street where I had two choices: take the bridge across the Nashua River to Canal Street—which would put me way off course—or take the walking path, with the river on one side and a steep embankment on the other, that would get me to the library and Pearson Avenue and back to Main Street, almost home.

I chose the path, tripping over discarded beer bottles and nearly colliding with a bum on the narrow snow-bound path. The cold air burned my lungs and I tasted blood in my throat. Sweat drenched my shirt and I unzipped my parka. But I kept running.

Then I just couldn't.

And that wasn't normal, because I was in top shape. I mean, way better than average. I did every sport I could from the minute I could. My mother had called me Fidget from day one. My brother accused me of living life with pedal jammed to the metal and not paying attention to any of the roadside signs. A gross overexaggeration, by the way. On top of that, I also ran to get rid of the toxic buildup of frustrations.

I know. Hard to believe that someone like me would need that coping mechanism. After all, I came from a reasonably well-to-do family. I got a top-notch education at local private schools. I could have stepped right into the family business if I'd wanted. And once I turned twenty-five next year, I'd come into a sizable inheritance.

But trust me, I was a snarl of frustrations. Guy troubles. Job troubles. Family troubles. They all wove together like a tightly knit scarf. And the mismatch of life patterns, expectations and needs tended to knot tension and choke. So I ran. And running had never failed me.

Until now.

Like cement that had suddenly turned to concrete, my legs refused to move, my lungs refused to fill, and my heart refused to settle. It pounded like a mad drummer out of step with the rest of the band. I'd probably pushed myself too far too fast after the bug that had flattened me for most of last week. All I needed was to catch my breath and I'd be okay.

Using the last of my strength, I hiked down an alley thick with shadows and scrambled over a wooden privacy fence to a small office building. Then gravity took over, pulling me down on the other side, just as the posse of wrestlers tromped by with all the finesse of stampeding cattle. Lucky for me a pile of garbage bags cushioned my fall.

With thick fingers, I managed to extract my cell phone from my parka pocket and press Speed Dial One.

"This better be important, Sierra," my brother, Van, barked at me.

"I'm in trouble," I managed to puff out, hand splayed over my hammering heart to keep it from flying out of my chest.

Immediately Van's voice deepened with concern. I had to give him credit. Even with all the grief I'd caused him over the years, he never gave up on me and was always there for me when it counted. "Where are you?"

"I, uh, I'm not sure." I forced myself to look around. Like teeth on an old skeleton, the fence seemed to fall away, spinning and blackening the world around me. My heart beat all out of synch. And my breath was as thin as smoke. "Near the library. Office building. Parking lot."

"Sierra?"

"Van. I don't. Feel so good."

He swore, and Van rarely swore. "Hang on, Sierra. I'm coming."

I tried to answer, but my suddenly thick mouth wouldn't cooperate.

They told me I died that night. But I don't remember any bright light calling me home or my life flashing in front of me. Just everything kind of fading away and the scary out-of-whack rhythm of my fibrillating heart pulsing in my head.

I didn't know it then, but I'd just hit the mother of all speed bumps.

Chapter 2

I huddled on the old burgundy leather couch that had once been my father's, flannel-clad knees up like a barrier, remote control in both hands aimed at the fifteen-inch television set across the room. The TV was loud enough to keep me awake, but not loud enough to disturb Mrs. Cartier downstairs. My rent was late. Again. My own fault for not closing cases. But I didn't want to give my landlady another incentive to kick me out.

The overhead light and the two table lamps were on, too, and I half wondered when PSNH was going to cut off my electricity now that the utility company's winter protection plan was over. A grown woman shouldn't be afraid of the dark—especially if she'd never been afraid of it as a kid. But then, I hadn't been myself for a long time—388 days to be exact.

For fifty-five long days after my heart stopped as I ran from Finn Murdock, I danced a daily reel with death, strapped to a hospital bed with machines feeding me oxygen and a steady stream of drugs that all but kept me alive. The doctors told me I'd need a heart transplant to live. The cold I'd ignored had turned into a fast-moving viral infection that had settled in my heart and led to complete heart failure, shooting me near the top of the transplant waiting list.

For fifty-five days, I prayed someone would die so I could live.

Then my prayers were answered.

Four days after the surgery, I started physiotherapy. Two weeks after the transplant, I was jogging a few miles a day on a treadmill. Three months later, after my breastbone had healed, I started weight training and, within a few months, I'd regained all the muscle tone I'd lost. Six months after dying, I was back at work. I could do almost everything I'd done before.

I was lucky to be alive. Everyone said so. And it wasn't as if I wasn't thankful. I woke up grateful for every new day I got. Honestly, I did.

But there was a dark side to this gift of life that no one seemed to want to acknowledge. No one talked about the identity crisis that came after. About how it sometimes felt as if there was someone else in my body with me. Even my once-a-month transplant support group in Boston didn't stray too long in woo-woo territory.

"Just act normal," they all said—the doctors, the shrink, my brother. But what was normal now? Craving flan when I'd never liked the creamy confection before? Acting like a mouse when I'd roared like a lion before? Crying like a geyser at every little thing when I'd never shed an emotional tear before?

I tried to act "normal," to pretend the changes weren't happening, to concentrate on healing body and spirit and finding the rhythm of the job I'd once loved.

I probably could have internalized all of the changes eventually. But the ghost was what put me over the top.

She started showing up five months ago, a face suspended just below the ceiling of my bedroom like some sort of death-heralding hologram. Each time she appeared, my heart pistoned like an overrevved hotrod, and cold fear needled up my spine and over my scalp until my teeth clacked and my muscles quaked. I didn't want to die.

At first I thought I was going crazy. I'd always been a live-for-the-moment kind of girl. The past was gone and there was nothing I could do to change it. The future wasn't there yet so there was no point worrying about it. Even my job was about capturing facts. My mother was the one into ESP, tarot and fortune telling.

I told myself the ghost was just a bad dream—the kind that feels as if you're awake when you're really asleep. But the more I tried to ignore her, the bigger she got, adding to herself every night. The head grew a filmy white body. And now…I shivered at the thought and pulled the lambswool afghan closer around my shoulders. I hadn't slept in my bedroom in over a month.

When she kept coming back, the thought that she

could be *her*—you know, my donor—occurred to me. Maybe she wasn't happy about how the organ lottery had turned out. Maybe she wanted to make sure I'd take care of her heart. Or maybe she just wanted it back because she was pissed she'd died and I'd lived.

None of these thoughts were especially comforting.

I'd even tried facing the mushrooming fear head-on, because that's how I'd dealt with problems before. I'd contacted the transplant coordinator, but she'd begged me not to pursue my curiosity further and regurgitated the ironclad rule of confidentiality, that the donor's identity could never be revealed to the patient or the patient's to the donor's family.

I'd done my best to do as everyone wanted me to do and simply ignored the dreams and the ghostly visitations and tried to get back to that elusive "normal."

But that was like asking someone not to think about a pink elephant. The ghost became all I could see. And really, how did one fight a ghost? I'd yelled at her, cursed her, tore at the cold threads of her spectral body with my fists. Still she came, every night, begging and crying. Frankly she gave me the creeps.

I flicked through the channels. To cut expenses I'd canceled my cable, so I had to make do with whatever network television I could pull in with the antenna. I sat through a lineup of comedies. I'd read somewhere that laughter was good for healing. At least it managed to keep me awake. But as the news came on, sleep tugged me into its dark fold.

No, please, no. I don't want to sleep.

I tried jerking myself awake, but it was too late, exhaustion won. I floated into the comforting blanket of blackness. I flew high and low, twisting and turning on some invisible current. I sailed in a series of maneuvers, steep turns and jumps. Lightness soared through my body, charging it with the almost-forgotten jolt of adrenaline-induced electricity. It'd been such a long time since I'd skysurfed.

On the wings of the dream, I drifted about, reveling in my freedom, until the deep blackness turned into a starry sky and the scene below me opened up into a familiar sight—Southern New Hampshire in March. I barely got the chance to orient myself before the skyboard beneath my feet disappeared, plunging me into the nightmare again.

I sank in a speeding rush, a scream ripping helplessly from my throat. Arms spread wide, hands splayed, legs braced, I battled to brake the fast descent.

I plopped behind a steering wheel and was driving north along the Everett Turnpike from the southern end of Nashua. Not Betsy, my beloved van. A rental, from the canned new-car smell of it. Was Betsy in the shop again? My gaze focused straight ahead into the black of night and purpose hummed through my body. Where was I going? Where was I coming from? Was I on a case?

The blinking lights on top of the orange-and-white construction barrels warned two lanes were narrowing to one. Although no one else shared the road with me, I signaled the lane change. When had I become so polite?

"There's a fault," I said, and the words surprised me. So did the huskiness of the voice. Fault? What fault? "A terrible fault."

Me, but not me. Outside, yet inside.

With a hand, I reached into a leather briefcase on the passenger's seat and extracted a sheet filled with neat boxes of computer-spewed data. As I looked at the unfamiliar figures, I shook her head. Fear rippled through me in an unexpected wave, draining my fingers and feet of warmth. "I was right. Oh, Wyatt, what should I do?"

Almost before I could wonder who Wyatt was, headlights blazed behind me. I shoved the paper between the seats and gripped the steering wheel with white-knuckled strength. With a sharp turn to the right and into the barrels, I avoided the ramming from the car behind me.

Sierra, girl, that's not *the way to handle this.* When had I lost my driving touch?

The car came at me again, engine growling. I fought to control the wheel, but my hands and feet didn't obey. Just like before when I'd almost died.

The surge of adrenaline scuttling through me rendered the March night in bold clarity—diamond-bright stars on an indigo canvas, the neon-white patches of snow on the embankment, the road shiny black, there, then gone—and I saw the inevitable before it happened.

The car careened off the road and took flight. I sailed forward. My head cracked against the windshield, exploded with pain. My body came to rest across the steering wheel like a shapeless shirt on a hanger. The sound of the horn blaring filled my head with an agonizing pulse.

From afar came the creak of the passenger door opening. I shivered in the sudden gust of cold wind.

No, please, don't. People will die.

The words echoed in my brain, but didn't make it out my mouth. Neither did muscles obey my commands to move. Papers from the briefcase swirled like dry autumn leaves churning on a breeze until black-gloved hands plucked at them. The rearview mirror swayed crookedly in my line of vision, drawing my attention.

Don't look, Sierra. Don't look.

A wide wound gashed the forehead. Red tears streamed down the cheeks. The mouth, bright with lipstick and blood, twisted open and a gush of breath rushed out.

Black hair. Dark brown eyes. China-delicate features.

"No!"

The face in the rearview mirror wasn't mine.

Then I was caught in a whirl of blackness, falling helplessly to the echoes of an unfamiliar voice. *There's a fault. People are going to die. Help me. Help me!*

I awoke in a sweat, gasping like a fish on dry land, trying desperately to escape the suffocating bonds of the afghan wrapped around me. The room stopped spinning, came into focus.

The ghost's gauzy white form hovered in front of the television, long hair fluttering as if caught in a breeze. Behind her translucent body, the screen crackled with the fire of a military jet that had crashed in some thick, green woods. As she floated toward the couch, the orange fire of the downed jet glowed where her heart should reside, and its black smoke filled her lungs, until every white line of her tortured face became a three-dimensional etching. Her arms stretched forward, reaching for my chest.

Blood cold in my veins, I scrambled against the fat

leather arm of the couch just as the ghostly fingers
scratched at my sweatshirt. I placed both hands protectively over my heart. "I won't give it back. It's mine
now. *Mine.*"

"Help me," the apparition pleaded. "It's started.
People are dying."

"I can't help you. I don't know what you're talking
about. Go away!"

The woman shimmered and faded. *Help me!*

I shivered, huddled in the corner of the couch. The
ghostly sobs echoed in my heart and left behind a com-
pelling hammer of time running out.

Wednesday, April 12

The next day I hid out in my office with the door
closed, hoping to avoid my brother, Van's, too-keen eye
when it came to sleepless nights. When a knock startled
me out of the chaos of my thoughts, I wished I'd had
the presence of mind to grab the phone and pretend I
was busy.

Too late. Van strode into my office and parked
himself in one of the two green leather wing chairs
opposite my desk. Even worse, the open door taunted
me with the freedom I couldn't reach. I braced myself
while Van took aim.

"You know what your problem is?" Van stared at me
through pinched pale-blue eyes.

I dropped my purple Gelly Roll pen on the desk
and leaned back nonchalantly in my chair. "I'm sure
you'll tell me."

Van ignored the sarcasm and plowed on. But then bulls were supposed to have thick skins, weren't they? And Van, despite his styled gray-salted brown hair, black Brooks Brothers suit, and polished wingtips, could still charge through life with the best of them. I toyed with the idea of waving a red cape in front of him, then decided against it. I was having a hard enough time trying to shake the unusual anxiety tightening my chest since this morning. Might as well hold my tongue and get this over with quickly.

"The problem with you, Sierra, is that you're afraid of commitment."

I bristled. Van's tone reminded me too much of Mrs. Craig, my third-grade teacher, and the way she'd looked at me over her glasses, down her long nose, exasperation dripping from every enlarged pore. "I want to see you after class, young lady." Which had meant I'd be deprived of yet another recess. Half the time the transgressions hadn't even been mine.

I studied Van, seeing Mrs. Craig in his place. A small smile quirked one side of my mouth. Part of my old daredevil spirit returned.

"How can you say that?" I asked, deliberately pushing one of his buttons. "I've had Betsy for eight years, and I haven't traded her in. That's commitment."

"I'm not talking about your mode of transportation, and you know it." Van glared at me over his rimless glasses.

"I come to work every day."

"But you aren't closing any files."

"Sure I am." But not lately. Not commitment, but something much deeper fed my fears. I'd tried time and again to explain to Van about my feelings of not quite being myself anymore, but Van wouldn't trade shoes even for the moment it took to understand. "Investigative work takes time and patience. It's all in the details. I've generated enough paperwork to keep Noelle busy."

"Sierra," Van warned.

The toro was goaded. "Well, how else could I justify keeping such a formidable assistant around?"

Van's mouth tightened and his nostrils dilated, fluttered, then returned to normal. "Have you exercised today?"

There he goes. I pretended not to notice. Elbows on the chair's arms, I laced my fingers across my lap. "I jogged through half an hour of *Good Morning America.*"

"Have you eaten?"

I shrugged, brushing off Van's question. "I had a bowl of oatmeal and a banana."

"Have you taken your pills?"

"Yes, Nurse Van. I've been a good girl."

His gaze sharpened, but he didn't charge at the red bait of sarcasm. Either he'd gotten much better at controlling his temper or I'd lost my touch at cape waving.

"I had to hire another investigator to get the video I needed for the workman's comp case," he said calmly. "Why?"

"I didn't have the time. I do have other cases."

I shuffled file folders I'd yet to open across my desktop. The fraud perpetrator in this case was a beefy teamster who wouldn't have taken kindly to being photographed carrying a piano when his back was supposedly too out-of-whack to work. I couldn't take the risk of being twisted into a pretzel. Not to mention the germ factor in that part of town. I shivered involuntarily.

"I've had a lot of backgrounding to do on the Grenier case. And I need the billable hours to pay the rent," I said.

"What about the Pendleton case?" he asked.

"Noelle's working on it." I rearranged my in-basket.

"What does a secretary know about finding a deadbeat dad?"

"Everything I do."

"Noelle's tied to the office." He paused and tented his hands over his lap. "What's really going on? You procrastinate until I have no choice but to get someone else to do the job. And you take more than enough breaks for both of us—"

"Got to stop and enjoy life once in a while. You should try it sometime—"

"But I must admit, when you apply yourself, your work can be exceptional."

I jerked forward in my chair, mouth open. "A compliment? From my brother?" I riffled through my agenda to find the day's date. "Excuse me while I mark the calendar."

"I'm trying to be serious here, Sierra."

"I know." Forearms on the desk, I leaned forward and did my best imitation of Van's scowl. I wanted to hug him to break this awful tension between us. But my family wasn't the touchy-feely type, and caring was carefully hidden behind criticism. *That* hadn't changed with my heart transplant. "That's the problem with you, Van. You're much too serious about everything."

"Life is serious business. You, of all people, should

realize that." He brushed away imaginary lint from his lapel.

"Naw, life's full of possibilities just waiting to be explored." A year ago I truly would have believed the words spilling automatically from my mouth. Now tension zinged through me, calling me a liar.

"You've never played by the rules." Van waved vaguely in my direction, indicating my Yankees sweatshirt and faded jeans.

Everyone had a weakness, and Van's was propriety. "It's much harder to catch a crook in action when you stick out like a sore thumb," I said. "Call it camouflage."

"We have an image to protect." Van's nostrils flared just enough to please me. Any minute now the steam would follow. A twinge of guilt plucked through me. I flicked it away.

"How many times must I explain this to you?" Van said. "Our father worked hard to build this firm to what it is today. Family values and propriety are big watchwords these days. A small, general law firm like ours has to capitalize on those family values to thrive."

"I'm a private investigator, not a lawyer." I yawned and stretched my hands behind my head. He should know better than to play word games with me. "And doesn't winning cases keep this sacred image of yours going?"

"Yes, but we have a history to live up to. There's a certain standard, a certain decorum our clients expect from us."

"I dress appropriately for the task." I leaned back in my chair and deliberately planted a scuffed basketball shoe on the desk. "Has anyone complained?"

Van wrinkled his nose. "Not exactly."

"Then what's the problem?" I snapped down my arms, jolted my foot off the desk and pretended outrage. "Is this about Betsy again?"

Van's nostrils widened but he managed to check his temper and keep his voice even. I had to give the guy credit. For a bull seeing red, he wasn't charging at the cape recklessly.

"No, it's not about your van," Van said. "Although I do wish you would park in the back of the building and not on the street where everyone can see that piece of junk. And don't try to sidetrack me, either. The problem is that I'm spending too much time worrying about you and covering for you. It has to stop. I can't bear to watch you waste your second chance at life."

"You think I'm wasting my life? You don't know—"

He cut off my rant. "I'll subsidize your share of the rent for one more month and that's it. If you don't start pulling your weight, I'll have to hire someone who will."

I cocked my head in stunned disbelief. Because he was my brother, I'd felt safe in Van's employ. Why the sudden change to tough love? "You'd leave me homeless and jobless?"

Van waved away my comment. "No, you'd move back home with mother."

"I can't do that!"

"I have partners I have to answer to." Van's bullish stubbornness came through in the stern set of his mouth. "I have a business to run."

"Moving back home is cruel and unusual punishment, Van."

"Nevertheless, I'm still your primary support person. And you've proven you can't handle your job full-time yet. Which means the show runs my way."

"Where do you get off telling me how to run my life? I'm doing fine. I don't need you watching over me every second. The obligation was temporary while I was recovering from the transplant. I set you free."

He leaned forward and reached for my hand. "Your nightmares are just dreams, Sierra. They're not real. You have to get over them and get on with your life."

Like a toreador who hadn't moved fast enough, I lurched as Van's implied horn gored my side. I snapped my hand from beneath his. *Damn you, Van.*

"I can't believe Dr. Katz broke confidence and called you," I said.

"He didn't call me. I called him."

Of all the asinine ideas Van had come up with since he'd assigned himself my primary support person this had to take top prize. Calling my shrink. Spying on me! "That violates my constitutional rights."

"I was worried about you."

"That doesn't excuse his actions." I stared at Van pointedly. "Or yours."

Van sighed. "Sierra—"

"You don't understand."

He thrust his hands forward, palms up. "Then make me."

"I see her die every night. Her death wasn't acciden-tal. It was murder. Someone deliberately ran her car off the road. He stole—"

"Sierra—"

I slapped the desktop with both hands. "You weren't there."

Van peered down his nose at me as if I were a witness he'd caught in a lie on the stand. "And you were?"

I shrugged and spun the chair to face the window. "I've tried to explain…"

"And I've run out of options with you. I need to be able to depend on you, or I'm going to have to find another private investigator to handle the firm's workload."

Incredulity stymied me for a moment and I forgot all about wanting to see steam come out Van's ears. My own brother was really going to fire me. Muscle tension cranked to near breaking, I faced him again. "You think making me pretend I don't have dreams is going to make them go away? You think pretending I'm the old Sierra will bring her back? Don't you think I've tried? I don't like who I am any more than you do."

Van dismissed my comment with a wave of his hand. "I think concentrating on your job, your family, your friends will do wonders for your sagging spirits. It's not like you to mope around an office all day. Once you're active, your nightmares will fade." His voice softened. "What's happened to all your energy?"

"I thought you didn't like all my 'energy.' Suicidal, you used to call me."

"Maybe. But there's a difference between careful and catatonic."

"Thank you, Dr. Martindale, for your expert psychiatric advice." I rolled the chair forward and gave Van my best intimidating glare. "But *you* don't have a stranger's heart beating in *your* chest. You don't know what it's like."

"No, I don't. I just want to see you happy again."

I narrowed my gaze and tapped my index finger thoughtfully against my lips. "I could leave, you know. My birthday's coming up in June. I'll have my inheritance."

"Sure, you could leave and live off your inheritance. But is that what you really want? To spend your life twiddling your thumbs?"

"I could go someplace where my unique talents would be appreciated and—"

"What? And prove you still have the guts to investigate?" Van shook his head, girding me with a knowing gaze. "That's why I'm doing this, Sierra. For your own best interest." Van rose gracefully for someone with an overfed girth and made his way to the door. "You have a month."

The door snicked closed behind him.

I spun the chair around to face the window. The shadows cutting through my neatly appointed office fell across me like solid bars. My shoulders sagged, and the sadness in my chest weighed like an unfulfilled obligation. The urgency returned. I fought the tears salting my eyes and the restlessness infiltrating my limbs.

Two floors below, the late-afternoon sunlight gleamed off the black asphalt and cars on the street. Part of me longed to run out into the sunshine, feel the wind on my face as I rushed down a dirt path on my mountain bike, feel the sweat trickle down my back as I zipped on in-line skates, feel adrenaline swamp my body as I parachuted from a Cessna. The taste of action had me salivating as it once had. I hated the fear that robbed me of my identity. Illogical, I know. But then, the definition of fear had everything to do with emotions and little to do with logic.

Van had backed me into a corner, and I didn't like cul-de-sacs.

He was right, though. I hadn't taken a risk since I'd caught Finn Murdock on tape. Truth was, I was afraid. Afraid to be myself. Afraid to die. But not taking chances wasn't giving me the security I'd hoped.

The pale reflection of myself with limp brown hair, sad blue eyes and haggard complexion didn't look like anyone I'd ever known. Or particularly wanted to be. Who had I become?

I had to do *something*.

I whipped the chair around and snagged open the bottom drawer of the desk. I snatched a foam basketball and, with an overhead throw, launched it in the direction of the garbage can strategically placed on top of the cherrywood credenza for just that purpose. Missed.

I'd woken up with a sense of restless urgency burrowing under my skin like some sort of parasite that no amount of scratching could release. Who was the woman who haunted me every night?

"Help me," the apparition had pleaded. "It's started. People are dying."

Had there really been a murder or was it all simply a paranormal delusion due to lack of sleep and the drugs I had to take on a daily basis as Dr. Katz insisted?

I lobbed a second foam basketball. The ball rolled around the rim and dropped to the carpet.

It's started. People are dying.

I had no choice. Not really. Not if I wanted this to end.

I used up my third ball. It rebounded off the back of the garbage can and joined its sisters on the floor.

One way or another, I had to get answers.

It's started. People are dying.

Chapter 3

"Noelle," I called to my assistant. I grasped the edge of my chair with both hands, half expecting a bolt from above to strike me dead on the spot for breaking the solemn promise I'd made after I'd woken up from the transplant operation to never risk this precious new heart.

Noelle popped her red head with its tightly wound chignon through the door. "Yes?"

"Find me *The Telegraph*'s Police Log for the week of March 9 of last year and any article of a car crash on the Everett Turnpike around that date."

"March 9? Are you sure that's wise?"

I shrugged and stooped to pick up one of the foam basketballs that littered the carpet. I raised my hands above my head and released a ball. It flowed in a perfect arc and swooshed into the garbage can on top of the credenza. "No, I'm sure that isn't wise, but that's exactly why I have to do it."

I'd once gambled every weekend by taking part in death-defying sports. I'd gambled every time I'd played a role or hidden a camera to prove a fraud. But as risky as my various activities had seemed on the surface, the risks were calculated and I'd prepared for them well.

I'd forgotten that in the past year. Hadn't Leo left me because I'd proved better than he was at tracking down information? The number of cases I'd closed got to him. Instead of praising me for how well I'd learned, he'd taken off with the contents of our joint account and our client list. His betrayal should have hurt more than it did. In truth, the skills he'd taught me were worth more than what he'd taken.

And if I wanted to own my new heart once and for all, I'd have to prove my right to it. I'd have to risk this investigation.

So why did it feel as if I was caught in a free fall from a cliff with my parachute still stowed on the ground? Of course, if the adrenaline was still flowing, it meant I was still alive.

Noelle brought the files and hesitated before placing them on my desk. Her wide green eyes said, "Are you sure?"

"Thanks, Noelle."

"Let me know if you need anything else." She left the door open when she returned to her desk, and her worried glance flicked back to me. Did everyone think I was on the edge of breaking apart?

Hands sweaty, I combed through the Police Log and newspaper articles and learned that my possible donor's name was Sofia James. Armed with that knowledge, I searched the Fort Worth *Star-Telegram*'s online morgue for her obituary.

The file was taking its sweet time to download, which wasn't helping the twitch of my nerves. If Van expected a higher output from me, I needed better equipment. This dial-up Internet connection was for dinosaurs. As the page formed on the screen, I worried about my heart's rapid race, about the feverlike heat that warmed my skin and dried my mouth. One shaking finger poised over the mouse, I talked myself out of closing the file half a dozen times.

But I *had* to know. Knowing was a matter of survival.

Still, knowledge would bring obligation. And obligation would demand action.

Later. I'd think about that later. First, get the facts.

Swallowing hard, I read the words as they appeared.

SOFIA MARGARITA CASTILLE JAMES

Sofia James, 27, of the Quarter Past Ten Ranch in Ten Oaks, died last Friday night in a traffic accident in Nashua, NH, while traveling on business.

Mrs. James had worked at Allied Defense for the past five years. She was a member of the Open Hand and Heart Literacy Program at St. Alban's Catholic Church in Fort Worth.

She received her engineering degree at the University of Texas at Arlington.

Her husband, Wyatt James, of Ten Oaks, and her parents, Antonio and Inez Castille, of Fort Worth, survive Mrs. James.

The Carlyle Funeral Home in Fort Worth is in charge of the arrangements.

Wyatt. The name the ghost had asked for guidance. I swallowed hard. Just a coincidence, right? Wyatt was a common name in the South.

The picture above the obituary started to appear, ripping my attention back to it. My damp palm strangled the mouse. My breath ceased to flow, caging fire in my chest. Then came the shocking moment when the lines finally filled in the blur of the picture.

No mistake.

No bad dream.

The possibility I'd put off for a year mutated into a living nightmare, bulging a goose-egg lump in my throat. The picture staring back at me on the computer screen was that of the ghost who came to me each night with a tale of murder.

If the ghost had been a real person, if she'd died on the night I'd gotten my second chance at life, then how could the rest of the horror not also be true?

It's started. People are dying.

What people? Dying from what?

I jabbed at the print button and growled.

I'd prayed for a heart. Sofia had died. Because of that, I'd lived.

I owed her.

"Sofia," I said to the woman staring back at me. "If I fix this mistake, will you leave me alone?"

A chill shivered over my scalp, bristled down my nape and rippled down my spine as if she stood behind me—as if she'd put her cold, dead hand on my shoulder and squeezed it.

I shook my head. *Get over yourself, Sierra. You know how to work an investigation. Start with the basics. Start with the facts.*

Still riding a wave of frustration, I yanked the phone off the cradle and called Ruth Hanley. She worked in Administrative Services at the Nashua P.D. Though I could be a Grade-A bitch when the occasion called for it, when it came to secretaries and assistants, I poured on the sugar. These people everybody ignored were the gatekeepers to information and access, and I made a point to cultivate their friendship.

"Sierra!" Ruth shouted, her voice sparkling. "How nice to hear from you. How are you feeling?"

"I'm doing great. Back at work as you can see. How are you? What about the twins and Larry?"

Ruth made a shuddering noise. "It's a soup of hormones at my house right now. Working here seems like a break compared to the refereeing I have to do at home."

"It's a phase. Your girls will be your sweet angels again once they leave for college." My mother and I hadn't exactly become friends after I'd left home, but the all-out warfare had mellowed to a tolerable truce. As long as we didn't spend too much time in the same room, we got along fine.

Ruth sighed. "I sure hope you're right."

"Hey, do you have time for coffee after your shift?"

"No, I wish I did. We have so much catching up to do. But I have to take Larry to a doctor's appointment."

"His back again?"

"Yeah," Ruth said. "As a matter of fact, I have to leave in about ten minutes."

I squeezed a foam basketball. "Do you think you could look up a police report for me?"

Ruth cleared her throat, then lowered her voice. "We've got a new chief, and he's still flexing his power muscles. He's really cracking down on the 'information dispersal,' as he calls it."

Great, just what I needed—a new chief on an ego trip. "It's really important, Ruth. You know I wouldn't ask for a favor if it wasn't."

Ruth's nails clicked on the hard surface of her desk. Knowing her loyalty to the department and her longing for adventure were fighting a battle in her mind, I gave her the space she needed. "I'd like to but I need my job."

"Okay, I understand. All I needed was a quick peek but I don't want to put you in an awkward position."

A phone rang in the background. A bark of laughter faded. A door slammed. "What do you need?" Ruth finally said.

I smiled at the small victory. I hadn't lost everything. "The details on a police report from a year ago."

"Do you have a date?"

"March 9. Sofia James. It was a single-car accident on the Everett Turnpike."

The sound of a file cabinet opening squealed through the line. For all the technological advancements available, police departments, because of tight budgets, still tended to run a decade or two behind. "Ah, here it is. What do you need?"

"No chance you can fax me a copy?"

"Not with the chief watching everybody's every move. With Larry out of work, I need my benefits, you know."

"Yeah, I hear you. Can you tell me who investigated?"

"Since it happened practically at our door, Officer Guy Stiver was the first responder. The state police, state Highway Enforcement Agency and the Hillsborough County Attorney's office assisted in the investigation."

Interesting. "Why so many eyeballs for a simple car crash? Did they suspect foul play?"

"Looks like they did for a while."

"But?"

"They finally determined the accident was due to motorist inattention. They think she fell asleep at the wheel and ran off the road."

"What about the air bag?"

"What about it?"

"Why didn't it deploy?"

"How did you know that?"

Because I feel her head crack against the windshield every night. "Must've read about it in the paper."

"Malfunction," Ruth said. "They looked at the rental agency, but the maintenance records were all in order. The poor girl just hit a streak of bad luck."

With some assistance. "Which rental agency?"

"Rent-a-Ride at the Manchester airport."

"Is there an insurance company listed?"

"Mutual of New England."

That was a nice bit of luck. The claims office was in Manchester, and I'd worked enough cases for Mutual to have a good source inside. "Any witnesses?"

"None listed. The accident happened at 1:43 a.m."

And the sidewalks tended to roll up early in this part of the world. How long had Sofia waited all alone in the dark for someone to notice her mangled car on the side of the road?

The transplant coordinator had woken me up at 4:00 a.m. with the good news of a heart's availability. I remember the rush of feelings—fear, joy, guilt. Shaking my head, I focused on my list of questions. "Where was she transported?"

"She was med-flighted to Boston." A beeping noise shrilled over the line. "Listen, Sierra, I've got to go."

"One more quick thing. Do they list a home address and next of kin for her?"

Ruth dashed off the information. "The chief's in the hall. I have to go."

"Thanks for all your help," I said. "Rain check on the coffee?"

"I'm holding you to that. I'll call you next week."

Well, there it was, I thought, the knock of my heart thumping in my throat. The first step. No turning back now.

"Noelle?" I called to my assistant, breath trapped high in my chest.

Noelle rolled her chair to the door and leaned back to peer into my office.

"Do we have any open files for Mutual of New England?" I asked as I formulated my next step.

"Two new cases came over the fax today."

"I'll take them." Needing to review the files would give me a reason to stop by the Mutual office tomorrow. I hated waiting when I was on a roll, but catching Claire Dagenais, my claims rep source, was easier with an offer of lunch.

Noelle frowned, then shrugged. "Okay."

I reached Claire just as she was leaving for a meeting and made an appointment with her to go over the files and lunch. Which left me with time to background Sofia and her family.

At six, Noelle walked into my office, pushing her arms through a fringed leather jacket. "I'm knocking off for the day. Need anything before I leave?"

I shook my head, then teased her. "Hot date?"

"Poker." Her sly smile reached all the way to her ears. "I'm on a hot streak. The petite size always fools them. These big boys think I'm helpless, and I clean them out every time. You'd think they'd learn."

"Does Van know about this?"

She glanced behind her into the hall, then whispered, "I won't tell him about your gamble if you don't tell him about mine."

I laughed. "Deal."

"See you tomorrow. Don't stay too late. Only one workaholic Martindale per office allowed."

I mumbled a good-night and turned my attention to the Internet.

Two hours later Van pushed his way into my office. "What are you still doing here?"

I looked up from the computer and blinked him into focus. "Working. Just like you wanted."

"What are you working on?"

I slid a file over the paperwork I'd gathered on Sofia. Van, for all his wanting me to get back to work, would not approve of this particular investigation. He'd fire me on the spot and send me packing to Mom's. Or worse, he'd call Dr. Katz. I didn't want to end up on some psych ward. I had to get this closed before Van figured out what I was up to. "Catching up on paperwork so you can bill some hours and keep your partners happy."

"There's no need to overdo it."

I snorted. "Like you're one to talk." I glanced at the Road Runner clock on the wall. "It's past your kids' bedtime. Do they even know what you look like?"

Van shook his head. "Go home, Sierra."

To what? An empty apartment? A ghost? *I don't think so.* "Sure, Van." Eventually.

Sifting through databases was a much better use of my time. Every piece of data I found put me one step closer to freedom.

Thursday, April 13

Thirteen, I decided, as I turned over the calendar page, was turning out to be a curse.

I'd fallen asleep at my desk, my arms crossed over a photo of Wyatt James I'd printed from an online copy of *Cutting Horse Weekly.* He rode a horse the color of a new penny. The tan hat, low over his brow, made it hard to see his face, but a quiet intensity exuded from the hard leanness of both man and beast. The accompanying article didn't say much, except that he'd won that particular competition and the purse that went with it.

How did he feel about his wife's heart beating in a stranger's body? Had Sofia talked to him about her suspicions? Had he acted on them?

I didn't think so. If he'd solved the problem, Sofia wouldn't be haunting me.

I stretched my arms over my head and yawned, surprisingly refreshed for having slept twisted in a pretzel. Must be the ghost-free nap. I rushed home before Noelle and Van came in. Refreshed or not, I wasn't in the mood for a lecture from either of them.

I did my duty to my heart by recording my weight and blood pressure, eating breakfast, swallowing my handful of pills and jogging through the morning news. The data I'd gathered on Sofia James simmered in my brain. I had facts—which needed double-checking—but I was no closer to understanding what had scared Sofia or why anyone would want to kill her.

Notebook and files in hand, I nosed Betsy into morning traffic. Investigating was not a deskbound job, so Van wouldn't miss me for a while. Since I had an hour to spare before my appointment with Claire, I stopped by the firing range near the airport—just for grins—and emptied a couple of magazines from my Glock into paper targets. I hadn't fired a weapon in over a year. At first the Glock felt foreign in my hand, but the hours of practice Leo had insisted on—even though I didn't usually carry a weapon on duty—had paid off, and conditioning took over.

Tap, tap, tap. Two in the heart. One in the head.

The groupings of holes on the targets were almost as tight as they'd been a year ago.

Like riding a bike, I thought, rather proud of myself as I climbed back into my van. Sofia hadn't taken everything away from me.

Snarled downtown traffic gave me a chance to play the observation games Leo had taught me. We'd be driving along and out of the blue, he'd say, "Close your eyes. Tell me the license plate of the car in front of us." We'd be in a restaurant and in the middle of a conversation, he'd say, "Describe the people at the table by the kitchen door." We'd be making love and he'd sometimes ruin the afterglow by saying, "Name three things I changed in the living room." Yeah, sometimes the constant training had gotten on my nerves, but it had paid off on many cases, because I'd noticed and remembered details. I was hoping all that knowledge was still floating in my brain and not concentrated in my old heart, pickling in a jar of formaldehyde in some hospital basement lab.

I lucked into a parking spot on Elm Street just a few doors down from the Mutual of New England building.

Claire wore the uniform of someone who was going places—black suit, white blouse and black-framed glasses that made her look serious but really didn't do much to complement her peachy skin and naturally blond hair. Being a claims rep was a temporary step for her, and I had no doubt she'd one day crash through the glass ceiling of this male-dominated industry and run the company.

I went through the files Mutual had faxed yesterday with Claire in her cubicle that smelled of the toffee she bought by the gross. Matter-of-factly I slipped Sofia's case into the conversation. "Hey, I have a couple of questions about an old case."

Claire turned to her computer, fingers poised over the keys. "Do you have a case number?"

"No. It's not one we did. The victim's husband asked me to take a second look."

Claire glared at me over the top of her glasses. "Is he thinking of suing?"

"No, there's some problem with the estate and he needs proof the death was accidental."

"We can just mail his lawyer a copy of the report."

I could imagine the frown on the random lawyer's face when that report showed up on his desk uninvited. If he called back to ask why Mutual had sent it, I'd lose a boatload of credibility with Claire. "I'll take it with me."

"Are you going to Texas?"

"Next week." The prospect loomed bigger with each new lead. As much as I'd wanted to know my ghost's identity, I had no desire to meet her family. I mean, what could I say? I knew how I'd react if a stranger showed up on my doorstep and claimed to have a piece of my loved one beating in her chest. There was no way my visit wouldn't open up old wounds and resentment. And I had enough of my own, thank you. If I thought outside the box, maybe there was still a way to avoid a trip to Texas.

"You know I have to do things by the book, Sierra."

Claire had a steel-trap mind and she'd hound me for

that lawyer's name until I came up with one. I'd have to stall. "I know. I'll e-mail you the firm's address."

I gave Claire the information she needed to locate the file. She typed, then scrolled through the results. Lips pursed, she shook her head. "I don't see anything that would indicate this was anything but an unfortunate accident."

"Why did so many agencies poke their nose into a simple accident?"

"There were questions because of the air bag, the seat belt and the paint transfer on the bumper."

I hitched in a breath as the remembered jar of bumper against bumper in my nightmare jolted through me. "A hit-and-run?"

"No, no. Probably just some parking lot mishap."

I stood behind her and pointed at the screen. "It says here that the air bag didn't deploy."

"Burned-out fuse."

"Wouldn't a warning light have gone off?"

"Who's going to bother getting it fixed on a rental? She was on her way back to her hotel near the airport. She had an early flight."

"What about the seat belt?" I asked. "It says it was nonoperative."

"A toll token got stuck in the mechanism and busted a gear, leaving no tension."

Accidentally on purpose? How badly had someone wanted to make sure the car accident was fatal? "What about tire tracks?"

"None other than hers in the snow."

"What about footprints?"

"Tough to sort them out after the scene was trampled by all the emergency personnel."

"So no foul play?"

Claire clucked. "Just another driver who fell asleep at the wheel."

"Alcohol?"

"Not a drop. No drugs, either, according to the blood tests." Claire put her computer to sleep. I hoped I could remember all I'd seen until I could write down the information. "Where do you want to go for lunch?"

"You pick." I hiked my tote over my shoulder and rose, noting that the final report's date was barely three months old. The slow wheels of justice might work to my advantage. "What happened to the car?"

"We totaled it." Claire grabbed her purse from the bottom desk drawer.

"Do you know where it went?"

Claire shrugged as we walked to the elevators. "Rent-a-Ride usually sends their wrecks out for salvage."

"Any chance the car's still on the road?"

Claire shook her head and pressed the elevator button. "Rent-a-Ride is cheap but they follow the rules."

"Which salvage yard do they usually use?"

Claire frowned. "Um, Shirley's Auto Salvage in Goffstown."

After lunch I made a detour to Goffstown and Shirley's Auto Salvage. An eight-foot privacy fence guarded the contents of the yard. Finding the rental car would be a crapshoot but I was used to playing long odds. With a window of three months instead of a year, parts could still be available. I took off my navy blazer before leaving Betsy and entered the office in the small building, wearing jeans and a T-shirt.

No Ed-the-Gruff-Mechanic manned the office, instead a pert brunette handled the phone and computer as if she had several extra sets of hands. "I'll be right with you."

I nodded, taking in the grease-free interior, the green plant on the corner of the desk and cheery yellow curtains at the window.

"What can I do for you?" the brunette asked. Her cupid mouth turned up, feathering sunshinelike rays around her eyes.

"I'm looking for a steering wheel and a front seat for a Taurus. Do you have any in stock?"

She turned back to her screen. "What year?"

I pictured the report on Claire's computer and gave it to her.

Her fingers zipped over the keyboard. "I have three. My mechanic's out at lunch right now. You'll have to wait, unless you want to pull the parts yourself."

"I'll take a look and see if there's anything that fits."

The phone rang and she flapped a hand toward the yard. "Okay, once you pass the gate, count three rows to your right, then go halfway down. They should be sitting right there."

"Thanks."

The phone's ringing became insistent, and the cheery lines at her eyes took a sharp upward turn. She waved me away as she answered. "Shirley's Auto Salvage. How can I help you?"

Walking through the cemetery of dead cars had a

certain sci-fi quality to it. Like dismembered robots, parts stuck out of piles of rusted automobile bodies. The breeze, moaning through the tunnels made by the piles of metal, had an eerie feel. My footsteps fell silently on the dirt roadway carved through the carcasses.

What was the germ factor in a place like this? I took out the hospital mask I kept in my tote and had it halfway on before I paused. This was crazy. There were no germs waiting to jump me. I took my meds. I boosted my immune system with vitamins. I was safe. I fingered the mask, swallowed hard and stuffed it back in my tote. Things I'd taken for granted before now required careful decisions, but I wasn't going to turn into an agoraphobic germophobe.

The pile of Tauruses wasn't where it should've been. I had to hunt down two more aisles before I came across it squashed between two behemoth SUVs. I hadn't really expected to find Sofia's car, but when the white Taurus with the crumpled front end caught my sight, recognition punched my gut. The VIN I pictured from Claire's report confirmed my instinct.

The doors were missing, as were most of the electronics, but the driver's seat was still there. So was the steering wheel.

I extracted an all-purpose tool from my tote and slid onto the dusty seat. The windshield was gone, so I was spared the sight of crazed glass haloed with blood. My overactive imagination still made me think I could smell her blood, though. Then I spotted the dark splotch on the dash. My stomach rolled. Sofia's. The rusted stains made her death that much more real.

Shaking my head, I forced myself to look past the blood. I didn't really know what I was looking for. I mean, if the experts had ruled Sofia's crash an accident, how was I going to prove otherwise? But the investigators didn't have the advantage of knowing about the black car that had bumped Sofia off the road or about the man who stole her briefcase.

I pried open the fuse cover and extracted the one that looked blown. I rolled it in the palm of my hand. Replacing a working fuse with a burned one would take the mystery man, what? All of five seconds?

I slid off the seat and crouched to get a closer look at the cracked plastic insides of the seat belt mechanism. Jamming a token in there would also take only a few seconds. And having some tokens would be perfectly feasible since she'd have to have driven through tolls from the south Nashua office of Allied Defense to the airport. Especially if she came to New Hampshire regularly on business.

In less than a minute the guy driving the black car could have ensured that both the air bag and the seat belt wouldn't function. And picking the highway to bump her off the road would ensure a crash at high speed. He'd wanted her briefcase, but he'd also wanted her dead. Why?

Sofia had asked Wyatt for help, and he'd once worked as a software engineer for Allied Defense. Could he have bumped off his own wife for some sort of profit? No matter how many times I reran the nightmare through my mind, I couldn't see the assailant's face.

Lost in my thoughts, I didn't notice the fetid scent

that pulsed hotly against my nape until a low, tongue-swallowing growl stood the hairs on the back of my neck straight on end. Moving my head in slow motion, I spotted the black jowls of a Bullmastiff vibrating with warning.

"Good doggie," I said in a soothing tone. I'd always liked dogs. For all my mother's neuroses, animals hadn't been one of them, and I'd grown up in a houseful of strays. Because of the threat of disease animals carried, the comfort of a pet was another thing I'd had to give up. And this beast was huge! "Your mistress said it was okay for me to poke around."

He growled again, thick slobber dripping from the sides of his mouth like venom and splattering on the knees of my jeans. That white poison had to teem with a trillion germs.

Because the doctors had had to cut the nerves from my heart when they'd carved it out and couldn't reattach them to my new heart, my heart didn't run on electrical stimulation like everyone else's; it ran on adrenaline produced by my body. I couldn't just leap up and run or I risked fainting. My best option was distraction until I could ease into flight.

After a Doberman had bitten me while I was on surveillance, Leo had run several drills with his Rottweiler on how to handle a future attack. I could do this. I squelched my recently acquired fear of germ-carrying animals and rose slowly from my crouch to face the dog. "Mess with me dog and you will regret it for the rest of your days. Now, go!"

His fawn coat shook with anticipation, then he

lunged at me. Screaming, I deflected his massive front paws with my arms. That knocked him off balance, body-slammed him into my chest and smacked us both to the ground. Instinctively, I curled up and covered my ears with my hands. Being ripped to pieces by 130 pounds of pure mean was no way to go.

He bounced to his feet and growled again. His yellow teeth were much too close to the exposed skin of my arms. Sticky slobber splotched against my hand. He was *not* going to bite me. Hard to exude confidence in this position but I gave it a shot. "Go home, dog!"

He didn't budge.

I spotted my tote knocked over on its side and the energy bar I kept there for emergencies. "How hungry are you, Mr. Death Breath? Trust me, I don't taste good. Not with all those drugs running through my veins." I inched my hand toward the bar until I reached it. I carefully opened the package and offered him the prize.

He sniffed the cranberry-and-almond bar, then gobbled it whole. While he chewed, I found my footing and armed myself with a tailpipe. Wielding the tailpipe as a sword, I backed away from him. He went for my tote. Using his teeth, he shook the contents to the ground and glommed onto anything edible—the handful of throat lozenges, the mints from the bank, the pack of gum. His search for food had knocked my forgotten can of pepper spray to my feet. Was it still good after a year-plus of no use? While he chewed the gum, I reached down for the spray, then continued backing away. If he was happy with gum, I didn't see the point of hurting him.

I'd gotten far enough away to turn around and get up to speed when he lunged at me again. I whirled, aimed the pepper spray and shot.

Whining, he fell back and batted at the burn with his paws. I booked it back to the office in record time.

The brunette took one look at me and said, "Oh, shoot. I forgot about Rufus. He didn't hurt you, did he?"

"No, but he ate my purse and I'd really like to get it back. By the way, I maced him. You might want to get him to a vet."

"You hurt my dog!" She raced around her desk and sped outside to Rufus's rescue. She lifted the whining beast into her arms as if he were a baby. Amazing, considering she couldn't outweigh the beast by more than twenty pounds. "Oh, my poor little puppy, what did the nasty lady do to you?" She glared at me. "He's just a big old galoot. He'd never hurt a flea."

Could've fooled me. "He tried to take a bite out of me."

"That's still no reason to hurt him. Look at him, he's crying." She kissed his slobbery snout. His eyes were running from the spray, and it did look as if he were crying.

I raked the contents of my tote off the ground and stuffed them in what was left of the bag.

The brunette crooned to the sniveling dog all the way back to the office. She carefully laid him on a beanbag bed in the corner, then grabbed tissues from the holder on her desk and dabbed them at Rufus's watery eyes.

"I usually tie him up before I let anyone go in there," she said in a crisp tone. "Did you find what you needed?"

"Yeah, I'll take the steering wheel and the seat belt mechanism from the front driver's seat." My sister-in-law's cousin was a mechanic. I'd have him take a look.

"George should be here soon." The brunette poured water onto a fresh batch of tissues and ministered to Rufus's eyes. "He'll pry them out for you. I'll print out an invoice for the parts."

"Great." Noticing the crusted slobber on my hands, I reached into my tote, brought out the sample-size bottle of antibacterial soap and slathered the gel up and down my arms. It would have to do until I could get into a soapy shower.

Once I had the parts stowed in Betsy's back, I aimed for home. No two ways about it. My snooping so far had raised more questions than it had answered.

There was only so much I could learn from a distance. As much as I hated to, it was time to make arrangements to meet the ghost on her own grounds.

Chapter 4

Wednesday, April 19

Ten Oaks. The thought whispered through my brain as the tiny speck of a town appeared on the flat horizon. An unexpected rush of homecoming set my heart thumping hard. Instinctively I let go of the gas pedal, and my foot hovered over the brake. I probably should've stayed home. Van would definitely have a cow when he found out I'd left town.

In theory I could have gotten someone else to investigate. I knew detectives all over the country, thanks to a female-P.I. online network I belonged to. A few even owed me favors.

My foot jittered on the pedal, urging me to press

ahead. *You can't quit now,* a hollow awareness soughed inside my skull.

Yeah, I know. Hearing voices was a bad sign. And thinking I heard *her* voice echo in my brain was freakier even than having her materialize in my bedroom.

But what choice did I have? No one was going to believe a ghost had sent me on this case. And without bringing up the ghost, what proof did I have that Sofia was murdered?

Perspiring even though the air conditioner was on max, I took the next exit without even consulting the map on the seat beside me. I drove through a sleepy town of red brick buildings that seemed oddly familiar. The feeling increased tenfold a quarter mile later when I spied a cluster of ranch buildings perched on top of a hill that overlooked acres of white fence.

The Quarter Past Ten Ranch.

Home. Tears smarted my eyes. Giddiness and grief tore through me like a summer storm. I pulled the rental over to the shoulder of the road and fought the gut-wrenching sob caught in my chest. Where was this coming from? I never cried—not even when the doctors had told me I could die without a transplant.

Was that it? Were these more of Sofia's feelings?

"You're freaking me out, Sofia." My grip tightened on the steering wheel, and I stared at the ranch buildings shimmering like a mirage in the sun. "Are you sure you want me to do this?"

People are dying.

Great, now my delusion was answering me. "Then how about a little help. Do you know who killed you?"

No.

"That figures. Why should you make this easy for me? How about a list of suspects, then? Some evidence?"

Dead silence.

"Let's just get one thing straight. If I'm going to investigate, then I'm running the show."

If there was such a thing as a mental shrug, I felt one nudge my brain.

How was that for crazy—extracting promises from a ghost?

Reluctantly, I pulled back onto the road and turned into the drive.

Tina had her foal, Sofia squealed as I drove past a field where foals practiced using their gangly legs. On the other side of the road, cows chewed their cud in the glare of the early afternoon sun.

"What no comments about the cows?" I mocked her.

Cows are business. Horses are pleasure.

Once I would have agreed with her. As a teenager I'd loved riding. Galloping full speed across a field and jumping over logs had been a total rush. Now I was sweating bullets imagining all the germs that teemed in the manure pile and in the three barns behind the big stone house. Uneasy, I glanced east and found Fort Worth's skyline under a cloud of haze. At least medical help was close by.

Those P.I. instincts I'd spent years honing screamed to stay away. Far away. That nothing good could come from raising ghost bones.

Stay, Sofia's voice insisted, prodding like a finger into the tissues of my brain.

"Since when are you such a coward?" I asked myself, ignoring Sofia's voice. "Investigating is what you do. You're good at it."

Were good at it, my evil twin whispered. Great. Now I had three voices playing tug-of-war in my mind—mine, Sofia's and self-doubt.

"Still am good at investigating," I countered stubbornly.

No one dared to object.

I parked by the house. Once I figured out what was going on, I'd call in the cops and let them tie up the loose ends.

Sofia's energy reached out to me as I stepped out of the car. The air was heavy with heat, weighing on my chest. Ordinarily a stone house this grand would have stirred my curiosity feelers—I had a thing for fine architectural lines—but my feet prickled with the need to run to the stables. Wyatt's name grew inside me on a wave of happiness, full and cresting.

Despite the dry Texas heat, cold dread sat heavily in the pit of my stomach at the prospect of walking into a ghost's world. I didn't really want to deal with Sofia's home or husband or her family. But if Sofia had a secret, this was where I'd find the information I needed.

"Okay, get a grip. It's just a bit of social engineering. Nothing to it." Pretexting was once a thrill.

As I knocked on the ranch house's massive front door, I was still rehearsing what I'd tell Wyatt James. "Hi, your dead wife's heart is beating inside my chest and I thought you should know she was murdered" was definitely not the right approach. The fib of my cover was for his own protection. I'd feel him out, see how far I could take the charade.

"Hello, can I help you?"

A small woman in her early fifties stood at the door. Her short brown hair was dyed and permed—badly—and framed her round face with tight curls. The amateur hairdo seemed at odds with the charmeuse of her peacock shirtdress that reflected taste and money. Her hazel eyes traveled over me with open curiosity.

I had the sudden urge to hug the woman. *Lorraine!* Whoever Lorraine was, she apparently wasn't a threat.

"I have an appointment with Wyatt James." I glanced at my watch and gave an apologetic smile. "My flight came in early."

"He's out in the barn, honey." She opened the door wide and the coolness of air-conditioning wrapped around me. "Come on in. I'll have someone run down and get him."

"That won't be necessary. Thank you. I'll find him."

Her brows rose to meet her bangs. "Those heels and that pretty suit aren't exactly barn wear."

I'd debated over what to wear for this meeting. Normally this would seem to call for jeans, blouse and boots, but something had kept nagging me to reach for the bright-blue, wrinkle-resistant suit that made the color of my eyes pop and brought out what curves I had. I'd propped my meager assets with a Miracle Bra and left my long legs bare. My instincts were never wrong when I dressed for a part, but now I was starting to have doubts. "They're sturdy enough."

"Suit yourself. It's the second building out back."

The woman shrugged, then shook her head as she went back inside. "City folk."

I headed toward the stable and my feet had started tingling again with a strange kind of eagerness. Shifting my new leather tote from one shoulder to the other, I swallowed hard. As a representative for a client who wanted to buy cutting horses, I'd have to show an interest in the animals I claimed I wanted to buy. I'd breathe shallowly. I'd wash my hands. No problem.

Fingers tight around the straps of my tote, I stood just inside the wide stable doors. The sweet scent of hay rode on the breeze funneling down the main aisle. "Mr. James?"

My only answer was the swish of tails and the curious looks from half a dozen equines, peeking over stall doors.

The soft thud of horse feet drew my attention to the corral behind the barn. In the middle of the ring, a horse and rider moved as one, foiling the strange-looking cow's every attempt to get by them.

I dropped my tote to my feet and grabbed the fence's top rail, caught up in the drama playing before me.

The intensity of the rider's total concentration made a marked contrast to the relaxation of his body as it flowed with the horse's hard stops and fast turns. I didn't need the picture I had in my tote to tell me the rider was Wyatt James. Not the way my heart was racing as if it wanted to fly right out of my chest and into his arms.

His full mouth hypnotized me for a moment with its improbable familiarity. The straight sandy hair poking out the back of his hat would feel soft to the touch. Those steely arms would hold me tenderly.

A metallic screech broke the spell of implausible awareness. My heart bumped heavily against my rib cage. Where had all this drivel come from? I'd never met the man.

"Knock it off," I warned Sofia under my breath.

Wyatt. A blinding rush of need, desire and longing swirled through me like a tornado and nearly knocked me off my feet. *I've missed you so much, my love.*

I grabbed the fence rail. "My way, Sofia," I mumbled. "You have to let me do this my way. Get out of my head."

The mechanical cow stood in the middle of the arena. Its lifeless eyes stared straight ahead. Wyatt pressed the button on the remote control in his hand, but nothing happened.

"Come on, li'l dogie." The husky timbre of his voice slid over my chilled skin like a caress. Familiar. Intimate. Too intimate.

He pressed the button once more. "Damn. I thought we had it this time, Ten."

He dismounted, dropping the horse's reins. The sorrel stallion lowered his head and snorted but stayed where he was. Wyatt strode to the steer, opened the panel on its side and stared at the mechanical insides while absently rubbing at his left side.

Scar. He had an old scar there. How could I possibly know that?

"Just a loose connection." Wyatt tightened a screw with a small screwdriver from his shirt pocket, then pressed the remote once more. The steer whirred to life.

Wyatt mounted the horse. With its mechanical whir,

the steer dodged right. Instantly alert, the horse played the steer with lightning-quick agility. Sinewy muscles flexed and extended with power and grace. Watching horse and man move arrowed an odd sort of pleasure right through me. With a press of the remote, the steer stopped and the horse halted.

"Great job, boy," Wyatt said and dismounted. The horse pawed in agreement. With a smile that packed a wallop of sex appeal, Wyatt extracted two pieces of carrot from his pocket and fed them to the horse.

My mind reeled with dizziness. The whole scene was like déjà vu. I shook my head. Sofia's memory. Not mine.

This was too freaky. I tugged on the hem of my jacket. After one last gulp of hesitation, I stepped to the gate.

Wyatt spotted me and walked the horse toward the gate. He checked his watch. Distractedly he wiped the horse's saliva from his palm onto his thigh and extended a hand through the fence. "Miz Martindale, I presume."

"You must be Wyatt James." I stared at his out-stretched hand, letting it float awkwardly in midair. Shoot, I'd have to do better than this if my cover was going to work. I gripped his hand firmly, wondering how soon I could get to the antibacterial gel in my tote. An unexpected current of awareness flowed, warm and strong like a pulse, keeping our hands fused for a moment too long.

The same intensity of concentration he'd fostered on the steer was now focused deep into my eyes, humming inside me like an overloaded circuit. Inviting green swirled into the wary brown of his eyes as if he knew me but couldn't place me.

I snapped my hand free. "That's quite a show you put on."

"A good horse makes it look easy," he said with an amiable drawl.

"Are all of your horses of the same quality?"

Wyatt let himself out of the corral and headed toward the barn. "Ten Bar None's got great cow sense, and more important, he seems to pass it on to his get. I'll give you a tour, if you like."

His once-over told me I'd gotten my attire all wrong. The suit had seemed so right at six this morning. He was old-fashioned. He liked women in dresses. He liked long, shapely legs. But this was business, not a seduction. How could I have planned this pretext so badly? Sofia's influence?

Enough. As long as I kept my cool, things would turn out okay.

"That's what I'm here for," I said with a salesman's cheer. "I'm fresh off the plane, so I'm not exactly dressed for it, but I'd love to see how your operation runs."

The horse's shod feet clattered on the barn's concrete floor. I hung back for a second but followed in.

An elderly stablehand looked up from his sweeping and rushed to take the horse from Wyatt. "In his stall or in the back field?"

"Back field," Wyatt said. "Make sure he gets a good rubdown. He's earned it."

The old man nodded. Wyatt turned to me. "You didn't come prepared to ride?"

I suppressed a shudder at the thought of being jostled

around on horseback. "I'm not a rider, just a buyer. My client wants to invest in the sport as a hobby." I laughed. "I know what you're thinking. More money than sense. But there you have it. He has some Canadian cowboy from Calgary lined up to ride the horse."

Something cold and wet touched my hand and I yelped. Looking up at me was an Australian sheep dog. "Hey, cutie. You surprised me." I bounced a pat on his head, hoping he'd go away, but he butted my hand for more.

"Jake, bed!" Wyatt ordered. His curiosity-filled gaze never left my face, making my nerves crackle. What had I done wrong this time?

Jake lumbered back to a nest of hay by the front door.

"Jake doesn't usually cotton to strangers," Wyatt said.

"Animals usually like me." I kept my tone friendly. "So, about that tour?"

As Wyatt showed me around and pointed out various horses' qualities, his gaze kept raking me with unspoken questions. I forced myself to keep on topic but my throat kept getting tighter. "Your horses have a very good performance record. You've had a National Cutting Champion, what, three out of the past five years?"

"They've got great lineage." Wyatt eyed me as if I were growing a horn in the middle of my forehead. "Doc Bar bloodlines. Makes them intelligent and easy to work with."

I asked a few more questions, but none of the information I'd gobbled up on cutting horses seemed to impress him.

Even though he'd only shown me half the animals he had available for sale he cut the tour short. "Why don't we go back to my office?"

We walked to the back of the house and entered directly into his office. The air-conditioned interior was much too cool after the afternoon heat, and I couldn't help the shiver.

Masculine lines dominated the room. Brown, hunter green with small splashes of burgundy formed the color scheme. Something in me sighed and wanted to flop in the big leather chair in the corner and tuck my feet under me. How well would that go over?

He hung his hat on a peg by the door, then fired up his computer and got out brochures of information about the ranch and individual sheets on the horses he had for sale. That strange feeling of déjà vu tingled up and down my arms. Only when his patter dried up did I realize I hadn't been listening. A muscle jumped in his jaw and his eyes darkened.

"Whatever brought you to my ranch, horses aren't it." Irritation coated his slow drawl. "What do you want?"

So much for Southern charm. "I don't know what you mean."

"You're not a very good liar."

And here I thought I was giving an Oscar-winning performance, even if I'd picked the wrong pretext. "I came to look at horses."

"And you've looked at them."

Yeah, so what now? The cover was to get me in—which it had—but I needed to find a way to talk about Sofia.

Tell him. The skin of my neck prickled.

Impulsively I reached up and set the wind chime at his window into motion with the tip of my index finger. I cocked my head as the pewter horses clinked and clanked in a tune that resonated like a long-ago echo. A shiver clawed up my back.

His eyes shimmered with something alive and dangerous, and something clicked inside me in a disturbing way. A need. A knowing. A fear.

The books in the bookcases on the far wall melded one into the other, creating a solid bar of psychedelic colors. Ice-cold splinters sliced into my bones. I'd have to hit him with the last thing he wanted—the truth.

He frowned at me. "Are you all right?"

I fanned my face and it occurred to me that a weak woman would get more out of this man than a strong one. "I'm not used to the heat. Between that and the flight, I must be a little dehydrated. Could I trouble you for some water?"

He reached into a small refrigerator behind his desk, pulled out a bottle of water and handed it to me. "About the reason you're here…"

I forced some water down. "Like I said, the horses aren't for me. They're for my—"

"Cut the crap. You're not here for horses."

I shrugged. "I'll admit that I don't usually buy horses. But when my clients want me to find something, I find it for them." Close enough to the truth.

"You're a personal shopper?"

"Yes." I plucked a lime gumdrop from the candy dish on his desk. He shook his head as if to dislodge a memory.

His glower deepened until it practically hid his eyes. "I feel I should know you."

Tell him.

Butt out, Sofia. I know what I'm doing. "This is my first trip to Texas," I said with a smile. "But I know what you mean." I set the bottle of water on his desk and reached for the picture of a pretty horse, more blond than red. "I like this one."

Sofia growled like a two-year-old before pitching a tantrum.

Wyatt frowned. "My reputation rides on matching the right horse to the right rider. Have your client send his rider along. That'll be more productive all around." He stood. "Now, if you'll excuse me, I have work to get back to."

I ambled back to the wind chime hanging like a sun catcher on his window. "Your wife. She gave you this."

His expression turned hard, his eyes cold. Who could blame him? I mean, if the nightmares made no sense to me, how could they possibly make sense to him?

"What do you know about my wife?" he asked, his voice completely stripped of warmth.

"Not much." I pushed one of the pewter horses with a finger. "I never met her. But Sofia gave you this at the office Yankee Swap where you met."

His jaw slid back and forth. "Are you trying to tell me you're some sort of psychic? Did my mother send you?"

Now there was a conclusion worth looking into. I gave a short, rough laugh. "No, your mother didn't send me. And I'm definitely not psychic or else I'd already have all the answers to my questions."

He advanced toward me with the slow predatory purpose of a jungle cat. "Then what are you driving at?"

Show him.

Panic welled, but I squashed it down. I shrugged off my jacket, folded it on the back of the chair and, with wood-numb fingers, started to undo the buttons of my blouse.

"What are you doing?" He caught my wrist, and my pulse beat steadily against his fingertips.

Swallowing hard, I freed my hand with a release move Leo had taught me and finished disengaging the top four buttons.

"A year ago your wife died and, because she died, I lived." I parted the folds of silk and exposed the skin of my chest where a nine-inch scar bisected my breastbone.

In slow motion, his hand reached up and hesitated over the scar, his gaze transfixed by the deep pink line on my chest. "Sofia…"

"She's haunted me since that night." My voice caught in my throat and the words came out no louder than a whisper.

His face shimmered behind the veil of mist stinging my eyes.

"I see her die every night."

Still he said nothing, but his breaths pumped out faster.

"It wasn't an accident."

At the scalding touch of his fingertips on my scar, my breath escaped in one long, silent rush. My heart hammered hard and strong, reaching forward, it seemed, to the warmth of the palm now pressing softly against the length of the flaw on my skin.

"Someone deliberately ran her off the road."

He ripped his hand from my chest, and I gasped as I stumbled back.

"The police investigated," he growled. "It was late. She fell asleep at the wheel and drove off the road." He grabbed my jacket off the chair and thrust it at me. "I want you to leave. Now."

I let the jacket drop to the floor.

"Her rental car was a white Taurus with a blue interior." Meeting his condemning gaze head-on, I fitted the buttons of my blouse into their proper buttonholes. "She was wearing a black suit and a black leather coat. On the passenger's seat there was a cordovan leather briefcase with the initials SCJ stamped in gold—"

"You read newspaper articles—"

"Those details were never released—"

"An accident report—"

"No—"

"Why are—"

"When they found the car, there was no briefcase inside because it was stolen by the person who ran her off the road."

Pain crazed his hazel eyes, sharpened the keen bones of his face. But now that I'd started down this path, there was no turning back. I had to make him believe. Needing a connection, I reached for his forearm, as if the truth could transfer itself with a touch. "When they found her, she was clutching a piece of paper in her right hand—"

He ripped his arm away, severing the hot pulse

zinging between us. "That's enough! The police investigated. The case is closed."

"How could I know she always wore a seat belt? How could I know it didn't function that night? How could I know the air bag didn't deploy?"

He grabbed my shoulders and shook me. *"Stop it."*

"How could I know she wanted your help to figure out what to do about a mistake?"

His features cemented, and his fingers dug into my skin. Between gritted teeth, he said, "Get out of here."

"I can't, Wyatt. She makes me relive the accident detail by detail every night. She begs for help." My throat worked as if I'd swallowed an apple whole and it had gotten stuck. "She says that it's started. That people are dying."

I braced myself, fearing that at any moment he'd throttle me. "What kind of person—" he started.

"A person who owes a debt of gratitude for another chance at life."

He spun me around and propelled me toward the door. *"Get out."*

"Did I touch a nerve?" I'd meant for the comment to be impudent, a way to deal with my frustration, but the tensing of his hands on my shoulders and his brittle silence told me I'd hit a mark. I sucked in a breath. "She's been haunting you, too!"

He swept my jacket off the floor, tossed it at me and yanked open the door.

Okay, so Wyatt James was a closed door. I slid on my jacket. I'd find another way. I was not going to let Sofia haunt me for the rest of my life. I'd just spent a long, exhausting day. I needed food, a shower and sleep before I figured out my next step.

No! Make him see!

I slung my tote over my shoulder. "You may not want to make peace with your wife's ghost," I said, "but I do." The rightness of my mission—it wasn't a case anymore—filled me with determined purpose. "It would be easier to find Sofia's killer with your help. You knew her intimately. You understood her. But either way, I *will* solve her murder. She needs that closure as much as I do."

I withdrew a card from my wallet, scribbled the hotel's address on the back and put it on Wyatt's desk. "If you change your mind, that's where I'm staying. Room 202."

As I started back to my car, the haunting jangle of the pewter horses galloped after me.

Three hours later I'd showered and changed into gray yoga pants and a T-shirt that read Chocolate Heals All Wounds—a present from Noelle. The wind had picked up, and rain lashed against the window like a boxer sparring, turning the afternoon sky black and my pitiful motel room dark enough to have to turn on the lights.

The TV was on, tuned to CNN, but the sound was turned down—an old habit. My laptop was propped on a pillow on the bed. I sat cross-legged before it, trying to figure out how best to infiltrate Allied Defense. Or at least run across some of Sofia's coworkers. My stomach growled, reminding me I hadn't had lunch yet, and the scrawny airline breakfast was long gone.

I debated hunting down some real food versus going to the fast-food joint across the road. I was supposed to watch my cholesterol intake but one burger wouldn't kill me.

The knock at the door didn't surprise me. I'd sort of been listening for it for the past hour. The peephole was filled with Wyatt James's imposing body—just as I'd expected. The hitch—I didn't know if he'd come to run me out of town or to help me. I opened the door, leaving the security slide in place, and skimmed his body for a concealed weapon. His jeans hugged his hard thighs, leaving no room to hide anything. No telltale bulge of a holster showed through his shirt.

"Talk," he said roughly.

He meant about Sofia, of course. I opened the door all the way and sat on the edge of the bed, leaving the chair free for him. He didn't move from the door frame, just stood there in silhouette against the lightning-crazed sky like some dark force of nature.

"Where do you want me to start?" I asked as a roll of thunder rumbled by.

"The beginning's good."

"From the night we both died? Or from the first time I saw her in my nightmare?"

His head dropped to his chest. After a moment he took off his hat, closed the door behind him and sat on the chair. He carefully placed his hat, crown-side down, on the round table at his elbow. I crossed my arms and rubbed away the urge to crawl into his lap and nest my head in the crook of his shoulder. He leaned forward as if bracing himself, his mouth firm and tight-lipped, his eyes so steely yet so tormented I regretted my story wouldn't ease his anguish.

His gaze speared me straight and steady. "Tell me about the nightmare."

I closed my eyes, both to shut off the misery etched on his lean face and to view the permanent videotape imprinted into my memory. "I fall into her body as she's driving along the Everett Turnpike. I see what she sees, do what she does, feel what she feels. There's a paper in her hand, and she's worried about the numbers. About some sort of fault." I snatched a tablet from my tote and drew the boxes and filled in the data I'd long ago memorized. "Does this mean anything to you?"

He studied the table I'd drawn, then shook his head. "It's data, but without context, it doesn't mean anything."

"You don't know what she was working on?"

"Classified."

I'd figured as much. "A black car comes up behind her and slams her off the road. Her car crashes into an embankment. The seat belt doesn't hold her. The air bag doesn't deploy. Her head cracks against the windshield." I winced at the burst of pain. My voice faltered, and I had to clear my throat. "Someone opens the passenger door and takes the briefcase. All the papers, except the one she jammed between the seats. After he's gone, she grasps the paper in her right hand. She was hoping someone would recognize what it meant."

His turn to wince.

I glanced down at the fingernails I'd chewed nearly to the quick because of Sofia's hauntings. "She used to say, 'People are going to die.' Then five days ago, she switched to, 'It's started. People are dying.' She wants me to fix her mistake."

He didn't say anything for so long that I wanted to scream.

"None of this makes sense, but…" His gaze went to my chest, staring at the scar hidden beneath my T-shirt.

"If you didn't believe me," I said, "you wouldn't be here."

"I'm listening. Don't ask for more."

"I'm going to need more. I'm going to need to talk to people who knew her, find out what she was working on, figure out what went wrong and how come nothing's being done about it. When I have a list of potential suspects, I'll start eliminating, then hopefully get to the who and the why."

"Call the police."

I barked a bitter laugh. "Yeah, that's going to go over real well. What do you think they're going to say when I tell them I dreamed Sofia was murdered? They're going to label me a nutcase, and that file's going to sit untouched."

"And you think that you can find Sofia's secret?" His tone clearly indicated his doubts.

"I'm a licensed private investigator." I dug out my badge and showed it to him. "Finding facts is what I do."

He examined the leather folder as if every inch of it was suspect. "What kind of cases do you usually handle?"

"Mostly insurance fraud and locates."

He frowned. "Locates?"

"Finding people."

Irritation flashed in his eyes. "How's that going to help you find out if Sofia was murdered?"

"Not *if*. She *was* murdered," I said with a confidence that narrowed his gaze. "The basic principles of investigation are the same."

He took his hat from the table and worried the brim. "But not the stakes."

"No." I curled my fingers into my palms to keep them from reaching for the stray strand of hair that had fallen across his eyes. "The stakes here are much higher. But I can't afford to walk away. I have too much to lose."

He stood up and nodded once. "Okay, then. Pack your bags."

Chapter 5

"Excuse me?" My spine stiffened at the deceptively quiet tone of Wyatt's command.

"You're coming home with me."

Home, Sofia sighed with longing.

Bad idea. I wanted to pick Wyatt's brain, not stay under his control. So I played on his old-fashioned sensibilities. "I'm not comfortable staying at the house of a man I don't know."

"You'll stay at the main house with my mother," he offered in such a low-key manner that I almost missed the stubborn set of his jaw.

"You don't live at the ranch?"

"I have my own place farther out on the property."

At least he wasn't a mama's boy who still lived at home. "I couldn't impose."

"You won't. It's a big house, and Ma would love the company."

Why would Wyatt offer his mother's home to a total stranger? I was an outsider, maybe even an enemy. That was it, of course. He was suspicious of my motives, and he wanted to keep an eye on me. Wouldn't surprise me in the least if he'd turned right around and hired someone to check my background. I'd have to tread carefully. I needed his input to get my search started, but I couldn't let him take over my investigation. "I'd still feel more comfortable here."

"I insist." Wyatt smiled but there was nothing gentle about it. Before I'd quite realized his intention, he'd taken my elbow and was leading me toward the door.

To my dismay my prickling feet were eagerly following him. What the hell was wrong with me?

His jaw tightened. "I've got a ranch to run, and I can't keep an eye on you out here."

"No eye needed. I'm a big girl."

"You said you wanted my help. You've got it. Where's your bag?"

"You Tarzan? Me not Jane."

Ignoring me, he grabbed the soft-sided bag on the bureau. "If you didn't want me involved, you shouldn't have come to me with your tall tale."

"It's no tale, and you know it or you wouldn't be here." I stepped in front of him and immediately regretted my decision. I wasn't into the he-man type, but there was something about him that pressed against me like some sort of force field and itched whenever he got too close.

No, not something. Someone.

Sofia.

I miss him. Her yearning unspooled into me, making my body feel like a cooked noodle.

Don't do this to me, Sofia. I need a clear head.

Time to play the pity note, I thought, focusing back on Wyatt. "Your ranch isn't exactly the best place for me."

He quirked a brow as if I'd insulted his family's honor. Considering the ranch had been in his family for five generations, could be I had. "Why not?"

"The animals." I took my bag from him and dropped it back on the dresser. "They carry germs, and the drugs I take lower my immune system."

He grabbed my shoulders and spun me around to face him. His eyes were fierce lances. "My God, woman, why didn't you say something sooner? That's why you didn't want to shake my hand or pet the dog."

"I just have to be careful, that's all."

He frowned, the hardness of his features bearing down on me like a car compactor. "You can't go around taking that kind of chance."

I snorted. "That's the whole point. No one's making me. I volunteered. For Sofia's sake." And for mine.

Immediately he released my shoulders. "No, you're right. I apologize." He swiped a hand through his hair. "My mother doesn't keep any animals in her house. You'll be safe there."

He was a man used to giving orders and having them obeyed without question. His old-world protectiveness would be charming if it was directed at anyone but me. I wasn't about to take orders from him. I already had a ghost trying to run my investigation.

"Look," I said, "if you're going to treat me as if I'm breakable, we're not going to get anywhere. I'm fine. Strong. Healthy. I can take care of myself. Always have. I have to be careful in crowds and around animals, but otherwise I'm just like everyone else. The best thing you can do to help me is answer my questions about Sofia."

He grabbed my bag again and started for the door. "I'll answer your questions—at the ranch."

"You're going to get in the way of my investigation, aren't you?" I asked, hands on hips.

He stopped and sliced me with a dark glare. "I am. You can let me help or I'll go around you for answers. Sofia was my wife. I can't let this go."

Which actually brought him up a notch in my esteem. A man with principles was a rare thing in my line of work.

Sofia's joy lit up my skull like fireworks.

Two against one wasn't a fair fight.

I sighed. Considering the state of my bank account, I couldn't afford to argue too hard. Still, the thought of sleeping at the ranch with the echo of Sofia's ghost all around me didn't exactly appeal.

"I'll get the rest of my things." I stuffed the sample-size bottles of shampoo, lotion and toothpaste into my toiletry bag, then gathered my files and laptop and crammed them into my tote. That he eyed my every move didn't endear him to me.

"I have a car," I said. "I'll follow you."

"I'll have someone pick it up."

He carried my bag to his truck where he settled me into the passenger seat as if he thought the rain would hurt me.

I snapped the seat belt in place. "I don't need special handling."

He nodded and said nothing as he climbed into the driver's seat and started the engine. Once on the highway, he asked, "It's been thirteen months since Sofia died. Why now?"

I stared out the window. Through the beads of rain glazing the glass, I admired the bluebonnets, Indian blankets and evening primrose smearing a wash of blues, oranges and pinks on the side of the highway. "The transplant coordinator convinced me I shouldn't attempt to make contact with the donor family. My shrink said that my nightmares about Sofia were paranormal delusions due to the drugs and to survivor guilt. And everyone else wanted me to pretend everything was just like before."

I slowly turned back to Wyatt. "I tried to please them all. I mean, I was alive. That should've been enough." I tried to laugh, but it came out more like a strangled choke. "If you knew me before, you'd know that pleasing others just isn't like me. Usually I don't give a hoot what anyone thinks."

I shrugged, wondering why I was spilling my guts to a perfect stranger whose every tense muscle told me that even though he'd asked a question, he didn't really want an answer.

"And like I said, Sofia wouldn't let it rest. I figured if I did this for her, maybe then things would go back to normal."

His attention riveted to the road, he said nothing.

"Why did Sofia go to Nashua?" I asked.

His jaw flinched. "On business. She worked as a

systems engineer for Allied Defense. She'd gone to the Systems Integration Lab for a test on one of her projects."

"Could she have stepped on some toes there?"

"Sofia?" He shook his head. "No, she wasn't one to make waves."

"Not even if she thought there was a good reason to? Some sort of mistake?"

"Sofia had a really hard time standing up for herself. She'd have made darned sure there was something wrong before she'd have said anything to anyone. Then she'd have been discreet as to who she'd tell."

"If she suspected something had gone wrong, who would she have told first?"

"She'd have come to me."

That seemed to fit my nightmare. Sofia had asked Wyatt what she should do. "You said the project was classified."

"She'd have couched her questions in suppositions. She'd never do anything to break the rules."

Unlike now when I was pretty sure she was breaking several karmic laws with her haunting. "Did she do that often? Come to you with suppositions?"

A small nod. "Often enough. She was a good engineer, but she wasn't a confident woman."

"What if the someone she trusted this time turned out to be the wrong person?" I asked, tiptoeing through the minefield of male ego.

Wyatt ground his teeth as he fought for self-control. "Sofia was always timid, meticulous, cautious to a fault. I questioned the seat belt, the air bag, the missing briefcase. But the investigators had a logical explanation for all of it." He jerked one shoulder. "I accepted all the theories because it was easier to believe the accident was an accident than to admit that my failure to listen to her sent her to her death."

Rain drummed harder, pelting the awkward silence of the cab. Nothing I could say would make him feel better.

"I won't fail her a second time." His guilt-darkened gaze pierced through me. "I need to do this. For my own closure."

The admission of guilt had clearly cost him dearly, and I found I couldn't deny him what I was seeking for myself. "Then work with me, not against me. Without understanding what was going on in Sofia's life a year ago, I can't figure out what happened to her."

Wyatt's jaw tensed so hard that it had to hurt, and his silent treatment was starting to saw at my nerves.

"The night she left," he finally said, "I was busy with a mare who was having a hard time foaling. I could see something was troubling Sofia but I brushed her off. I asked her if it could wait. She said it could. There was time, and she wasn't sure anyway. I kissed her, and she left. Two nights later when the phone rang…"

Oh, Wyatt. Sofia's tears tightened my throat.

"Her death wasn't your fault," I said gently, my fingers tingling with the need to hold him.

"If I'd listened to her, maybe I could've saved her."

Sofia's sobs made it hard for me to focus.

"It wouldn't have made a difference," I said. Whoever had wanted Sofia dead was bent on doing the job right.

He concentrated on the highway as if a blizzard raged outside. "She was a gentle soul. She didn't deserve to be murdered."

"No, she didn't." Between his grief and Sofia's my emotions felt wringer-washer battered. I raked a hand through my hair to ground myself. "Any more thoughts about the data sheet I showed you?"

He shook his head. "Without knowing what she was working on, there's no way to say what the data means."

"Then finding out what she was working on is our first step." I fished a pen and a pad of paper from my tote. "Do you know any of the people she worked with?"

"A couple."

"Can you introduce me?" Introductions usually fared better than cold calls.

"It'll take a few days to arrange," Wyatt said. "I haven't kept up with business associates."

Two days was too long to wait for progress. I was on a tight budget and a tight schedule. I mean, it wasn't like I could bill a ghost. And Van had already left two messages on my phone. I couldn't put him off indefinitely. "Did you clear her office?"

"She worked in a classified area. Someone there handled the task. All her personal effects were given to her mother. There wouldn't be anything work related."

"Her mother? Why didn't you collect Sofia's things?"

"Inez insisted, and it wasn't worth the battle."

That either made him a strong man or a pushover.

He's a good man, Sofia insisted.

I folded the pad of paper to a fresh page. "Maybe

there was a personal computer, an organizer or a diary of some sort."

"Engineers usually use special work journals and those become part of the work files. Property of the company."

"You never know, though. Do you think her mother still has Sofia's things?"

He snorted. "Inez Castille lives for her daughter. If anything, whatever she was given of Sofia's is enshrined."

Now there was dysfunction for you. Refreshing, though, to find out other families were as crazy as mine. "Could we pay Mrs. Castille a visit?"

No! The slide of Sofia's fear slalomed right through me.

Wyatt's jaw worked. "I'm not exactly welcome there."

"Why not?"

He flicked me a strange look. "Inez didn't approve of Sofia's marrying me. She didn't approve of my donating Sofia's organs, even if I was just honoring Sofia's wishes. Sofia'd already signed her donor card. Technically the doctors didn't need my permission."

"I see."

"No, I don't think you have any idea what you're getting into."

"Even if there aren't any work-related materials, maybe there's a personal journal where she wrote her thoughts about what she was feeling about her work. It's worth a shot."

Please, no, Sofia begged, but didn't deny the possibility of finding personal writings.

I could detect no emotion in Wyatt's face, yet his

gaze seemed to penetrate deeply, and I certainly didn't like the piano wire of tension it twisted in me.

"Sofia was murdered." I was losing patience with him. "We have to start somewhere."

"Hang on." An undertone of threat rumbled in his sandy drawl.

He snapped on his signal and took the exit with too much speed, forcing me to hang on to the door handle.

A sense of unease reared up in the pit of my stomach. With each step I took, I was closing another door, miring myself deeper into Sofia's world. And the last thing I wanted to do was get completely lost in a place not mine.

Wyatt whipped over the overpass, down the ramp and onto the highway in the opposite direction. "Don't say I didn't warn you."

Sofia's parents lived in a gated community on the southwest side of Fort Worth. The guard waved Wyatt through. So much for security. The house was an immense mustard-colored brick box with a pair of two-story-tall, white Tuscan columns supporting the narrow porch cover. Someone had sculpted the shrubs hugging the house to perfection. Caladiums and a riot of red impatiens massed the flowerbeds. An S-shaped brick path led up the small incline to the front door still bearing a black wreath.

That couldn't be a good sign. Maybe Wyatt was right and this visit wasn't such a good move.

Leave, Sofia said, her voice so feeble it sounded as if it were coming from the far end of a long tunnel.

Wyatt knocked on the door and waited, his face impassive. "Let me do the talking."

"Maybe she'd respond better to a woman."

"She doesn't respond well to people in general."

I'd play it by ear. If Wyatt wasn't getting me what I needed, I'd jump in.

Inez Castille looked very much like her daughter. She'd swept her black hair into braids and twisted it into an elaborate do. In spite of her death-white skin, her head and neck had a regal bearing. Her eyes were the same deep brown as her daughter's. But the similarities ended there. Though her haunting was disturbing, I thought of Sofia as soft. This woman was hard-edged and sharpened with anger. More than a year after her daughter's death, she still wore a mourning-black dress.

"Inez, could I talk to you for a minute?" Wyatt asked.

Inez stared at her son-in-law with a decided lack of enthusiasm and started to slam the door in his face.

Wyatt reached out and caught the door. "I'll take only a bit of your time."

"You've already taken too much from me." Her voice was both thick and hollow as if she were already halfway dead.

"I just want to look at a few of Sofia's things."

Inez frowned. "Why?"

"To help her."

"Help her! Help her!" Inez screeched, intensifying her Spanish accent. "Where was this helpful attitude thirteen months ago when you allowed those butchers to dissect my daughter?"

"I would rather talk inside." The muscles of his jaw spasmed, but his voice remained gentle and calm. "Please, Inez."

She glanced nervously over Wyatt's shoulder as if she was gauging the neighborhood's reaction to her visitors. After a long moment, she allowed us in, treating me as if I were invisible.

All the window shades were drawn, making the inside of the house dark and depressing. The air was still and lifeless, and I couldn't help reaching for the heaviness in my chest.

Inez picked up a photo of Sofia from a small table in the vast entrance hall. With a shaky breath, she hugged the frame to her breast and looked up at Wyatt, her gaze so icy I shivered. "I have no interest in hearing anything you have to say."

Light flickered from the living room where a television was on. I spotted the outline of a man in a black velveteen recliner. His corpulence had spread and molded to the contours of the chair. Seemingly unaware of the visitors or his wife's distress, he flicked through the channels with such speed, I doubted any of the pictures racing by registered, then he stopped on CNN at what looked like coverage of a plane crash.

"I need to look through Sofia's work things," Wyatt said.

Instantly suspicious, Inez bristled. Stiffly she snapped the frame back on the table and seemed to grow a couple of inches as she assumed battle position. "Why?"

"Because I need to know what she was working on when she died."

"Why?"

Wyatt's fingers twitched at his sides. "Because there's a chance her death wasn't an accident."

"Are you saying my daughter was murdered?" Inez's voice became piercing. "My Sofia?" Her lips trembled. "Who would do such a thing to such a sweet angel?"

"That's what I'm trying to figure out."

"Why now after all this time?" Sharp nails of rage spiked her voice. "Why now when time has finally dulled the edge of pain on my bleeding heart?"

"Because—"

"Of her? You have found a new woman, and you dare invite her into my home. Are you expecting my blessing?" Inez shot me a look of pure hatred. "Who are you to defile my daughter's memory?"

The woman was insane. I could barely hear Inez through the whooshing of blood past my ears. My skin went cold as if someone had shot my whole body with Novocain. "I'm the woman Sofia's gift of a heart gave life to."

Before the sentence was out my mouth, I knew I'd said the wrong thing.

Inez gasped, bringing both her hands to cover her mouth and half sinking to the ground. Her eyes rounded, then narrowed with spuming fire. She rose up again and curled her hands into fists. "You are the one my daughter's body was violated for?"

"Four others got a chance at life because of her generosity." Every cell in my body prickled with static energy, skipping over my skin and leaping through my hair.

"She was carved like an animal, separated from her soul." Inez placed a hand on my chest and crimped my T-shirt in her grasp. For the briefest of moments, I couldn't move.

"No!" Fear, wild and stark, galloped through me. Mine? Sofia's?

Darkness blanked through my mind, and for a moment I thought I'd pass out.

Instinctively I surrounded Inez's fist with both my hands and pushed. But it was as if I were watching the scene from outside myself. I had no strength. Every movement took a massive amount of effort.

"That's enough." Wyatt grasped Inez's wrist, forcing her to release her hold of my T-shirt. "This won't get us anywhere. We're here to help Sofia."

Inez, still blind with fury, continued to spear me with hatred. "Who are you to think you can replace my daughter?"

I blinked, jerking back into myself, and rubbed at the throbbing at my breastbone. What was happening to me? Why were my muscles so weak? Was my heart failing? "I'm not—"

"You are *not* Sofia. I spit on you." Despite Wyatt's interference, Inez's aim was true and spittle landed on my cheek and burned like a brand.

Shocked, all I could do was stare at Inez's face contorted into an ugly mask of rage. A rumble grew inside me like a dormant volcano coming to life.

"That's enough, Inez," Wyatt said.

Inez whirled on him. "And you? Have you no shame? Sofia gave you everything—her soul, her body, her heart—"

"And I gave her everything in return. Is it so hard to believe she loved me?"

"She deserved better."

"And if she was murdered," Wyatt said, "she deserves to have her killer punished."

Inez yanked open the front door and showed us out. "Do not darken my doorstep again. If I so much as smell you in the neighborhood, I will have you arrested."

The door slammed on our backs. I was never so glad to leave any place in my life. Even the hospital seemed like a vacation compared to the preview of hell that was.

In the truck I reached for the antibacterial gel and rubbed it over my face and hands. My heart finally returned to a normal rhythm.

Wyatt's stiff posture telegraphed his anger. I couldn't blame him. I'd put him in this difficult position. He had to feel damned on both ends. "I'm sorry," I said. "I shouldn't have put you through that."

"I tried to warn you."

"You did."

"Inez isn't a pleasant woman."

"I gathered that. How did Sofia feel about her?" Given Sofia's fear, odds were their relationship wasn't exactly Hallmark TV movie material.

For the longest while my only answer was the *flick-flack* of the wipers. "She married me in part to get out of her mother's clutches."

"You're kidding, right?" Was Sofia so weak she'd needed someone to run interference between her and her mother?

His grip tightened on the steering wheel. "Sofia loved me, don't get me wrong. She was a gentle, giving, compassionate woman. But she couldn't handle her mother's volatile moods. Inez is very old-fashioned.

Marriage was the only acceptable way for Sofia to escape home."

Escape? How bad was Sofia's home life?

At the flash of headlights in the rearview mirror, Wyatt swung into the right lane. A deep red Cadillac pulled up next to the truck and slowed. The electric window on the passenger's side slid down. A Hispanic man wearing sunglasses leaned over from the driver's seat and mouthed, "Hey, Wyatt, pull over."

Wyatt grimaced, then nodded. "Reynaldo Castille. He's one of Sofia's cousins." Wyatt drove onto the shoulder and stopped, but didn't turn off the engine or get out of the truck. "Rey's a little twerp with a puny brain and an inflated ego. And he's Inez's lapdog. Don't ask me why. Sofia found him amusing. I think he's a royal pain. If I don't stop, he'll dog us all the way to the ranch. The less we have to do with the Castille clan, the better."

Rey parked ahead of the truck, then sauntered over, pulled off his sunglasses and leaned against the door. The overpowering scent of his sandalwood cologne invaded the truck. Wyatt flicked the air vent to high.

Chewing on a toothpick, Rey nodded at Wyatt and leered at me. I shivered, feeling the need for a soapy shower. Rain washed down his slicked-back hair as if he were a duck. He reminded me of the black racers that slithered through the grass behind my mother's house, and I took an instant dislike to him.

"Have you no manners left, Wyatt?" Rey asked. "Are you not going to introduce me to the beautiful lady at your side?"

"No."

Rey shrugged his indifference. "Inez sent me. She wants to make sure there will be no repeat of today. She doesn't want her daughter's eternal soul disturbed."

"No problem."

Rey splayed his hands up in surrender. "Hey, if Inez thinks your new woman is a problem, man, I gotta believe her. It's much easier to do as she wants than—"

"Don't threaten me."

"It's no threat, my friend. You leave Inez alone or I'll have to take back the last piece of Sofia."

Talk about overreaction. I was beginning to think that the whole Castille clan was running a few quarts low. Because of grief? Or had they always been that way?

The storm outside had nothing on the one raging in Wyatt's eyes. "Inez got everything. There's nothing left. Her daughter wasn't even cold in the grave before she burst into my home and packed all of Sofia's things away. What more does she want?"

"A heart for a heart." Rey looked pointedly at me, dark eyes shining bright. I wanted to scratch them out.

Wyatt's fist wrapped around Rey's shirt and dragged him up until their noses practically touched. The low grit of his voice rolled like the Bullmastiff's growl in the salvage yard. "She has nothing to do with this. Leave her out of Inez's delusions."

"I am sorry you choose to be so difficult." Rey pushed himself off the car door and nodded at me. "*Señorita*, perhaps you could change your boyfriend's mind. He does not realize what a passionate woman Inez is. When she wants something, nothing can hold her back."

"You could," I said. What a piece of slime.

Wyatt shot me a warning look but I ignored him. There were three types of people in this world—nice, difficult and wimps. I had Rey pegged as a wimp who liked to hide behind others, and the only way to deal with a wimp was to strip him of his mask.

Rey shuddered with exaggeration. "I do not want to incur her wrath. My aunt is a very powerful woman."

"Um, does that make you a weak man?" I asked.

Rey's face reddened and his eyes narrowed. He spit out his toothpick. "Sofia was like a sister to me. There's a hole in my heart that's just starting to heal. Leave the dead buried, Wyatt. You've already hurt Inez enough by taking her only child." He glanced at me. "I am sure you have grown attached to Sofia's heart. It would be a shame to have to give it back."

Rey's smile was predatory, as if carving living organs out of bodies was a pleasurable occupation. With a salute, he stalked back to his car and roared off in a spray of water. His juvenile posturing reminded me of high school boys peeling out of parking lots to impress girls. He was a threat I could handle.

Wyatt checked the traffic. "You can't go around questioning a man's *cojones*. Especially not someone like Rey."

"He deserved it."

"You insulted his pride. He won't be able to let that go."

"He's just a bully. More bark than bite."

"For an investigator, you've got lousy instincts." Wyatt jammed the truck into gear. "Rey takes great pleasure in plucking wings off butterflies, kicking dogs and drowning kittens."

A prime example of the milk of human kindness. "So we don't bother Inez. We'll get what we need elsewhere."

"It's not that simple. Not when it comes to Sofia." As he eased onto the highway, Wyatt shook his head. "By insisting we visit Inez, you opened up a giant can of worms that would have been better off left sealed."

"For who? For you?"

He glowered at me as if he wasn't used to being challenged. "For everyone."

"Except Sofia."

An arrow of pain compressed his features. Direct hit into his Achilles' heel. "Except Sofia." The windshield wipers slapped madly at the rain. "And now you."

"You can't really believe he'd take Sofia's—*my* heart out of my chest. That would be murder."

"That would be justice in Inez's mind. If she feels we're desecrating Sofia's memory with our investigation, Rey is crazy enough to stop it."

"Sofia's dead. We can't hurt her. All we'll do is put her killer behind bars. Doesn't Inez want to know who killed her daughter?"

His jaw flinched. "As far as she's concerned, I killed her by taking her away from the great future Inez had mapped out for her. Now that you've told Inez that a part of Sofia lives in you, she won't be able to let it go."

"Inez spat on me. Told me I wasn't Sofia."

"If Inez feels you're a threat to the gift her daughter gave **you**, she'll have Rey take back what she feels belongs to her."

A shiver scraped down my spine, and I splayed my hand protectively over my chest. "The heart belongs to me."

Chapter 6

"**M**a!" Wyatt called to the quiet house when we walked through the massive front door of the Quarter Past Ten ranch house.

He plopped my bag on the entrance hall's green flagstone floor and strode toward the kitchen.

Sofia's awareness was like cotton on my brain. I shook my head to clear my thoughts and nearly bumped into Wyatt as he paused outside the empty kitchen.

"Ma?"

"In here, Wyatt," came the muffled answer from the back of the house.

Wyatt doubled back toward his office. "What are you doing in here?"

"There was a problem with the feed store. No one

knew where you were, so I took care of it." Mrs. James, an apple-green apron tied around her waist over the same dress she'd worn that morning, rose from the massive chair, rounded the desk and batted Wyatt's chest with a file folder. "Close your mouth, son. It's not very becoming. I wish you'd let me take over the accounting. You know I love to do sums."

"It's all done on the computer, Ma." He took the folder his mother handed him and glanced inside.

"How do you think I took care of Mr. Landry's concerns? Fired up that machine of yours and followed the arrows. Any two-year-old could do the same." Pride shone in her eyes and a satisfied smile graced her lips.

"You knew how to turn on the computer?" Wyatt asked.

"Don't look so stunned."

He frowned. "Accounting's a little more complicated than—"

"Don't you dare say 'in your days,'" she warned, shaking a finger at him. "I'll have you know this brainless mother of yours has been treasurer of more clubs than you can count for longer than you've been alive. I have kept up with the times."

He held up his hands in surrender and laughed. "I give."

"You're just like your father." Mrs. James shook her head. "Women are a lot stronger than they look. We are not simple pretties to be put under glass." She turned to me, curiosity barely contained. "I'm sure your guest would agree. Most modern girls have jobs now. What do you do, honey?"

"I'm a private investigator." I bit back my amusement. Seeing six-foot, Mr. Hear-Me-and-Obey, brought down a notch by his five-foot dynamo of a mother was just what I needed to unwind the knot in my chest. In spite of my reservations about being in Sofia's territory, I had to admit, I liked Wyatt's mother. She had an energy my own mother devoted only to her paintings.

"A private investigator!" Mrs. James clapped her hands in delight. "Now that sounds wonderfully challenging."

"Actually, it mostly falls under the hurry-up and wait category. Although, I'm not anchored to a desk, so that's a plus."

Mrs. James tucked her hand under my elbow and guided me out of Wyatt's office. I wasn't surrendering; I was just being polite. "You're staying for dinner, aren't you, uh, what is your name, honey?"

"Sierra Martindale."

"Sierra, how unusual! Call me Lorraine. When Wyatt gets caught up with the horses, he tends to forget his manners. I'll bet you haven't seen hide nor hair of a dining room since your plane landed this morning."

Lorraine slanted her son a disapproving look.

"We've been otherwise engaged," Wyatt said. "Which reminds me, I've invited Sierra to stay with you for a few days."

"I told him I didn't want to impose," I said.

Her eyes shone. "It's most definitely not an imposition. I love company. And Wyatt's friends are always welcome."

Lorraine led me into the kitchen. At the rich scent of simmering stew, my stomach growled.

She smiled widely. "Food first, then we'll see to a room."

She pointed to a solid oak table surrounded by six chairs with sunflowered cushions. "You look like you've had a long day, so we'll keep it casual tonight."

I sat, feeling as if I was caught in some sort of warp. Not time. I knew I was still in the present. But it seemed as if I'd stepped into someone else's skin. Sofia's skin? She'd liked it here. Felt comfortable. But for me, it was something that didn't quite fit, as if the suit was too tight.

The front door burst open. "Hey! Anyone home?" a female voice called.

"Tracy! In the kitchen," Lorraine called, a smile brightening her face. "Set another place for your sister, Wyatt."

Sofia's energy spiked shards of hostility into me. Why didn't she like her sister-in-law?

A tall woman bounded into the kitchen. Her jeans and T-shirt showed off a lanky wiriness brimming with energy. Her sandy hair was cut in a chin-length, carefree but feminine style, and her fresh-faced rosiness didn't require any makeup. As Lorraine squeezed Tracy into a hug, Tracy's green eyes flicked to Wyatt and a serious look passed between them.

"What are you doing home, Tracy?" Lorraine asked. "I thought training went on for another week. You should've called ahead. I could've made those brownies you like."

"And what, ruin the surprise?" Tracy reached to the counter and swiped a chunk of crusty bread from the cutting board. "I'm on a two-day leave, so I thought I'd pop in and snag a homemade meal."

"I'm so glad you're home." When Lorraine hugged her daughter again, a thorn of envy stabbed my heart.

Because my own mother wasn't the hugging, stay-at-home, cookie-baking type? I'd made peace with that years ago.

As Lorraine served heaping bowls of stew, the phone rang. "Get that, Wyatt." She handed a bowl to Tracy. "Tracy, this is Sierra, Wyatt's new friend. She's a private investigator."

"Nice to meet you." Like her mother, her curiosity was open. "So where did you two meet?"

"He's helping me with a case," I said.

Wyatt handed his mother the phone. "That girl Carly from the Boys & Girls Club."

Lorraine took the phone and Tracy plopped at the table next to her brother. She leaned toward him and whispered, "Has Ma seen the news yet?"

Wyatt hiked a brow in question. "No, she's been busy."

"Good. I was afraid she'd freak."

"Freak about what?"

Tracy bit into the bread and chewed. "The crash in New Jersey."

Lorraine dropped the phone back onto its cradle. "Crash? What crash?"

"Everything's fine, Ma," Tracy said, affecting a bored tone.

Wyatt turned on the small television mounted under the counter. He flashed through channels until he landed on a news segment featuring crackling flames, billowing black smoke and the debris of an airplane on what looked like a marina. My stomach turned queasy.

Sofia's agitation beat like frantic wings inside me.

I stared in horror at the TV screen, remembering

that the first time Sofia had told me about a fault there'd been a burning jet glowing behind her. She'd worked for a defense contractor that built avionics and countermeasures for the military. Was that the connection?

Pilots were dying. My pulse thumped with the intuition. Keeping a polite expression plastered on my face for Wyatt and his family took all of my control. Was that how this related to Sofia? One of her company's products?

Sofia's anxious energy twisted inside me, telling me I was on the right track.

A reporter stood at the edge of a field, keeping a Coast Guard cutter framed behind her. "Two Air Force fighter jets collided last night off the coast of New Jersey. The Coast Guard has recovered the bodies of the two pilots." The reporter tipped her microphone toward a uniformed man. "We have with us Major Davis of the Fighter Group at Atlantic City International Airport. Major Davis, can you tell us what happened?"

"Two F-22s collided about sixty miles southeast of Atlantic City over the Atlantic Ocean," Major Davis said. "At this time, it's too early to comment on the cause of the accident."

"Turn that off, Wyatt." Lorraine took a seat and reached for Tracy's hand. "That's not the type of airplane you fly, is it, honey?"

"They're safe, Ma," Tracy assured her. "I knew this would upset you."

Lorraine passed the salad bowl. "I'm not upset."

My fingers itched to check out my hunch that this crash and Sofia's fears were connected.

"You're a pilot?" I asked Tracy. Taking a cue from everyone else, I dug into the hot food.

Tracy nodded, her smile a bright beacon. "Air Force."

"Ma thought Tracy's career choice was a grand adventure until planes started falling out of the sky last week," Wyatt said.

Lorraine's fears would grow exponentially if she knew Sofia's suspicions—that an error was causing these planes to drop out of the sky. "Are the two crashes related?"

"Two different planes, so I don't see how. It's just unfortunate they went down so close together." Tracy turned to her mother. "It's nothing to worry about."

My watch beeped, and Wyatt cocked an eyebrow in question.

"Could I trouble you for a glass of milk?"

Wyatt nodded, and I followed him to the fridge.

At the counter, back to everyone, I palmed a handful of pills I'd retrieved from my tote and swallowed them down with the milk, aware of Wyatt's watchful gaze.

The touch of his fingers was light on my shoulder. "You okay?"

I nodded. "Maintenance."

"Did you let Carly do your hair again?" Tracy teased her mother as Wyatt and I sat down again.

Lorraine patted her curls. "She's getting better, don't you think? Someone has to encourage the poor girl."

Their conversation buzzed around me as I watched the genuine care and concern weave with the laughter. This was the kind of family I'd dreamed of when I was little, eating a peanut-butter-and-jelly sandwich by myself in front of the television.

As much as I'd prefer to work alone, I needed Wyatt. I was caught between the rock of ticking time and the hard place of access he could open because Sofia was his wife. I speared a piece of potato, suddenly aware of a growing hollowness smack in the middle of my body.

I looked up and caught Wyatt staring at me. I wrestled up a small smile. His skin paled beneath his tan. He pushed himself away from the table and said, "I need to go check on the stock."

Something had spooked him, and I had this odd need for him to stay. "Wyatt—"

He cut me off. "We'll talk after you're settled in."

"Soon," I insisted. Now that the crashing jets had given me a potential direction, I wanted to explore it. The faster I solved Sofia's problem, the sooner I could go home.

He nodded and left.

"Your son's very old-fashioned," I said.

Tracy roared. "That's Wyatt, all right. You should've seen the fit he pitched when I signed up for the Air Force."

"He gets that from his father." Lorraine shook her head. "After Waylon—that's my husband—died, Wyatt felt he had to take over the ranch and become the man of the house."

Why didn't that surprise me? "Wyatt was married…"

"Yes, such a tragedy." Lorraine clucked. "Sofia died in a car accident last year. Losing her nearly broke him."

"What was she like, Sofia?"

Sofia drew in a breath, her fear at the answer sliding through my gut.

Lorraine eyed me as if she wondered what my intentions toward her son were. "She was a lovely woman, and she loved Wyatt. Adored him, really."

Sofia's sigh of relief rattled through me.

Tracy stood up and refilled her bowl. "Sofia was a dead weight."

"Tracy!"

"You don't think they were suited?" I asked.

"What Wyatt needed was a Quarter Horse—sturdy, self-reliant, with enough horse sense to set him straight when he got too bossy," Tracy said. "What he got was a colicky thoroughbred. High maintenance, time consuming and clingy. For crying out loud, the woman jumped at her own shadow. And when was the last time you saw Wyatt laugh? I mean *really* laugh."

Sofia growled in outrage.

Lorraine stared at her bowl and finished the last bite of stew. "Don't speak ill of the dead."

"She practically choked the life out of him," Tracy said with no trace of apology.

Lorraine gave a small smile. "Sofia was a lovely woman. It's just that Wyatt had already given up too many dreams for responsibilities that weren't his."

The stab of Sofia's sense of betrayal pierced my chest, and I rubbed at the pain with the heel of my hand.

Tracy slathered butter on a slice of bread. "Sofia was one more albatross he didn't need."

"I wish…" Lorraine shrugged. "His father raised him with a steady diet of tradition and responsibility. And although Wyatt loves horses, he doesn't care much for cows."

"That's because he got gored by a longhorn when he was fifteen," Tracy added with a chuckle. "That's why he's working on that mechanical cow. He wants as little to do with the real thing as he can."

I couldn't help the smile. Wyatt could shoulder responsibility he didn't want, bury his ambition and face a ghost, but he avoided cows. That little quirk somehow made him more endearing.

Lorraine got up to clear the table. "Why does Wyatt need a private investigator?"

"It's more that I need some information from him to close a case."

"Oh." She clearly wanted to ask more.

Tracy skipped right over politeness. "What kind of case?"

I shrugged. "Client-investigator privilege."

"I can't imagine what kind of information Wyatt could have that you'd need. He hasn't done a lick of work he's cared for in three years." Tracy shook her head and took her bowl to the sink.

The force of Sofia's anger snapped the fork out of my hand and it clattered on the tile. *Get out of my body, Sofia. I won't let you use me like that.*

"Dessert anyone?" Lorraine asked, no doubt seeking to put an end to the thick conflict choking the kitchen.

After dinner, Lorraine led me up the stairs to a cozy guest room with dark furniture and light, lacy coverings. I listened halfheartedly to instructions about towels and extra blankets. I thanked Lorraine and closed the door, welcoming the silence and solitude.

My phone rattled in my tote. Van. Again. I sighed.

Better to get this over with. I sat cross-legged on the bed and answered.

"Where the hell are you?" Van barked. I could definitely hear the steam coming out of his ears.

"I'm safe. I'm fine."

"That's not what I asked. You didn't even tell Noelle where you were going. How can I protect you if I don't know where you are?"

Honestly, I hadn't thought anyone would miss me that soon. "I'm working. That's what you wanted. I'm following a lead on a case. I don't need your protection."

"Which case?"

"Van, you're going to have to trust me."

"I'm responsible for—"

"No, I'm an adult now. You have to give me room. You promised me a month. Let me have it."

The silence thrummed with his frustration. "Check in, okay. Not for you. For me."

Cutting the cord was hard. He'd felt responsible for me since our father died when I was twelve. My mother was a decent parent—when she was on planet Earth. Otherwise, chaos reigned around her. Artistic inspiration could strike at any time, spiriting her to her own little world of oils and canvas, stranding me at school or leaving dinner on the stove. "I promise I'll check in every day. Quit worrying, will you?"

"You're a bad habit, Sierra," Van muttered. "How long do you think you'll be gone?"

"A couple of days."

"Do you have enough medicine?"

I couldn't help smiling. "Yes, Van. And I was fed a home-cooked dinner tonight. Beef stew with real vegetables. The way my hostess cooks, I'll probably gain a few pounds."

For once the pause wasn't filled with tension. "It's nice to hear life back in your voice."

I drew in a long breath. "Van?"

"What?"

"Thanks for caring," I said, suddenly feeling maudlin. "If you gave up on me...I wouldn't have a compass."

He cleared his throat. "Yes, well, you make sure you come back in one piece."

We hung up, and I shook away the sticky web of useless sentimentality. What had gotten into me? Maybe Tracy was right. Sofia was too soft, and this close to her essence, her weakness was infecting me.

I fired up my computer, searched for the two aircraft crashes involving military jets, then got down to work. The more I read, the more vital it became for me to find out what Sofia was working on and if her company was involved in these crashes. I wanted to have a solid argument ready before I told Wyatt of my suspicions.

A knock thumped against the door. "Come in."

The door opened, and Wyatt stood there filling the frame like some sort of advertisement for cowboy virility. The diffuse light of the room softened the hard planes of his face. Crazy the way I wanted to run my fingers over his jaw.

I rubbed at my heart that suddenly felt too full.

"I talked to Paul Farr," Wyatt said.

I cleared my throat. "Who's that?"

"Sofia's old boss. He's agreed to meet with me tomorrow after work."

Thursday, April 20

The Watering Hole was a dump. A hitching-post rail separated the dance floor from the rest of the bar. The main floor was crammed with small wooden tables on which a decade of patrons had carved their initials. Peanut shells cracked under cowboy boots, and the air reeked of stale beer and sour sweat.

The bartender's face glowed red and blue from the glare of the neon beer sign behind the horseshoe-shaped bar. Barmaids in black skirts that were too short served drinks to raucous cowboys unwinding from a long day of riding desks at the nearby Allied Defense plant.

The smoky light brought out the green in Wyatt's hazel eyes and gave his sharp face a bad-boy edge that invited bedroom fantasies I had no right to entertain. I forced myself to focus on the crowd, playing Leo's what's-his-story? game.

"Can you drink?" Wyatt perused me in a way that knifed heat to parts that hadn't felt any warmth in a long time. "I mean with the pills and all…"

"I could probably drink you under the table. But since I'm working, I'll stick to soda." Actually, I'd never done much drinking. Adrenaline had been my drug of choice but Wyatt didn't have to know that.

I focused on the task. "Now, remember, take your time. Ease into the subject. Do the good-old-boy network thing, and I'll be the meek arm-candy."

"Meek? You?" Half a smile teased his lips, reviving those improper fantasies.

"What? I can do meek. You just play your part."

"Here he is." Wyatt's body tensed as he spotted our contact entering the bar and raised a hand in welcome.

"Play it cool," I whispered to him.

"As a cucumber."

A twinge of guilt niggled at my conscience. Pretexting came as easily as breathing to me but not to Wyatt. I was asking a man, honest to a fault, to go against his grain. But, for Sofia, he was willing to endure the ill fit. What would it be like to be loved so unconditionally by someone?

Earth to Sierra, pay attention to the situation at hand. No side trips to the moon. Right. The contact.

Paul Farr had a ruddy face. The loose skin of his jowls hung past his jawbone. His dark eyes were mere slits. And his sparse, greasy black hair was neatly spread out over his shiny pate.

"Paul looks fierce," Wyatt said as the man threaded his way to our table, "but he's fair, hardworking and honest."

"Good to know."

Wyatt made introductions. Paul ordered a draft beer, then turned his attention to Wyatt. "So what do you really want, James? It's been three years since you quit your job and not once since then have you invited me for a social drink."

Paul wasn't going to make this easy. I shot Wyatt

a meek smile and nudged his thigh with my knee under the table.

"Something's come up, and it looks like Sofia's death might not have been an accident."

I cringed. Amateur! I'd told him to ease into the conversation, not plow right into it.

"What are you saying?" Paul's eyes widened to shiny black marbles. "Murder? Now, Wyatt, I know how much Sofia meant to you, but you're taking your grief in the wrong direction."

"There's a new report that says the air bag and seat belt were tampered with. Her briefcase was missing."

"Do you realize what you're implying?"

"Yes, I do." Wyatt concentrated on the pale ale in his glass as if it held all the answers. "I want to know what was in her briefcase. What she was working on."

Paul studied me with a bulldog's fascination for a bone. "Who's your friend, again?"

"The private investigator who uncovered the fraud."

Ack, I'd told him not to say that. Now I'd have to salvage the situation.

"Well, it was nice seeing you again, James." Paul scooted back his chair.

Whoa, not so fast. "We still have a few more questions." I flashed him a friendly smile that had hooked more than one slippery fish before.

"Why should I answer them?"

Paul fell into the "difficult" category. People like him wanted to argue every point and always needed to know why. Pushing back wasn't going to help me break down the brick wall. "Because Sofia was one of your employees, and if she was murdered because of what she was working on, that means anyone else who's working on the same project could also be in danger."

Paul grunted as the barmaid served his beer and placed a bowl of peanuts in the middle of the table. "It's been a year. If there was anything to your theory, it'd have shown up by now."

"It is showing up right now," I pointed out. "You must have seen the news about the F-117 and the F-22 crashes."

Wyatt snapped his head in my direction. His dark glower said he wasn't pleased I'd kept my suspicions from him.

Paul's body stilled, alert like a buck caught in crosshairs, not sure exactly what he'd walked into but aware of danger. "The crashes aren't related."

"I think they are," I said. "What was Sofia working on before she died?"

Paul spoke to Wyatt. "I can't talk about what Sofia was working on. It's classified."

"I understand," I said, refusing to be ignored. "But withholding information about a murder makes you an accessory."

That got his attention. He cracked a peanut between his pale, wurstlike fingers. "I probably shouldn't even be seen talking to you. If security found out I was talking to a P.I. I could lose my job."

Paul needed to look at the big picture. "There's evidence that someone rammed Sofia's car off the road and stole data she was carrying. That's not going to look good for you, Paul. Not when the military starts putting the crash pieces together and it all leads back to those missing data sheets. As her boss, you were responsible for the data. Now, if I can find out who took the sheets and what they did with them, that would help you out of your jam."

"How?"

I shrugged one shoulder. "Armed with the information, you'd have time to go back and check if that data is the reason for the crashes and prepare yourself for the investigation."

He squeezed another peanut between his fingers. "I'd like to help, but protocol—"

"That's your choice, of course." I sipped my soda. "You can know exactly where to shore up your defenses and prepare an offense. Or you can scramble and be on the defensive once the blame lands at your feet."

Paul's eyes sparked and his mouth flattened, but he didn't say anything.

"We're not asking for secrets, just a direction," I continued. "That way you can leave the scut work to us, go about your business as usual and still come out looking like a hero for finding what went wrong and who killed Sofia."

"And if there's no relation between Sofia's death and the crashes, I risked my neck for nothing."

"Then you'll know for sure," I countered. "And when the military investigation hits your door, you can close the file with proof before Allied Defense makes the news with negative media suppositions that could hurt the company. Again, you come out the hero."

Paul pointed a thumb at me. "Is she for real?"

"She's for real. And she has a point, Paul. This is win-win."

Never taking his gaze off Wyatt, Paul chomped on a nutmeat. "Sofia was working on the HART. That's all I can say."

"HART?" I asked.

"High Amplification Radar Terminator," Wyatt explained with the quiet authority of someone who belonged in that world. "It's an instrument that allows for complete cloaking. The stealth aircrafts avoid radar detection because of their shape and their material but there's still a weak image left behind. The Russians have managed to build a device that can enhance that faint image. The HART makes the aircraft completely invisible."

"So an error with the HART would affect only the stealth fighters?" I asked.

"I can't confirm or deny that information," Paul said too fast.

"Originally," Wyatt said, "the military had planned to install the HART on the Raptor, the B-2 bomber and the stealth fighter."

Wyatt was proving useful after all.

Paul's jowls flapped as he squirmed in his chair. "I can't talk about where it might be installed."

But Paul's nervous shifting revealed so much more than words. I'd bet what was left in my savings account that the HART was on all three types of aircraft.

"So if the HART was in testing when Sofia was killed," Wyatt said, eagerness spiking his voice. "It would have to undergo qualifications testing, then advanced flight testing. That puts installation right around the time of the first crash."

I cheered silently. Wyatt had worked for Allied Defense. He knew the way they operated. As much as Paul wanted to keep his secrets, he was an open book.

Paul took a long draft of his beer but said nothing— which, of course, told me a world.

"Was she working off the old Trinity program?" Wyatt asked.

"Wyatt…" Paul hedged.

"Okay, okay," Wyatt relented. "Why was she in Nashua?"

Paul crunched on peanuts. "The Integration Lab was running a final test before we shrunk the components down to fit the military specifications. She asked to be invited. Everything went better than expected—"

Wyatt lifted an eyebrow. "She *asked* to be invited?"

"Yeah, there's nothing unusual about that," Paul said.

"We're talking about Sofia," Wyatt said. His voice was calm, but his fingertips were red with pressure against the glass.

Paul's eyes disappeared in the folds of his face. "What are you getting at?"

"To speak up, she must have thought something wasn't right."

Paul downed the rest of his beer and knocked the glass firmly against the table. "Everything passed with extreme confidence."

"Or maybe that's what you were meant to believe."

Paul barked a laugh. "What you're suggesting would

require quite a conspiracy. As much as the government is a pain in the butt to work with, I don't think anyone would resort to killing off a systems engineer to fudge test results. There's too much at stake. And they'd have to kill off too many people to make it work. Including me."

"What specifically was she working on?" I asked.

Paul slanted me a glance as if I were an annoying bug, then turned back to Wyatt. "Integrating circuits that use clockless logic technology with COTS technology."

"Which means?" I asked.

Impatience reddened Paul's face. "The new chip is small—less than two millimeters. The clockless logic allows it to use less power, improves reliability and gives it faster cycling. Integrate that with commercial off-the-shelf technology, and you've got state-of-the-art and affordable avionics. Everybody wins—the Air Force, the suppliers and the public that foots the bill."

"Everybody but Allied Defense," I pointed out.

"We win, too. It's a cooperative effort. No one's losing on this one."

Paul slapped some bills on the table. "Any other details about her job are not in the public domain."

"Thanks, Paul." Wyatt pushed back the bills toward Paul, who ignored them. "You've been a great help."

"Yeah, well, I just hope you're wrong."

"Hey, who took over Sofia's job?" I asked.

"I don't want you talking to my people." Paul hefted his bulk from the chair. "Wish I could say it was a pleasure. Next time, James, try to make your invitation a true social call."

"Will do."

Wyatt stood and shook Paul's hand. "How's Glenda doing these days?"

Paul eyed Wyatt suspiciously. "She just got herself a promotion to manager."

"Avionics Management?"

"Electronic Systems."

"Does that mean you got a promotion, too?" Wyatt asked.

"I'm moving up to the third floor."

"VP?"

Paul beamed and nodded.

"Congratulations," Wyatt said. "Is Glenda still into cutting?"

"She's looking to buy herself a new horse."

"Send her my way, then. I've got a fine crop of prospects. I'll give her a good deal."

The chair scraped against the floor as Paul pushed it in. "Don't even think about asking her any questions. I've already stuck out my neck for you. Don't make me regret it."

After Paul left, I said, "Well, that was interesting."

"Paul was a friend when I worked for Allied Defense," Wyatt said.

"I know. I'm sorry." I twirled my glass on the table. "But whoever killed Sofia had to know her intimately—where she worked, what she worked on, where she'd be. Either they surveilled her until they knew all her habits or they already knew her and made an opportunity. In my experience, the culprit in a business environment is usually internal. We have to list all the possibilities before we can start eliminating."

He slung down what was left of his beer. "So where does that leave us now?"

"We know what she was working on. We have a better idea of the timeline. And if someone killed her to stop her from slowing down the HART project, then we have a why. It all points to business, Wyatt, so that's where we keep digging. We have to find out who took over Sofia's job."

He scrubbed a hand through his hair. "Glenda will know. If she's looking to get back into cutting, she's bound to be at the Classic this weekend."

I wasn't a cruel person. I knew how much all this digging into Sofia's death was costing him. But he'd asked to be involved. And maybe the answers would free him. I wanted to hold his hand, but I couldn't let his problems become mine. And I couldn't afford to get attached to him—especially with all these unwanted feelings Sofia kept throwing at me. So I did what I always did when things got too touchy-feely, I made light of the situation. "Looks like Glenda's about to become my new best friend. And this time, *I'm* asking the questions."

Chapter 7

Friday, April 21

The next afternoon Wyatt and I sped by the bronze statue called *Will Rogers Riding into the Sunset*, standing outside the Will Rogers Memorial Complex in the heart of Fort Worth's Cultural District. We snaked our way through the squirming human mass and the echoing din. The smell of sweat and perfume competed with the pungent scent of arena dirt, horse and cow.

Animals and crowds.

A double whammy for the immune challenged. What was I thinking coming here? My hand dipped inside my tote, feathering the edge of the hospital mask. Not so great for blending in and extracting information.

You took your pills, I reminded myself. *You took your vitamins. You're strong. Just do your job.*

Though Wyatt had a young horse entered in a class later in the afternoon, he trekked with me through the complex, searching for Glenda McCall, his former supervisor and the woman who now managed Sofia's business area. Considering he knew what she looked like and I didn't, I had no choice but to tag along.

"I don't think we're going to find her sitting," I said as Wyatt scoured the arena seating.

"If she's trying to get back into cutting, she's going to want to watch the competition. Especially the young stock, because that's what she's most likely to be able to afford."

He so did not get the way a woman's mind worked. "My point exactly. There's no competition going on right now. Looks like they're setting up for whatever's coming next. If she's here, she's probably in the exhibit hall."

"Glenda's not much into frills and things."

"She's still a woman. She's going to want to check out the merchandise." Even someone like me who shopped mostly from the Lands' End catalog couldn't resist taking a peek at so many vendors crammed into one space.

Wyatt slanted me a doubtful look as he wound his way around the arena boards at a ground-eating pace.

I hitched one shoulder. "You never know when you might find a bargain."

"You might have something there." Wyatt swerved, changing directions.

The Amon G. Carter Exhibits Hall was filled with every imaginable stock-related item from horse trailers to cowboy-decorated night-lights. In the squeeze of people, my throat constricted and my palms grew sweaty.

The mental huff of exasperation gave me the impression Sofia was rolling her eyes. She was right. I wasn't going to die of a germ invasion today. Not that I was going to take her word for it. Delusions by definition weren't trustworthy.

Wyatt came to a halt in the middle of the aisleway. People streamed around us as if we were rocks in a river. "There she is."

In a booth filled with silk shirts, a woman bargained in a strident voice with the owner of the booth. Boy, had Wyatt ever pegged Glenda wrong. The woman dazzled in an expensive way with her custom-made jeans, bronze-sequined shirt and boots with fancy stitching.

Both the pull of friendship and new mistrust seemed to tug at Wyatt as he greeted his old supervisor when we reached the booth. "Glenda."

Glenda whipped around, her face scrunched in annoyance until she recognized Wyatt's solid frame blocking the booth's exit. She crunched him into a bear hug. "Wyatt! It's so nice to see you again."

When Glenda stepped back to admire Wyatt's admittedly fine form, I hooked an arm possessively around his waist. He stiffened at my touch, and a nice shade of red crept up his neck at my boldness but he didn't move away. And just as I'd expected, Glenda's brown eyes warmed with curiosity.

"Hi, I'm Sierra."

"Oh, nice to meet you." She extended a hand, and I had to shake it. I swallowed hard and reminded myself that I had antibacterial gel in my tote. "Glenda McCall. Wyatt used to work for me before going into ranching full-time."

"He's told me you used to ride." I purposefully didn't give her any other information about me.

"Haven't really kept up since my son was born."

"How have you been doing?" Wyatt asked Glenda. The fingers of his right hand rested lightly on my shoulder in a way that warned me not to take my pretext too far. I leaned in closer and regretted it when a sigh of contentment rustled through me and fogged my brain. I shook my head to clear Sofia's sticky gush of emotions.

"Good, good." Glenda's mouth ran through every possible manifestation of a smile before she settled on a teeth-baring number. "And obviously you're doing well, too."

He ignored her sideways poking into his personal life and jabbed her back with an intrusion of his own. "I was talking to Paul yesterday. I hear congratulations are in order."

"Yeah, I finally got the promotion I've been gunning for. They're moving me to the bunker this weekend." She snorted. "Took long enough. Had to bend over backward in ways Paul never did to get to a band-four pay grade."

"Bet Jack's proud of you."

"Somehow I doubt it." Her hand scrunched the shirt she was still holding, wrinkling the jade satin. "He left me last winter. He's been fighting me for custody of Justin ever since."

"I'm real sorry to hear that."

"Yeah, well, I can blame all the overtime." Regret strained Glenda's voice. "Jack said he got tired of eating alone."

Couldn't say I blamed the guy. Eating alone wasn't one of my favorite things. And marriage was supposed to mean you'd have someone to share meals with. Even Van, who worked ungodly hours, still ate a late dinner with his wife every night.

"Paul says you're thinking of getting back into cutting," Wyatt said.

Glenda flicked away a stray wisp of auburn hair. "Yeah, now that I'm single again, I'm considering it."

"If you're serious, give me a holler and come by to check out my new crop of prospects."

"Thanks. I'll do that." She glanced at my arm casually looped around Wyatt's waist, to his fingers brushing my shoulder, then back to his face. "It's good to see you out and about. I was worried about you after Sofia…passed away."

I latched on to the opening I'd been waiting for. "Especially considering he just found out she might have been *murdered*."

"Murdered?" Her gaze hopscotched across Wyatt's face. "What would make you think such a damn fool thing?"

"Some new evidence that came to light when he was settling with the car rental company," I said in my best drama queen voice. *"Her car was run off the road."*

"You're kidding!"

I shook my head and leaned toward her to whisper, "Her job killed her."

"No." Glenda shook her head like a bobblehead doll on a bumpy road. "That's impossible."

I jerked a shoulder. "They say the data she was carrying was stolen."

"That wouldn't make a difference," Glenda pooh-poohed with a sour-grape twist of her mouth. "It would all be transmitted electronically anyway."

"Unless there was a mistake to hide."

Glenda honked out a dry laugh. "Too many checks and balances. That could never happen."

"What Sierra means," Wyatt said, "is that a competitor might have stolen the data Sofia was carrying for their own use. You know how Allied Defense is always a target for spies."

Glenda bit her lower lip in thought. "No, you're wrong on this one. No disrespect meant, Wyatt, but Sofia wasn't important enough to kill."

My well-honed instincts for a lie zeroed in on all the anxiety Glenda's body language shouted—the eyes that flitted away, the shifting weight, the hand that kept trying to cover her mouth.

An icy shudder barreled through me as Sofia realized a close ally might have betrayed her, and Wyatt skewed me a worried look.

I ignored him. "Sofia was still working on a secret project."

"The HART." Wyatt's low-key voice masked the tension stringing his body tight. "That's got to be high on the compromise list."

Glenda threw her chin up and shored up her defenses with crossed arms and hiked shoulders. "But she wasn't high up enough to have enough pieces to put together. Whatever she had would do a spy no good. Not without heftier slices of the pie."

"She was run off the road." I dug my fingers into Wyatt's solid side so I wouldn't slap the snooty bitch. "Deliberately."

Glenda curled her lip. "You know, she had enemies outside of work."

"Sofia?" Wyatt shook his head. "Everybody liked her."

Nose in the air, Glenda plowed on. "Not long before she died, she was telling me about the trouble she was having with one of the families she tutored."

"Who?" Wyatt asked, a touch of outrage sharpening his tone.

"I don't know their name." She heaved an impatient sigh and fluttered her hand. "It's one of the Mexican families she was teaching English to. Her father'd helped them relocate up north. Their teenage daughter wasn't happy about being uprooted from her friends and committed suicide. Sofia told me the girl's father blamed her."

Sofia's tantrum broke and a roar filled my head. *No!*

"How could that be her fault?" Wyatt's growing irritation had him tightening his hold on my shoulder.

"Well," Glenda huffed, "considering how your mother-in-law reacted to Sofia's death, I'd think you'd know all about misplaced blame."

That was a low blow.

"Did Sofia say she felt in danger?" I asked.

"She said she was scared of the father."

Wyatt's expression hardened. "She never said anything to me."

A wave of sadness rolled through me. My hand reached for my chest at the quick-changing swing of Sofia's emotions that were starting to feel like a runaway amusement park ride. This couldn't be good for my heart.

"Of *course* she didn't tell you," Glenda said. "She knew you'd worry too much."

The pinch of guilt heightened the fine lines around Wyatt's eyes. He nodded distractedly, then glanced at his watch. "The three-year-old class is up soon. I've got to go get ready. It was nice seeing you again, Glenda. I was serious about looking over stock."

Relief sagged Glenda's shoulders now that the fire was turned down from under the frying pan of tough questions. "I'll do that."

"Why don't you join me, Glenda?" I still needed to find out who had taken Sofia's place, and I couldn't let Wyatt chase her off just because he was uncomfortable with the scum she was stirring up. "I've never been to a cutting competition before. I could use a guide."

"Sure, I'd, uh, love to." Glenda dropped the shirt she was holding on the table, and it promptly slid to the floor. "Wyatt, I've been hearing some good things about the way this young mare of yours is working."

"We'll find out before the afternoon's out." Wyatt strode toward the exhibit hall exit.

I didn't let go of his waist until the pull of the crowd forced me to—mostly because I wanted Glenda to believe Wyatt's and my relationship was more intimate than it was.

Once we got to the stable area, Wyatt stopped. His

worried glance told me he didn't want me where germs teemed. Though I was more than happy to oblige him, I wished I hadn't told him about my fear. I didn't need him going all protective on me.

"I'll see you after the class," he said.

I leaned into him as if I were going to kiss him. A shudder rippled through his hard chest, momentarily distracting me with a strong need to taste him.

"Glenda's hiding something," I whispered into his ear as Glenda gave us space to smooch. Doing it for real was tempting.

"Glenda's solid stock," Wyatt whispered back, tickling my ear. "She's had to work hard to get where she is and get past the old-boys' network."

"She's wound up tight."

"She's going through a divorce."

"What she said about Sofia's volunteer work is a lie."

"Just how would you know?"

The stir of Sofia's anger still roiled in my gut. "Doesn't matter. I'll bet if we check it out, there's going to be nothing to the story."

"Then we'll check it out." His fingers rounded against both my shoulders and he pushed me away. "Can you stay out of trouble for an hour?"

I scoffed at his arrogance. Something both visceral and contrary flashed through me, and before I could stop myself, I nipped his earlobe with my teeth. "You betcha, cowboy."

Rubbing his ear, he mumbled a curse, then shook his head as he stalked toward the stall area. I chuckled.

Turning toward Glenda, I pinned on a goofy smile, pouring on the ditzy-blond act with a hair flip and giggle, though I was neither ditzy nor blond. "I can't wait to see Wyatt ride. He looks so hot on a horse."

Glenda raised an eyebrow and slanted me a questioning smirk.

Wyatt's class was due to start in about thirty minutes. Glenda led me to a spot by the boards where we watched the action on both sides of the split arena. I kept her talking about surface things and waited for her guard to slip.

"There he is!" I twisted my face into a dopey, lovestruck expression, which came surprisingly easy looking at Wyatt. I jumped up on my toes and waved at him on a pretty copper mare with a bold white blaze down her face. His slow smile gave my heart an unexpected lurch. He knew this was a pretext, didn't he? Of course. I'd shown him that while I was hanging all over him for Glenda's benefit. He was just being a good sport.

Wyatt walked the mare inside the warmup ring at one end of the arena. He did look hot astride a horse. The long legs wrapped around the horse's barrel, the flex of his thighs under the leather chaps, the promise of power waiting to fly free cranked up my temperature.

Sofia's desire-heated voice whispered across my brain. *Foreplay.*

Yeah, I was attracted. I hadn't felt anything like this for a man since Leo—even if it was all Sofia's memories. But doing anything about it would be plain stupid, and I prided myself on being smarter than I looked. Besides, Wyatt really wasn't my type. Too uptight. Too controlled.

Glenda pointed to the milling cattle at one end of the

ring. Two riders were settling them. "The cows are all yearling heifers. They're chosen for their uniformity of weight and size."

"To keep the competition fair?"

Glenda nodded. "Right. The first eleven cutters are going to work this herd, then a fresh bunch is going to be brought in for the last twelve cutters." Glenda jerked her chin at the five tables set up between the show ring and the warmup ring. "The judges sit over there. They can't see each other or the scoreboard. The highest and lowest scores get thrown out and the middle three are added together."

"I'm surprised at the number of people cramming the stands." The whole competition sounded kind of boring to me.

Glenda tipped back her head and laughed. "People get hooked on this. You'll see. It's exhilarating to watch. Even more fun to do."

Soon the first rider was allowed in the ring. Two herd holders kept the cows from moving up the fence. Two other riders were positioned behind the cutter to keep the cow being worked from running off to the far end.

"He's going to have two and a half minutes to work," Glenda explained. "He might get to cut two or three cows."

"In two and a half minutes? That doesn't seem like enough time to even get to one."

"A cutter's happy if he can work a cow for thirty seconds."

This sounded more boring by the second. I needed

to bring the conversation back to Sofia and the HART. "So you worked with both Sofia and Wyatt?"

"Good people, both of them."

"Must be hard to replace good workers like that?"

"When it comes to work ethics, yes, but the job itself, anybody trained in their field can do. Programming takes some imagination, but engineering is pretty straightforward."

"Who's taking over Sofia's job?"

Glenda shushed me. "The competition's starting."

Well, shoot. Now I'd have to wait for the next lull to get my answer.

The rider entered the herd and separated one cow from the others. He dropped his rein hand to the horse's neck, signaling for time to start. The horse hunkered down and a charge of electricity zapped through the whole arena. The horse ran, stopped on a dime, reversed directions at a dizzying pace, drawing screams, shouts and whistles from the crowd. I got caught up in the excitement of the surprisingly quick action. The rider's second hand touched the rein.

"Oh," Glenda roared. "He's going to lose three points for that touch."

The buzzer sounded and the crowd applauded.

Halfway through the first group of cutters, Wyatt entered the arena riding Tara Ten Tall, when something—or someone—caught Glenda's attention. Her smile slid like a Popsicle in hot sun. I scoured the crowd but couldn't see what had spooked her. Her mouth recovered fast enough, but her eyes remained clouded. "I've got to run to the ladies' room. Be back in a flash."

Oh, yeah, there was definitely something going on with Glenda. Not that I could prove anything right now. Hunches just gave direction. I'd follow her and see where it led.

I let her slip into the crowd, and in spite of her sequined shirt, I almost lost her. Then she lurched sideways and disappeared.

Some quick maneuvering through the thick crowd brought me close to the spot where Glenda had disappeared. I soon realized someone, hiding behind one of the concrete pillars in the hallway, had yanked her out of the stream of people. I couldn't see who was there, but the hand crimped like a manacle around Glenda's shirtsleeve was definitely male. Using a nearby pillar to hide, I edged my way closer until I could hear their exchange.

"I told you never to contact me in public." Glenda gritted her teeth, and her eyes darted about like a trapped sewer rat.

"You aren't meetin' your end of the bargain, darlin'." The voice was deep, masculine and condescending.

Glenda tugged her shirtsleeve free and crossed her arms beneath her chest. "What do you want?"

"Have you seen the headlines?" Gingerly the man crooked up the corner of the paper he was holding and read. "'Air Force Jet Lost over Persian Gulf.'" He jettisoned the paper, and it scattered over the floor where passersby trampled it.

Another death.

"So?" Glenda's fear peeled off her, raw and open.

"It's the fourth jet in just over a week."

My spine tingled with that Novocain feeling again. *Stay out of me, Sofia. Let me do my job.* I shrugged her out but still went cold. Cold enough to see my next breath frost the air. Cold enough for my scalp to crawl. Glenda knew. She knew about the fault that was making the airplanes crash.

Glenda paced in a tight, dog-on-a-leash half circle. "Have they detected a common thread?"

The man stepped forward to get into Glenda's face, but his black cowboy hat shaded his face. With a hand around the collar of her fancy shirt, he stopped her agitated pacing.

"We're talkin' about the government here." He guffawed. "They couldn't find their own asses with a road map. It'll take them years. By that time, the blame will point to them. And you can be sure they'll keep that particular fact nice and quiet. All you have to do is keep up your end of the bargain to make that happen."

"But—"

"I don't think I'm makin' myself clear here. Take care of the details you were hired to deal with, or I'll make sure you lose what's most precious to you. Do you understand?"

Rey had used those same words with Wyatt. Was there a connection?

Glenda swallowed hard. "Yes, I do."

He let go of her collar. She backed up in a careful motion and rubbed the skin of her neck.

Could Glenda have sacrificed Sofia for whatever she was trying to save?

"You're scared," the man said. "And scared people make stupid mistakes."

"I've got everything under control," Glenda assured him.

"See that you do."

"The pilot?" she asked, her voice clipped and precise. She didn't sound worried so much about the pilot's health as to how his status would affect hers.

"Dead."

"Natural causes?"

Interesting question. To ask it, she had to know the man was capable of killing. Someone that cold would think nothing of using Sofia as a pawn or a convenient fall guy.

"Let's just say you didn't have to break one of them fancy nails of yours on this one." He shook his head in disgust. "I don't know why you were trusted in the first place. When push comes to shove, women just don't have the balls for business."

Glenda shot him a look of hatred, pure and undiluted. He laughed uproariously. "Loosen up, darlin', or you'll pop a spring."

Nose high in the air, Glenda pivoted on her fancy boot heel and clipped her way toward the ladies' room. He fell in behind her, giving me a clear view of his broad back. He caught Glenda's elbow and spun her around. I slunk to the next column for a better look. If I moved closer, they'd see me but this far I could barely hear their exchange above the rumble of voices.

"Remember, I can't afford any popped springs," the man said.

As his meaning hung in the air, Glenda wrenched her arm free. "You can't afford to kill me off right now, either."

"No one's indispensable."

Glenda's throat worked. "Someone's asking questions about Sofia James."

Now she was willing to use Wyatt and me to get herself out of a tight spot.

"Who's askin' questions?" the man asked, but he didn't seem surprised. Did that mean that Wyatt and I were under surveillance? By whom?

"Her husband and some woman," Glenda said.

"Toss 'em some tainted crumbs."

"Like what?"

"Use your imagination, darlin'. That's what got you in this mess in the first place."

What had Glenda done that someone could blackmail her into betraying a friend, her employer and possibly her country?

A strong stink behind me made my nose itch. Recognition of its owner hit me a second before Rey tapped me on the shoulder. Shoot. I should've paid more attention to what was going on around me. Multitasking was a basic P.I. skill.

Rey! Sofia went positively giddy.

"Hey, pretty lady." Rey's snake charmer's smile dazzled. "Where is your lover?"

My gut tightened at the thought of Wyatt as a lover. But I didn't bother to dignify Rey's taunt with an answer. That would only have fed his wimp ego. When I glanced in Glenda's direction, she was plowing through the bathroom door, and her tormentor was striding toward the exit.

"Hey, yourself." I shifted to widen the space between Inez's lapdog and me. "You don't look like the rodeo type."

His smile widened, showing off orthodontic-perfect teeth and a well-chewed toothpick. "I am a man of many talents."

I'd just bet. The breadth of those talents probably came printed on a rap sheet. "Are you checking up on Wyatt?"

Rey splayed a hand over his bony chest. "I have Wyatt's and your best interests at heart."

"Yeah, I'm sure."

"All is not as it seems."

"Why don't you enlighten me, then?"

He tipped his head. "There are forces in motion to right wrongs."

"Such as?"

"I am not at liberty to reveal."

"Then how can I believe anything you say? After all, you like to hang out with fifty-something women instead of girls your own age."

"Ah, your eyes trick you." Surreptitiously, he flashed a knife at me. "Walk with me."

Rey? Sofia startled and her frown bit into my forehead.

For a second my breath stuck in my throat. The lapdog had some teeth after all. That was the problem with wimps. They had the courtesy patter down but they'd stab you in the back every time. Basic rule of survival dictated that one never leave the protection of a crowd. Once the thug had you alone, you were as good as dead.

I held my ground in the crowd buzzing around us. "Here's fine."

"There are too many ears."

I narrowed my gaze at him. His dark hair, eyes and black pants and shirt gave him a demonic look he no doubt cultivated for intimidation purposes. But I wasn't falling for it. Deep inside, wimps were, well, wimps, and their revenge came at the hands of others. "Just what is it you have at stake in Sofia's death? Or at least in it staying uninvestigated?"

He shook a finger at me. "I was right. You are the instigator of all this trouble." He poked the tip of the knife into my side. "Walk with me. You will get some answers."

I snorted. "You're not going to stab me in the middle of a crowd. Too messy. Tell me what you really want."

His smile blinded as the tip of his knife pierced the first layer of skin under my last rib. "I want you to go back to your home but I have a feeling that is not going to happen. So I have a proposition for you—for our mutual benefit."

My radar of suspicion went haywire. Wimps didn't care about mutual benefit. If we were going to talk, we'd do it on my terms. I twisted my torso out of the line of the knife. At the same time I shoved Rey's knife hand away from me. I grabbed his wrist and wrenched it until he had no choice but to let go. Then I quickly dropped the weapon into my tote before anyone could wonder what they might have seen.

"Okay, let's walk." I led him toward the exit.

We strode outside and sat on a bench near the *Midnight, the Outlaw* bronze. The strong sun beat on our backs. The foot traffic milling in and out of the building still gave me witnesses should he try something else. But if he had an accomplice perched somewhere, we made open targets.

Rey spit out his toothpick. "I allowed you to take my weapon only because I did not want to create a scene."

"Sure, Rey, whatever you say. What did you mean by 'forces are in motion to right wrongs'? Who do you work for?"

Rey's face turned serious. "Sofia's death was a tragedy. But it is merely a cog in a bigger concern. For her death to mean anything, the greater good must be served."

"You're really good at spewing out a lot of words that don't mean much."

His dark eyes burned hot with temper. "Your investigation is interfering."

"With what?"

"Something bigger."

"Spell it out, Rey."

He shook his head. "I cannot."

I threw up my hands. "Then I can't stop looking, either."

"You are making life difficult not only for yourself but for Wyatt, also."

There he went with the subtle threats again. "Just what is Inez involved with?"

"Inez?" Faint lines of confusion wrinkled his brow. "She is simply a grieving mother."

Was his concern for Inez based on guilt? "Did you kill Sofia?"

He shook his head, and sadness flitted across his eyes. "No, she was like a sister to me. I could never harm her."

So he said. But how often did people tell the truth? In my business, not often. "Yet you threatened to cut her heart out of my chest."

He shrugged. "I needed to make a point with you and Wyatt. Keep your nose out of Sofia's business and there will be no need for me to hurt you."

I slapped my thighs and made as if I were leaving. "Well, I'll gladly stop investigating if you give me a good reason. So far all I've heard is a lot of hot air."

"I am trying to help you."

I shook my head. "Frankly, I'm not seeing a whole hell of a lot of help."

His nostrils flared. "Tell me what you know."

"What do I get in return? You promised me a 'mutually beneficial proposition.'"

His dark eyes studied me with a note of pity. "You get to live."

"Okay, well, in that case." I stood up. "I'm so glad we had this little chat. It cleared up the whole situation for me."

His hand snaked out and trapped my wrist hard enough to cut circulation. Surprising strength for someone so wiry. "We are not finished."

"Wyatt's class is going to be over soon. If your goal for this conversation was to warn me, then I got the message." With a twist of my arm, I freed my wrist.

He fisted his hands. "Tell me what you know."

Hands on hips, I gave Rey the Cliff's Notes version. A gamble, I know, but maybe he'd give something away. "Sofia was killed in a deliberate hit-and-run accident. The data she was carrying was stolen. Now pilots are dying."

He looked up at me. "Yes, and to find the truth, the people responsible for those deaths must be made to feel they are getting away with murder."

"What people?"

He took a deep breath. "People even more danger-ous than me. People with no scruples at all. If they get wind of your investigation, they will not warn you. You can ease your conscience by knowing that when the right time comes they will pay for what they have done."

"Are you saying you're law enforcement?" I asked, a sudden lightbulb going off in my head. That would certainly skew everything. And I'd be happy enough to let all this go.

No! Sofia's fear landed like a medicine ball in my stomach.

She wasn't being reasonable, but I had no control over the situation. I could leave. I could go back home, but Sofia would keep torturing me.

Rey flashed his white teeth. "I am saying that I cannot allow you to panic the people responsible for Sofia's death. You have my word that her death will have meaning."

I didn't trust him. He was too oily, too cagey. "I'm not sure your word counts for much."

"All you will do is stir the pot."

I shrugged, but I was starting to feel in way over my head, "Maybe the pot needs stirring."

Rey got up and his duck-slick hair glinted in the sunlight. "The decision, of course, is yours. I had hoped you would see reason for the sake of Sofia's heart beating in your chest. But I see I was wrong." His dark eyes narrowed. "Next time we meet, I may not be able to protect you."

Chapter 8

Saturday, April 22

At breakfast Wyatt informed me he had business to
deal with. Which was just as well because I was sure
he wouldn't approve of the way I planned to spend my
day. I hadn't learned much more from Glenda or from
my late-night online exploring of Allied Defense's Web
site. Social engineering would mean another two-day
delay. With Van on my case and my funds running low,
that really wasn't an option. If I was going to get
anywhere, I needed solid information. The kind that I'd
get only by eyeballing where Sofia had worked.

"Don't worry about me." I slanted Wyatt my most
innocent look. "I have plenty to keep me busy."

His gaze contracted to laser intensity. "Whatever you do, stay out of trouble."

I raised my glass of orange juice at him. "But of course."

I let Lorraine stuff me with an omelet oozing with vegetables and cheese, then excused myself.

Lorraine is going to worry. The thought crossed my mind as I slid behind the wheel of my rental. *So is Wyatt once she tells him I'm gone.*

But that couldn't be helped if I was to solve Sofia's problem. I pointed the car east on the highway.

Armed with a map, a large bottle of water and some snacks from a Mobil station outside of White Settlement, I hopped onto the loop that would take me around the Allied Defense plant. The terrain was flat. The trees were sparse. That gave me a clear view of the plant and its sprawl of sand-colored buildings.

At the first exit past the plant, I circled around and drove by for another pass. Then I wound my way through side roads for a closer look. The east-side front gate was closed and manned by armed guards. So was the south-side entrance. I'd need a badge or an official invitation to get through either. Some sort of military reserve base lined the whole north side of the plant. Depending on how solidly it was guarded, getting through that way was a possibility. But as I explored the west side, I came upon a city park that bordered the plant on its northwest corner for a few hundred yards.

My arms got scratched from the thick choke of mesquites, and I didn't even want to think about what kind of creepy crawly things my hiking boots squished or how many germs the dirt sticking to my skin carried. I made my way to the edge of the woods and found a clear view and an easy way into the site. Sort of. I didn't know if the plant had always had a busy network of patrols or if they were added after the 9/11 frenzy, but sneaking past them was going to be tough.

Sofia hovered around me like an annoying mosquito, and I really wanted to swat her.

"How about a little help here, Sofia? The patrols, what do you know about them?"

Sofia shrugged.

Great. "Okay, walk me through this. Where did you work?"

Building 100.

"Which one is that?" I peered at the plant through the pair of miniature binoculars hanging from my neck.

On the other side of the assembly building.

"Okay, hang on." I fought my way back out of the woods to my car and drove around to the parking lot of the bar outside the plant entrance where we'd met Paul on Thursday. In the lot, I arranged the map around me to play the lost tourist in case someone wondered why I was parked there for so long.

"Which floor?" I asked Sofia, raising the miniature binoculars to my eyes and focusing on the building with the flower boxes out front.

Basement bunker.

"Basement as in an underground location?"

A psychic nod.

"I thought you couldn't build basements in Texas because of the soil."

Expensive but not impossible.

I groaned. Getting to Building 100 from the city park would mean going by a row of outer maintenance buildings and coming all the way around the mile-long assembly building to midway around the other side. Cutting across the base would be much shorter.

"How busy is the base?"

A frizzle of confusion.

"How well is it guarded?" I scanned the base but couldn't see any outward activity. Which didn't mean it wasn't guarded.

A growl of frustration.

"Did you notice *anything* while you worked here?"

A haughty huff.

Just what I needed—a ghost with an attitude.

I ignored her pressure to call Wyatt. I didn't need any more complications. "Are there exits that lead directly out of the building from the bunker?"

Stairs or the elevator.

"Windows?"

The building is spy-proof.

"I don't suppose you noticed security cameras."

Sofia sniffed.

This wasn't looking good. "Where's the Human Resources building?"

Same building. First floor.

That might be doable. *If* I could get into the building. I hadn't learned the name of Sofia's replacement from Glenda, and the organization chart on the Web site left much to be desired. Probably on purpose.

"If you could walk into that building and into your

work area," I asked, "what would you need to check your numbers?"

My engineering journals.

"Where would I find them?"

In the project drawer.

A black pickup truck barreled into the bar's parking lot, and the driver stared me down as if I were a would-be burglar.

I went back to looking confusedly at the map and forced a flinch when the driver knocked at my window. I rolled it down a couple of inches.

"Can I help ya?" His breath smelled of coffee, and crumbs from his lunch speckled his dark brown mustache.

"I think I'm lost," I said with bubblehead breathiness and a Boston accent.

"Where you looking to get ta?"

"The Stockyards." Pronounced with the required dropping of the *R*.

"You're not as lost as you think." He gestured with his hands as he pointed out his directions. "Get back on 183 going north. Up the road a spell, you'll see signs."

I beamed him my best smile. "Thanks."

I fired the engine and took his advice, then turned around on the Jacksboro Highway to get back to the plant. I spent the rest of the day getting a handle on the security patrols. Unfortunately, the park still looked like my best entry point.

Just as I was despairing about getting into Sofia's work area, I saw my chance. There was no time to lose, so I found a phone book and went shopping.

Sofia's energy percolated around me like coffee in my grandfather's old stove pot.

"Do you have a better idea?" I said out loud and got a strange look from a fellow shopper at Target, my last stop.

Sofia's sigh was filled with confusion.

Preparations done, I found a small restaurant a short drive from the park and ordered a bite to eat.

With the tinny plink of a Mexican tune playing in the background and grease and cumin scenting the air, I checked in with Van. I didn't want to risk him calling me at an inopportune time. Before I even got "hello" out, he lit into me. "You've been gone four days, Sierra. Where are you?"

"It's better if you don't know." Especially considering what I was planning to do.

"How can it be better for me when I'm worrying myself sick? I'm going prematurely gray over here."

"That'll make you look distinguished. A plus for a lawyer, I hear."

He grumbled. "That's not funny. How long is your couple of days going to stretch?"

I hated lying to him but I really didn't know. "A couple more."

"You are going to be the death of me."

"I hope not. Listen, I have to go. I just wanted to check in like I promised."

Knowing that if he pushed too much, I'd conveniently forget my promise, he relented a bit. "Do you have enough medicine to last you through?"

"I have enough for a couple more weeks." I swirled

the straw in my glass of water. "I'll be home before then." I hope.

"Sierra." Van stretched my name out on a resigned sigh. "Take care of yourself."

"You, too, Van."

My next call was even harder to make. Knowing I'd be out late, I didn't want Wyatt to worry and put out an APB on me, so I felt obliged to check in at the ranch, too. Which was starting to give me a handcuffed sensation—not good for an independent woman.

Just like Van, Wyatt's bark bit me before I could say anything. "Where the hell are you?"

"Not that it's any of your business, but some place called Casa Angelita. The chips are a little too salty but the salsa's nice and hot."

Wyatt swore, which took me a little by surprise. I didn't think he had it in him to throw words like that around. "I told you to stay out of trouble. That place is a drug den."

My gaze circled the cheerful red-covered tables filled with parents and kids. Of course, there was the sniffling skinny guy wriggling by the hostess stand as if he had fleas in his big brother's pants. "It's a family place."

"With a little extra takeout on the side."

"That's okay, I brought my own."

He wasn't amused. "I'll be there in fifteen minutes."

"Wyatt, no—"

But he'd already hung up. So much for trying to be nice. I could leave and keep him guessing, but I was afraid he'd make more trouble looking for me than if I just waited for him. I flagged the waiter and had him set another place and double my order of burritos. By the time Wyatt stormed into the cantina, the burritos were landing on the table.

"Just what are you up to?" he asked, his mouth tight. He ignored the food.

I gave him a short synopsis of my day and my plan to visit Sofia's work area.

"That's breaking and entering," he said in a low, harsh voice. "Do you know the kind of trouble you could get into if you got caught?"

I shrugged. "I'll just have to make sure I don't get caught."

He thumped a finger on the tabletop, making the salsa bowl jump. "You could go to prison."

"It's a risk I'm willing to take."

"There are guards with guns running around there." A blue-norther had nothing on Wyatt's voice when it came to ice. "They'll shoot first and ask questions later. The risk is too great."

He couldn't seem to remember that I hadn't asked for this case but had been drafted into it against my will by a damn ghost.

"I'm not planning on dying tonight." I attacked my dinner as if I, indeed, needed sustenance for the long run. "You should eat up before the food gets cold."

Something in his eyes flared. "Is this how you run your business?"

I sawed another bite off my burrito with the side of my fork. I wasn't going to let him get to me. "I'm always aware of the legal ramifications of my actions,"

I said, voice even. "I work mostly for lawyers and insurance companies. So I have to. But this is different."

"I don't see how. If you mess up, Sofia's killer could go free, and you'll end up behind bars. Somehow I doubt industrial spying comes with a slap on the wrist."

I threw my fork at the plate. So much for keeping cool. "It's a matter of life and death. Pilots are dying, Wyatt."

"I get that, and I'm all for—"

"And if Sofia is right and there's an error with the HART, then they're being used as pawns in a game of national security proportion."

"Now you're just being plain dramatic," Wyatt said.

Lucky for him we were in public and slugging him would bring me more attention than I wanted at the moment. "Don't you want to know what's wrong with the airplane your sister straps on for a living? Don't you want to stop them from dropping out of the sky? Isn't Tracy worth the risk?"

Sofia gasped.

Wyatt's jaw flinched. "Don't play the guilt card on me."

Low blow, I know, because his shoulders were already stooped with the weight of all the guilt he'd taken on.

"The error Sofia died for is somewhere in that plant," I said. "Getting to it is the only way we're going to get to the truth. No one's going to invite us in there. No one's going to hand it to us." I pointed in the direction of the plant. "Someone there has too much to lose if we uncover the truth."

Wyatt pinched his temples with one hand as if he had a major headache coming on. "Okay, let's say for the sake of argument that we do this. The place is huge. There's no way we could get to the information we need without attracting attention."

There wasn't going to be a "we" but he didn't need to know that yet.

"There's a big move happening tonight," I said. "And that makes it the perfect time to sneak in unnoticed. The movers are on a dinner break right now."

"How do you know they haven't quit for the day?"

"Because of the stacked cube-farm parts waiting outside the building. They all have to be up and filled before folks show up for work on Monday."

Wyatt turned a knife over and over on the plastic tablecloth. "How are we going to know what to find and where to find it?"

I took a long drink of water. "I have Sofia."

His whole body jolted as if I'd shot him. "Sofia is dead." And so was his voice.

"Yes, she is."

He stared at me long and hard.

"I know you loved Sofia, Wyatt. But I need her to stop haunting me. I want her voice out of my head, her fears out of my bones, her face out of my dreams. Finding her answer is the only way I can do that. Can you understand that?"

Giving him a chance to collect himself, I forced another bite of food onto my fork. "I have a plan."

Wyatt shook his head. "I don't want to hear this."

"That's fine by me."

He swore under his breath. "You're more trouble than a green horse." Growling, he jabbed his elbows on the table and rubbed his eyes. "Give it to me."

So I did. Unedited.

The dark erased the warts that daylight accentuated. Even bathed in security lights, the whole plant took on a softer look, a deceptive tranquility. The breeze whispering through the trees in the park behind us provided a soothing background symphony in complete opposition to the tension coiling neat rows of knots into my muscles.

In the privacy of the dark, as we lay on our bellies silently watching the static scene in front of us, the smell of the loamy earth only inches from my nose had my skin crawling with the imagined germs invading my bloodstream.

Block it out, Sierra. Mind over matter.

I wasn't sure which was worse, my obsession with the dirt seeping into my pores or how highly aware I was of Wyatt beside me. The warmth of his body. The steady rhythm of his breath. That wasn't helping the tension.

But mixing pleasure with business was always wrong.

Sofia lay down beside me, sandwiching me between her and Wyatt. His side was broiling hot; hers freezing cold.

"Once the next security Jeep goes by, I'll have fourteen minutes to reach my first aim point," I said.

Wyatt braced binoculars to his eyes. "I'm not liking this."

"Tough."

The Jeep puttered by on the narrow ribbon of road that hemmed the plant and disappeared around the assembly building. I rose to my feet and hiked the backpack to my shoulders.

Deep lines sculpted Wyatt's face as he watched me prepare. "It doesn't feel right, you going and me staying here."

I didn't have time to smooth ruffled male-ego feathers. The window of opportunity was small and it wouldn't open this easily again.

"I've got it covered. Besides the uniform I got is too small for you." I'd made a concession to his desire to help by having him stop at a Radio Shack and buy a communications system for us. I inserted the earpiece and twisted the wire-thin mic in front of my mouth. "Testing, testing. One, two, three."

"Coming in loud and clear." Brisk disapproval guttered through his voice.

"Look," I said, "the best way you can help me is keep an eye on the patrols and give me a heads-up if I'm cutting it too close. It's harder to hide two people than one."

"You're a woman. You're going to stick out."

"Times have changed. Even in Texas. And social engineering is what I do for a living."

Without giving him a chance to argue further, I scanned my intended path. Starting slow, I took off trotting for the maintenance shed, my first goal. Hugging the meager shadows along the side of the building, I caught my breath and took a survey of the area around my next goal—the assembly building.

"I'm at the shed," I whispered.

"Got you in my sights." A heartbeat thrummed. "Coast looks clear."

Keeping as low a profile as I could, I made my way to the assembly building. When the guards at the rolling doors had their backs turned for a cigarette break, I took a chance. My heart hammered hard until I made it safely to the other side.

"I can't see you anymore," Wyatt said.

"I'm on schedule."

I blended with the shadows of the building until I reached the staging area for the cube-farm wall sections.

"I'm going in now, Wyatt. I'm going to have to hide the earpiece till I get inside."

"I hate this."

"I know." He was used to taking on the protector role. That was a habit he was going to have to break. "I can take care of myself."

I stowed my backpack behind a trash barrel.

My opportunity to flow into the work pace came up a few minutes later. As if I belonged, I reached for one end of a panel a mover with a compact body was struggling to heft. "Here, let me give you a hand."

"You're new?" Sweat darkened his dirty-blond hair.

"Tonight's my first night."

He laughed. "Hope you got a good back."

"Like a mule."

The armed guard at the loading dock didn't even glance my way.

I let my carry-partner lead the way to the freight elevator and up to the second floor. The stink of new

beige carpet—that perennial favorite of industrial buildings—fouled the air. Banks of fluorescent lights gave
the room—with all the size and charm of an airplane
hangar—a look of midday.

"What number?" A supervisor with a clipboard asked.

"G-15," the mover answered.

"Over there." We duck-walked to the appointed
spot. I followed him to the door, then turned in the
opposite direction.

"Where you going?" my partner asked.

"Ladies' room. Shouldn't have had that extra cup of
coffee with dinner."

He nodded and kept heading toward the freight
elevator.

I reinserted the earpiece. "Okay, Wyatt," I whispered
into my collar. "Directions to HR."

"Turn right, then take the stairs to the first floor."

Donning transparent Latex gloves to hide my prints,
I sneaked down the stairs, staying aware of the location
of the security cameras. With my cap low, my hair
hidden and my body size beefed up with padding, iden-
tifying me wouldn't be easy, but I wanted to give the
least amount of data to work with.

"Where to now?" I asked Wyatt as I neared the
bottom of the stairs. On the first floor, only the security
light at the end of the corridor shed any light.

"Turn left and go toward the front of the building. It's
the office with all the glass windows."

Glass windows and security doors. From the folds
of my padding, I extracted a small maglite and a code-
breaker device. I stuck the maglite in my mouth and

inserted the device's leads into the lock. Sweat wormed its way down my back. My pulse kicked into overdrive as the device took longer than expected to punch out the code.

Holding my breath, I opened the door, entered and relocked it.

"Personnel files, Wyatt?"

"Try the file cabinets in the cubicle at the back."

Staying low, I wound my way there, unlocked the cabinet. My lock-picking skills weren't as rusted as I'd thought. Then I pawed through the files.

I looked for Glenda's and Sofia's, photocopied the contents and stuffed them into my shirt. "I still need to know who'd taken over Sofia's position," I told Wyatt. "I'm not finding an organization chart in the files. I'm going to try the computer." I sat at the farthest computer station from the door but all that got me was more frustration. The thing was password protected, and I didn't have the time or the technical ability to hack.

As I pondered my next move, footsteps plodded out in the hallway. I pressed the computer's sleep button but the screen remained bright and a droning whirr kicked up. The shadow of the guard loomed closer. Shoot, he was going to see the glow from the computer screen. Pulse pounding in my ears, I sank below the level of the desk and pulled the plug. The computer screen went black.

The guard paused at the door and flashed his light all over the office.

"Look up Paul's file," Wyatt said. "Whoever took Sofia's place was hired before he was promoted, so they'd be in his supervisory responsibility list until he moves up to his new job."

"Good idea."

When the guard's footsteps retreated, I headed back to the files and got what I needed.

I paused next to the office door and listened for the guard. Nothing.

"Where to next?" I asked Wyatt and double-checked the hallway.

"Stairs. At the end of the corridor."

I was halfway down the stairs when I heard a metal door clang two floors up and laughter drift down. I had to force myself to act slowly and with care as I reached the basement bunker door. I used the code breaker to get into the bunker. Like the first floor, the basement was mostly dark. The cube farm created an eerie landscape silhouette against the dim glow of the security light.

I readied my maglite. "Which one was Sofia's cube?"

"Three rows over, five cubicles down."

Two desks, two sets of shelves and two file cabinets crammed the small space of the beige cubicle. "Which desk was hers?"

"The one on the right. But someone else has probably taken it over."

"And taken over her project, too."

I crouched beside the cabinet, maglite between my teeth, and groped for my pick set.

"Try Leann's desk," Wyatt said. "Employees aren't supposed to keep keys at their desks, but not everyone follows the rules. Look under the phone."

"Nothing."

An Important Message from the Editors

Dear Reader,

*Because you've chosen to read one of our fine romance novels, we'd like to say "thank you!" And, as a **special** way to thank you, we've selected <u>two more</u> of the books you love so well **plus** two exciting Mystery Gifts to send you — absolutely <u>FREE</u>!*

Please enjoy them with our compliments...

Pam Powers

Lift here

Peel off seal and place inside...

How to validate your Editor's
"Thank You"
FREE GIFTS

1. Peel off gift seal from front cover. Place it in space provided at right. This automatically entitles you to receive 2 FREE BOOKS and 2 FREE mystery gifts.

2. Send back this card and you'll get 2 new Silhouette *Bombshell*™ novels. These books have a cover price of $4.99 or more each in the U.S. and $5.99 or more each in Canada, but they are yours to keep absolutely free.

3. There's no catch. You're under no obligation to buy anything. We charge nothing—ZERO—for your first shipment. And you don't have to make any minimum number of purchases— not even one!

4. The fact is, thousands of readers enjoy receiving their books by mail from The Silhouette Reader Service™. They enjoy the convenience of home delivery...they like getting the best new novels at discount prices BEFORE they're available in stores... and they love their Reader to Reader subscriber newsletter featuring author news, special book offers, book reviews and much more!

5. We hope that after receiving your free books you'll want to remain a subscriber. But the choice is yours— to continue or cancel, any time at all! So why not take us up on our invitation, with no risk of any kind. You'll be glad you did!

GET TWO Free *MYSTERY GIFTS...*

*SURPRISE MYSTERY GIFTS COULD BE YOURS **FREE** AS A SPECIAL "THANK YOU" FROM THE EDITORS*

The Editor's "Thank You" Free Gifts Include:

- *Two NEW Romance novels!*
- *Two exciting mystery gifts!*

Yes! I have placed my
Editor's "Thank You" seal in the
space provided at right. Please
send me 2 free books and
2 free mystery gifts. I
understand I am under no
obligation to purchase any
books, as explained on the
back and on the opposite page.

PLACE
FREE GIFTS
SEAL
HERE

300 SDL EFZF   **200 SDL EFX4**

FIRST NAME	LAST NAME

ADDRESS

APT.#	CITY

STATE/PROV.	ZIP/POSTAL CODE

(S-B-08/06)

Thank You!

Accepting your 2 free books and 2 free mystery gifts places you under no obligation to buy anything. You may keep the books and gifts and return the shipping statement marked "cancel." If you do not cancel, about a month later we'll send you 4 additional books and bill you just $3.99 each in the U.S., or $4.47 each in Canada, plus 25¢ shipping & handling per book and applicable taxes if any.* That's the complete price and — compared to cover prices starting from $4.99 each in the U.S. and $5.99 each in Canada — it's quite a bargain! You may cancel at any time, but if you choose to continue, every month we'll send you 4 more books, which you may either purchase at the discount price or return to us and cancel your subscription.

If offer card is missing write to: The Silhouette Reader Service, 3010 Walden Ave., P.O. Box 1867, Buffalo, NY 14240-9952

BUSINESS REPLY MAIL
FIRST-CLASS MAIL   PERMIT NO. 717-003   BUFFALO, NY

POSTAGE WILL BE PAID BY ADDRESSEE

SILHOUETTE READER SERVICE
3010 WALDEN AVE
PO BOX 1867
BUFFALO NY 14240-9952

NO POSTAGE
NECESSARY
IF MAILED
IN THE
UNITED STATES

"Rolodex."

"Not there." Ice stippled my right side as if Sofia was hanging over my shoulder.

"In the program coffee mug."

Sure enough, there was a key under the variety of pens.

I opened the cabinet and slid out a drawer. "What am I looking for?"

"An engineering journal. It's a soft-sided brown book."

"Got it."

"Look for December and January of last year and the HART program number I gave you."

"I don't see anything past with that program number."

"Then they must be in the Mosler safe."

"Where's that?"

"In Paul's office."

I followed his directions to Paul's office, growing tenser by the minute, expecting a guard to come by on his rounds. Boxes waiting to be moved to Paul's new office hid the safe. I maneuvered my way around, disturbing as little as I could. The safe looked like a bulky file cabinet. "The code breaker isn't going to work on this spin dial."

"Look on his secretary's desk," Wyatt said. "She can never remember the combination, so she writes it down on the back cover of her agenda."

Armed with the code, I punched in the numbers. Just as I grasped the engineering journal bearing Sofia's name and the correct date and program, the elevator binged into place in the hallway. Steps echoed on the bare linoleum. The code buttons crunched. The door slid open.

Shoot. Not good.

I stuffed the journals and the data file under my shirt,

doused the maglite and frog-walked my way out of Paul's office.

"Sierra? What's going on?"

"Someone just walked in."

One set of lights went on, then another. I lost my cover of darkness.

My breath came too fast. My head was going light. My heart throbbed violently. I recognized the pressure on my chest as panic that would have me gulping for air if I gave it a toehold.

Sofia, stop it!

Her fear was paralyzing me. So I blocked it out, swallowed it down and forced my attention to my feet, to keeping them moving, one in front of the other. I hadn't come this far just to get caught.

Using the concealment of the maze of cubicles, I kept out of the intruder's way.

Rounding a corner, my sleeve caught a protruding piece of metal and ripped.

The plodding footsteps halted. "Who's here?"

Cold fear sparked my nerves. Paul's voice. A flash-fire of pain burned along the cut on my upper arm.

A warming overhead fluorescent light pinged. Paul grunted and went on his way.

I reached the stairs, made my way back to the loading dock and stuffed the Latex gloves into my pocket. I spotted a pile of protective padding and grabbed it to hide the cut on my arm and the blood seeping through the sleeve. The guard nodded at me as I dumped the padding in the truck. I headed toward the staging area, then, seeing the coast clear, trotted to my waiting backpack.

I reversed my previous course and snaked my way past the assembly building. "See any patrol Jeeps?" I asked Wyatt.

"Clear," Wyatt said.

I was just crossing the road to the shed when a white truck with some sort of blue swash turned the corner, its headlights seeking me out.

"Hurry," Wyatt yelled.

No way I could outrun the truck, as lumbering as it was, and movement would draw the driver's attention to me. I dropped and rolled onto the grass, then remained as still as a speed bump while it rumbled by, its wash kicking up dust into my eyes. Once it turned the next corner, I slithered my way to the shed. Timing the return of the patrol, I trotted to where Wyatt waited.

"That was a rush," I said, hands on knees to catch my breath. Man, had that ever felt good. I'd missed this adrenaline kick that spiked my blood and gave me such a high.

Wyatt grabbed me by both arms. "That was the most idiotic thing I've ever seen anyone do in my life." The look in his eyes bore both the dark remnant of fear and the light spark of relief. "You could have gotten yourself killed."

Then he leaned toward me and captured my mouth fiercely. At the hot insistence of his kiss, a shudder ran from my scalp down to my knees, turning them to mush. Even worse was the way I sought to deepen the kiss as naturally as if I'd known him forever.

Attraction wasn't supposed to happen. Not between us.

How easy it would be to use Sofia's familiarity with Wyatt to allow this to go further, to keep the adrenaline rushing. Too easy. Besides, I'd never been the one-night-stand type. When it came to relationships, I wanted long-term and steady. I wedged a hand between us and pushed myself away, regret yawning in my chest.

"Sofia…" I breathed.

That magic word had him withdrawing. Slipping back into memories? Steadfast in his love for the woman who'd given me a second chance at life. He needed someone, but not me. I'd forever remind him of his loss.

"You're bleeding." Face tight, Wyatt had body and emotions clearly back under lock and key.

"It's just a scratch."

He stuffed his hands in his back pockets. "Did you get the files?"

I patted my stomach, then pulled them out and transferred them to the backpack. "Got them."

Giving me a wide berth, he grabbed the backpack. "Let's get out of here before anyone notices anything's gone."

Chapter 9

"About what happened out there…" Wyatt stood outside his office door, one hand choking the doorknob. Moths bumped drunkenly against the spotlight throwing yellow light over the yard.

"Heat of the moment," I said, refusing to look into his eyes. The kiss was just a kiss, and the discharge of adrenaline rush had felt pretty damn good. "Don't worry about it."

Wyatt scrubbed a hand through his hair. "I wasn't talking about the kiss. I was talking about the idiotic risks you take."

Sofia gasped as if Wyatt had sucker-punched her.

I glared at Wyatt, the remnant of adrenaline still frizzling through my veins. "Let's get something

straight. There's nothing idiotic about the way I do
my job. The risks I take are calculated, and I'm damn
good at what I do. I'm not one of your Southern belles
who need a man's protection." Tonight I'd proven
that the old Sierra was still alive. I wasn't going to
let her go.

"Sofia brought you to me. I'm not going to let anything
happen to you while you're investigating her death." He
jammed the key into the lock. "No more solo outings."

"Back off, Wyatt. I already have a pain-in-the-ass
brother. I don't need another."

In one quick move, he backed me up against the wall
and caught my face between his palms. "Since we're
setting things straight. What I'm feeling right now isn't
the least brotherly, Sierra."

Static sparked along my skin like the air before a
lightning strike as he leaned against me. He captured
my mouth and plumbed it as if he had all the time in
the world. Pleasure thrummed in my throat, but somewhere deep inside reality kicked in. Like Leo and Van,
Wyatt wanted to control my life.

I came up for air. "Sofia…"

He shook his head. "This is between you and me."

No kidding, I thought, still looking for breath. There
wasn't an inch of space between us, and everything I
was missing pressed hot and hard against my belly. For
the first time since Leo, I wanted a man—this man—
and knew on an impossible level that we could rock
each other's world. How could that be when we were
so wrong for each other?

Dimly on the edge of my consciousness, I became

aware of Sofia's distraught sobs hiccupping through my heart. Talk about wake-up call. Obviously her memories were causing my reaction to Wyatt.

"Whoa, cowboy." I slipped out of Wyatt's hold and made a time-out sign. "I don't mix business with pleasure." Another wise lesson learned from Leo. "Try that again, and I'll clock you. Got it?"

"Got it." Scowling, he shoved open the door and snapped on the overhead light.

Ignoring him, I marched over to his desk and dug the copies I'd made out of the backpack. "Let's get this stuff spread out and see if it tells us anything."

I noticed the stronger grate of static between Wyatt and me, as if Sofia had firmly wedged herself between us.

When Wyatt's desk didn't prove large enough, I moved everything onto the floor. I liked to get the big picture without having to juggle. Wyatt hunkered down beside me, his knee striking mine like a match every time he reached for another piece of paper. He was doing it on purpose. I wasn't going to give him the satisfaction of a response.

I liked to work things out by talking out loud. Sounds ridiculous but sometimes the sound of my own voice clicked something I'd missed by just eyeballing it. "From the org chart in Paul's file, it looks like Leann Rice took over Sofia's work and they got a new hire, Candace Howard, to fill Leann's spot."

"Leann was a friend of Sofia's," Wyatt said. "And her cubicle mate. She'd only been on the job for six months, though."

"There was a hiring freeze for everyone but entry-level

personnel," I said, reading from the hiring memo. "Do you think Leann was aware of the data discrepancies?"

Long frame bent over a fan of papers, Wyatt shrugged. "Coming in in the middle of a project always takes some adjustment. She might not."

"Can you make heads or tails of any of this?" I handed Wyatt Sofia's engineering journal.

Wyatt thumbed through the pale green pages. "A lot of technical stuff. It's going to take me a while to decipher it. The phase Sofia was working on was integrating a smaller, lighter and more power-efficient piece of equipment. Looks like the HART uses signal intelligence Trinity software architecture so it'll be interoperable with the avionics already in the aircraft."

"And what does that mean in English?"

"That the software they're using is based on a program I wrote years ago. The problem could be with the integration of the software with the existing hardware component."

I tucked a stray strand of hair behind my ear. "So you'll be able to figure it out?"

"Maybe," Wyatt said.

"Would Sofia have noted anything about the integration process in the journal?"

Sofia's filmy body materialized against the black of night at the window. She floated over to Wyatt, wrapped her arms around his shoulders and read her journal.

"I'll have to go through her notes." Wyatt rolled his shoulders, dislodging Sofia's hold.

A stricken look etched her face and she disappeared. Her agitation waved needles of static through me. For as much as she got on my nerves, I felt sorry for her. Being caught between two worlds like that couldn't be easy, especially when the man you loved couldn't see you. That someone had killed her wasn't her fault. She didn't want to haunt me any more than I wanted to be haunted. And she couldn't stay away any more than I could go home. We were stuck with each other until this case was solved.

After a couple of hours of staring at print, a low-level headache pressed against my temples, my neck ached and my eyes burned.

"Here's how it looks." Wyatt stretched the kinks from his body. "The HART successfully completed its first flight on the stealth fighter on September thirteenth."

"Six months after Sofia died," I said.

He nodded. "It operated flawlessly at a demonstration for the Defense Department and some other key government officials. Qualifications testing was scheduled for completion by the end of September, and then it would move on into the advanced flight-test phase."

"How did it perform in the advanced phase?"

He flipped through Sofia's journal, then the test results from her files. "I don't see any mention of the results. They're probably in later journals." His gaze skewered me. "And no, we're not going back for them."

I stared him down. The window of opportunity had closed—not that I was going to admit it to him. I stabbed a finger at a memo from Paul's file. "It says here that Allied Defense was scheduled to deliver HART systems to a third of the stealth fleet by the end of March of this year. Meeting this date was a key business event for the year."

"And in April, airplanes started crashing," Wyatt said.

Lorraine came in, bearing a tray of flan and a pitcher of milk. "I thought you might like a bite to eat before I went up to bed. I can heat up some leftover stew if you want something more substantial."

"We're fine, Ma," Wyatt said, his irritation at the journals seeping through.

"Thank you." Reaching for a bowl and spoon, I couldn't help a stir of envy for Wyatt. I tried to picture my mother bringing me a late-night snack and my mind went blank.

Lorraine peered over my shoulder. "What are you working on?"

"Making order out of chaos," I said.

She pulled out a couple of sheets from Glenda's file. "Look at this, Wyatt. This woman got a bonus for meeting all her target dates. And she works with numbers. Imagine that."

I glanced at the memos and compared them to the ones I'd been looking at in Paul Farr's file. "Good catch, Lorraine."

Lorraine narrowed her gaze at Wyatt. "I told you I was good with sums."

Wyatt sighed. "Tell you what, Ma. Since you're so fired up to take over the accounting, we'll go over it once this is over, and you're welcome to it. It'll give me more time to work on other things."

Like his silly-looking mechanical cow?

Wyatt strode to his desk and searched the piles of

papers. "Ma, did you throw away a sheet with handwritten numbers on it?"

"You know I'd never throw away anything of yours without asking first. Speaking of lost things, you need to remember to close your window if you're going to have the air-conditioning running."

Every muscle of Wyatt's body tensed. "Which window?"

"The one behind you." She rubbed her hands along her apron. "I'm going to call it a night, Wyatt. I want to go to the early service tomorrow. I don't suppose I could talk you into going with me."

"Maybe another day, Ma." Wyatt walked his mother to the door, then as it clicked shut, his gaze met mine. "The data sheet you wrote for me is gone." He examined the window, then held up a toothpick he found impaled in the carpet.

Rey.

Why had he threatened me at the show? Because he'd needed the data sheet? Did he work for one of Allied Defense's competitors? "Where did you say Rey worked again?"

"I didn't," Wyatt said. "But he works for Sofia's father's company."

"What does he do?"

"Antonio's a garbage man. I'm sorry—a recycler. I'm not sure what Rey does there."

"And this is picking up more stink by the minute." I grabbed a pad of paper and closed my eyes to recall the numbers on the sheet.

As I finished transcribing the last row, Wyatt said, "We have a problem."

"What?"

He spread the journal pages open wide and showed me how the page numbers skipped. "Six pages are missing."

"As in removed?"

"As in cut out." He fingered the nearly invisible cuts.

"But why? Wouldn't it be obvious in any sort of review or audit that someone had ripped pages out?"

"If the deception was uncovered during a government audit, it could mean a jail sentence. But with Sofia already dead, she'd be the fall guy, and dead people can't defend themselves."

I massaged the stiffness from my neck. "So if pages are missing, it means someone inside Allied Defense removed them."

"The same person who had her killed?" He shook the bonus memos Lorraine had found.

"To protect their bonuses?" I asked.

"Seems farfetched. There's always some sort of incentive to meet target dates."

"But this time it's significant if someone was hellbent on getting that bonus and messed with the data to meet the deadline."

"Possibly."

I laid out the time line for him. "Sofia went to Nashua in March for some sort of software/hardware integration test at the lab. She doesn't like something she sees. Someone picks up on her concerns and kills her before she can make them known.

"The program goes on as if nothing was wrong. Allied Defense meets all its target dates and zips through the tests with flying colors. Congratulations are passed around. Bonus checks are inked. The following March, the HART goes into one-third of the stealth fleet. Three weeks into April, four have fallen out of the sky."

"With so many accidents, why haven't they grounded the fleet?" Wyatt rasped out. "Can't they see the pattern?"

"The midair collision was judged pilot error. And the other two airplanes were different types. Grounding the whole fleet is a drastic measure, especially when we're fighting an active war at the moment."

Missing pages. Performance bonuses. A murdered engineer. Crashing airplanes.

Like an invisible umbilical cord each piece led back to the HART.

But who was behind the information suppression?

The closest players were those above Sofia in the food chain.

I closed Glenda's file with a snap. "Guess we need to have another chat with Paul and Glenda."

Sunday, April 23

I figured Wyatt and I had had enough togetherness for a while, so I made myself scarce. He needed to learn I couldn't have him hanging around me all day. He'd agreed to get in touch with Paul and Glenda, and that's all I wanted from him today.

I used my business account to run a financial on both

Paul and Glenda. Since today was Sunday, I wouldn't get results back until late Monday or Tuesday. I did more research on the previous crashes to see if anything had been reported on the cause of the accidents and came up blank. Either it was too early for results or no one was telling.

At dinnertime, I ventured back downstairs. I had to say that I'd regained a healthy appetite since coming to Texas. Van would be pleased.

"Something smells really good," I said as I walked into the kitchen. The little cabinet-mounted TV, was on but the sound was turned down low—as if Lorraine needed it more for company than for its programming content.

Lorraine inserted beaters into a hand mixer to mash a potful of potatoes. "I'm glad you're taking a break. You're working too hard."

"It's a tough puzzle to piece together."

"How did you get involved with it?" Butter and milk went into the pot.

"Long story."

"I've got time." She whipped the potatoes until they were fluffy.

"What are your thoughts on death?" I asked as she transferred the potatoes to a serving dish. Wyatt had thought I was a psychic sent by his mother when we'd first met, so I figured she might be more open than the average person to the paranormal.

Lorraine skewed me with a quizzical look. "Well, I'm not sure. The church speaks of Heaven, and it's comforting to believe that it exists."

"Do you think there's life after death? That we

somehow survive our bodies and live on in a different state?"

Lorraine paused, steamer of green beans hanging in midair. "Are you talking about ghosts and such?"

"Maybe. I'm not sure." When someone invaded your mind, that went beyond ghostly haunting, didn't it? Or maybe Sofia was nothing more than a delusion that I'd somehow manifested like a child's imaginary friend to fill some void. But the fault with the HART seemed real enough, so maybe I wasn't quite ready to have a straitjacket fitted.

Lorraine's gaze flicked to the door, then back to me. "I've seen Waylon since he's died."

"Your husband."

She nodded and color crept up her neck. "He's come to me at night, and we've had conversations."

I filched a piece of cucumber from the salad in the bowl on the counter. "I hear Sofia."

Her eyes went wide, not with fear as I'd half expected, but with curiosity. "I thought there was something familiar about you from the second I saw you in that blue suit. That was Sofia's favorite color."

"I got her heart."

She passed me a handful of cutlery. "I wondered why someone healthy like you was scarfing down so many pills."

I set the table. Lorraine had noticed more than I'd given her credit for. "Antirejection stuff."

She nodded and went back to transferring the green beans to a serving bowl. "Yes, I've read about that."

"She asked me to find who killed her."

"Well, now everything makes sense. I always knew there was something wrong about the way she died, as careful as she was with things like seat belts. Since you have a part of her, she could reach you most easily."

I'm glad that made sense to someone, because I was more confused than ever.

Lorraine pressed an intercom button. "Wyatt? Come carve the chicken, please."

"Be right there."

A few minutes later Wyatt strode in and went to work on the chicken with the efficiency of someone who'd done the task often. As he sliced into a breast, he stopped cold and swore.

"Did you cut yourself, honey?" Lorraine rushed to his side.

Wyatt turned up the volume on the television and moved aside. Orange flames. Black smoke. Pieces of debris scattered along what looked like a marina. I wrapped an arm around Lorraine who gasped at the images on the screen.

Not again, Sofia whispered. Her anguish squeezed the tissues of my brain.

"An Air Force stealth fighter plane, roaring low over a crowded Maine air show, crashed into a waterfront neighborhood, exploding in flames and destroying one house," a reporter said, her blond hair whipping in the wind. "The pilot ejected safely and four people on the ground suffered minor injuries."

"Maine?" Lorraine squeaked, shaking in my arms. "Oh, God, no. Tracy."

"She probably hasn't been on base long enough to

enter the flight rotation yet, Ma." Wyatt crossed over to the phone and dialed. "No answer."

I tried to reassure Lorraine. "They're probably on some sort of alert."

The reporter continued, "The pilot, identified as Captain Erik Lamphere, is a twelve-year veteran who has been flying the F-117 stealth fighter for four years. He was making a display circuit over the Pierce Air Force Base runway where more than six thousand spectators were gathered for the annual air show. Witnesses said the airplane went into a steep climb, then slammed into a storage building shortly after 3:00 p.m.

"The explosion and fire gutted one house, destroyed a dock and damaged several fishing boats. The area was quickly sealed off, even to residents. Lamphere landed about sixty feet away from the crash and was airlifted to Boston. The extent of his injuries is unknown.

"The F-117 is usually considered a reliable jet. It is the fifth military airplane to crash in the past month. Stealth fighters were used during both Persian Gulf Wars because of their radar-absorbing materials."

Wyatt punched off the television. Our gazes collided.

"The pilot lived," I said. I had to talk to him. He was flying. He could tell me what had gone wrong—if the HART was involved.

Wyatt nodded.

I yanked the phone off its cradle and, using a calling card to mask my location of origin, I dialed information and asked for the numbers of the major Boston hospitals. It took me three tries to find the right one. When

I finally reached someone who seemed to know what was going on, I pretended to be Erik's distraught sister. "What's his condition?"

"He's in Intensive Care," a nurse answered.

"Oh, God." I let a strangled cry escape. "How bad is it?"

"His most serious injuries are to his back."

"Is he—" I gulped "—awake? I mean…can he talk? Is he going to know me?"

"He has brief periods of lucidity," the nurse assured me. "He's under heavy sedation at the moment, but he should be stable enough to transfer to a private room tomorrow."

"Okay, I'm going to fly up. Tell him to hang on, please."

"I'll do that."

I hung up and turned to Wyatt. "I'm flying to Boston."

"I'm going with you."

Chapter 10

We caught the last flight out of DFW to Logan. The possibility of getting something concrete from the downed pilot throbbed between us like a cyst in need of lancing.

As the 737 lifted off, Wyatt ripped the in-flight magazine from the pocket in front of him. Sardined as we were in these coach seats, his shoulder rubbed mine going down and back up. The last thing this thin air needed was a spark.

"What if the pilot won't talk?" Wyatt's voice had an edge like a machete.

I squeezed myself closer to the window. "He will. I'll make him."

"What? You're going to rough him up?"

"No." I glanced at the magazine bunched in Wyatt's fists and smirked. "I thought I'd leave that up to you."

"Smart-ass. You know you're playing with a stick of dynamite."

I'd thought about that. A lot. I had every intention of living to a ripe old age—thanks to Sofia's heart. No way I was going to let it blow up in my face. I shrugged. "I'll deal with it when I see how much fuse it has."

Soon, I told myself, I'd get my life back. The only question was—which life?

Don't go there, Sierra, I cautioned myself.

Sofia hadn't said a peep since we'd boarded. Closer to heaven like this, I'd thought she'd be right in my face. But even her regular cold static seemed to have died down.

Wow, was that when "crazy" went into the shrink's notes? When the patient started missing the voices in her head?

Are you there, Sofia? Are you okay?

Right, like there could be something wrong with a ghost. But still, the answering silence was unnerving. What if she was gone for good?

I snorted silently. As if I'd get that lucky. She wasn't done; she'd be back.

As the 737 leveled off, I let the facts of the case tumble around in my mind. I juggled and twisted and turned over the pieces of the puzzle, hoping a clear picture would emerge. No aha moment lit a bulb over my head.

I'd just have to dig harder.

I steamed breath against the window. As the mist evaporated, the vast expanse of black outside rumbled to the drone of the engines. Skydiving would help. Everything was clear and sharp when the ground was rushing up at you. Every cell of your body came alive. Worries that had seemed so huge before shrank down to nothing. It was life in its purest essence. Too bad I was afraid to risk strapping on a parachute.

I sighed, suddenly melancholic. Out of nowhere a sprinkling of lights appeared, shook, then vanished. Like life, I thought. Short, but oh, so precious.

"I've always liked flying," I mused. "Up here it seems like the possibilities are endless. Like nothing is impossible. Like the world is a blank slate."

Wyatt offered a noise of agreement and stuffed the magazine back into the pocket before he mangled it to shreds.

"If anything was possible," I said, "what would you do?"

In the dim light of the plane, his cheeks were dark and shadowed and his jaw cut a sharp silhouette. "I don't know. I've never thought about it."

"You've never dreamed?"

He shrugged, reclined the seat and crossed his arms over his broad chest. "I have dreams."

"Like what?"

"The ranch."

Before the transplant, I'd lived my life on a knife-edge. I didn't have a death wish but I'd wanted to experience as much of life as possible. Did Wyatt feel as if he was experiencing life to its fullest? Did he take risks? Was his marriage to Sofia everything he'd dreamed marriage would be?

I know I had no business asking, but curiosity was

an investigator's gift and curse. "Did your mother ask you to take over the ranch after your father died?"

His jaw tightened. "She didn't have to. It's tradition. The oldest son takes over. The ranch isn't going to die on my watch."

"Did you ever consider that she might have wanted to run it herself?"

"She's earned her retirement."

So okay, he hadn't even considered it. I already had a foot in where it didn't belong, might as well stick the other in, too. "She's not as helpless as you make her out to be, you know."

He grunted a noncommittal noise and closed his eyes.

Coward. As if that would save him from me. "If the ranch wasn't there, what would you do?"

"Why all the questions?"

"Because for some reason it matters." His gaze met mine, green swirling in the brown of his irises, and something sparked. "What would you do?"

"I'd probably go back to writing code." A small smile quirked his lips. "I've been working on that mechanical cow. It's going to be better than the real thing, especially for youngsters just starting. Safer. And eventually I'll be able to have it programmed for specific drills." Passion for the challenge lit his eyes for a moment, then his smile drooped as if allowing himself to want anything would bring him disappointment. "Still needs some tweaking." He elbow-nudged me. "What about you?"

I let out my breath slowly. "I'd stop being afraid. I'd live again like I used to. I'd have a real connection with my brother and mother instead of this feeling of obligation."

"You? Afraid? Of what?"

In the dark it was somehow easier to admit that I wasn't perfect. "Of my heart rejecting me. Of always having this feeling that I'm not alone in my body."

"Sofia?"

I nodded. "I know it sounds crazy. But sometimes I think of her and I get nervous. Something in my body changes, like there's someone else watching me, and I'm not myself."

"That's enough to scare anyone."

"Sometimes I'm afraid she's going to take over my body and that I'm going to disappear." A ripple of cold mist filled my chest, made my heart pound.

Is that you, Sofia? No answer. Maybe it was just the recycled air filling my lungs with germs. No wonder people got sick on airplanes.

He reached for my hand and squeezed it. "No way. You're too damn stubborn. She wasn't half as strong as you are."

The solidness of his hand over mine eased the knot in my chest. Sofia didn't voice any objections, so I let my hand rest in his.

"Do you miss her?" Stupid question. Of course he missed her; she was his wife.

"All the time." He took his hand back, pain etching his face. "You don't expect someone so young to die. One day she was there. The next she was gone."

"It's supposed to hurt." I thought of Leo and the way he'd loved me one night and been gone the next. Even with my own heart dead and decayed, there was still a tender bruise left on my psyche.

I shifted in my seat, trying to find a more comfortable position. Fatigue tugged at my eyelids, but instead of giving in to sleep, I watched Wyatt through lowered lashes.

I could understand why Sofia fell for him. He was principled and determined to see things to their end even if he didn't agree with them. He provided a safe refuge from chaos. And if my visit to Sofia's parents' home was any indication, her life there hadn't been a picnic. Wyatt had been her knight, riding off with her into the sunset.

But I didn't need a hero. Especially one who liked to boss me around, fix things his way. And he worried way too much. That would drive me crazy.

Still…

Admit it, Sierra, you like the way he looks. I sighed.

I liked the blunt cut of his hands, that his palms were rough with calluses. I liked the steadiness of his hazel gaze when he looked at me. I liked the way the solid feel of his body against mine could make me forget all about Sofia, even if for just a few seconds. And, yeah, I liked the way his kiss had knocked the knees out from under me.

But business and personal didn't mix. I'd learned that lesson the hard way. And even Leo would agree that I didn't make the same mistake twice. So I closed my eyes tight and sought a reprieve in the oblivion of sleep.

Two hours later, as the plane started its descent, I woke up with my head snugged into Wyatt's shoulder and an airline blanket draped over me. Good thing Sofia was AWOL or my train of thought would upset her. Avoiding Wyatt's gaze, I got my stuff together.

We'd both taken overnight bags so we didn't have to stop at Baggage Claim.

"Garage," I said as Wyatt started toward the exit to catch a cab. "I have my car."

Betsy waited where I'd parked her. Wyatt raised a doubtful eyebrow when he saw her patchwork body.

I unlocked the doors. "She's a cantankerous old witch, but I can't seem to give her the boot. Nobody gives her a second look when I do surveillance."

Wyatt threw our bags into the back. "She looks like she's going to fall apart any minute."

"That's part of her charm." I turned the ignition. All I got was a choked cough. "Unfortunately, she doesn't always pick the best times for a dose of extra attention. Come on, Betsy, you beautiful girl. I really need you to take me to see someone special tonight."

"We're going straight to your place."

I cajoled Betsy into starting and nosed her into the nearly deserted streets of Boston toward the hospital. "I know it's way past visiting hours, but I can talk my way in to see the pilot."

Wyatt shook his head. "You really are something. He'll be sleeping. We can wait a few more hours to see him. Besides you need some rest."

I stifled a yawn, fighting the weariness that had settled into my bones. "I had a nap on the airplane. I'm good."

"You look like you need another week's worth."

"Gee, thanks."

But the depth of my exhaustion panicked me a little, because I didn't want to think about organ rejection, about dying.

So don't think about it. Keep moving.

I hit my flasher to signal for a turn toward the hospital.

"Don't even think about driving to the hospital until tomorrow morning," Wyatt warned. "Or I'll tie you to your bed and make you beg me to set you free."

"You wish." Grumbling, I reluctantly took I-93 and drove to my apartment in Nashua on the top floor of an old Victorian. Sneaking in to talk to the pilot would be easier during visiting hours.

As I unlocked the door to my apartment and flicked on the lights, I tried to see my space through Wyatt's eyes and was a little embarrassed that it seemed to shout of loneliness. Plain vanilla walls. No photographs. No pets. No plants. Nothing all that personal. I could leave in a flash and have no worries about anything requiring feeding or care.

And I must have left the heat on because the living room was stuffy and warm. Real smart to jack up my heating bill when my checking account was in the red. Or maybe the flushed face was because I was alone with Wyatt in my tiny apartment.

"You can have the bed." I pointed toward the small room in the alcove. "The sheets are clean. I'll take the couch."

"I couldn't take your bed."

"It's not a sacrifice, Wyatt. I haven't slept in it in months."

"Why not?"

I shed my tote and bag as I headed to the bathroom. He followed me.

"Why not?" he insisted, arms braced on both sides of the door frame.

"Didn't I tell you about Sofia haunting me?" I asked as I squeezed toothpaste onto a toothbrush. I was going for normal, trying to hang on to the illusion that this was just another investigation. Didn't work. Just the thought of him sprawled in my bed without a stitch of clothing on had me working up a sweat. Where was Sofia's ice-cold splash of reality when I needed it?

Maybe her silence was a good sign. Maybe I was coming back into myself. Maybe she'd finally given up on me being able to fix the problem with the HART.

Wyatt looked at me long and hard. Sweat trickled down my neck.

"Okay," he said finally, "I'll take the bed." But he made no move toward my room.

Tension. Awkwardness. The zing of it raw as I finished brushing my teeth and reached for a facecloth. What was I supposed to do about the pull I felt around him? About him? I knew him well, yet not at all. And when he looked at me, how could he not think of Sofia? I didn't need this. I just wanted to work. Close the case. Get back to my life. I'd have to ask Mrs. Cartier if she'd let me paint the walls. Red maybe. Or emerald green. Something vibrant. Something wild. Adventurous.

I slung the wet facecloth on the towel rack and started for the door but Wyatt's body blocked the way. That snake of sweat had wound its way down my spine and pooled at the small of my back. Even my palms were damp.

For a second, I thought he felt sorry for me and my delusional state. Then the glint of something else flashed in his eyes, and my face flamed.

"Get some sleep." His eyes never lost their intensity.

He didn't kiss me. But the way he looked at my mouth, the way his breathing sped up, made me think he wanted to. And that stoked me with need.

But sex required a surrender I wasn't yet ready for. Especially not with Wyatt. And who knew when Sofia would decide to pop back in.

A pounding at the door startled me and broke the spell. "Sierra, I know you're in there."

"Van?" I brushed by Wyatt and ripped open the front door. "What are you doing here at this hour?"

Van bulldozed his way inside, and Wyatt, standing sentinel behind me, puffed up in protector mode.

"You look like shit," Van started, then broke off when he spied Wyatt. "Who the hell is this guy and what's he doing here?"

"Thanks for the compliment. I can't look that bad. If you hadn't barged in, I'd be in the throes of passion right now."

Behind me, Wyatt's whole body jerked in surprise.

Van eyed Wyatt as if he was going to lunge for his throat. Like I needed two Neanderthals raking me over the coals.

"I don't think I want to hear this," Van said.

"That's what you get for barging into my home at this time of the night." I crossed my arms under my chest. Unbelievable. It was almost 3:00 a.m. and he'd taken the time to put on a suit. "What are you doing here?"

"I told Mrs. Cartier to let me know the minute you came home."

I hoped my landlady hadn't sold me out for back rent. "What the hell for?"

"You've been gone for almost a week, that's why." Van plopped onto the couch, buried his face in his hands, then looked up at me. "I've been worried sick about you. Doesn't that mean anything to you?"

It did. And if he was a little more open-minded, I'd tell him about Sofia and the HART, but I couldn't take the chance that he'd stop me. He'd had Mom committed once when she went through a stretch of depression after Dad died. Yeah, she'd been suicidal, but I know he'd do it to me in a heartbeat if he thought it was for my own good. "Wyatt is a client, Van."

Van popped back up. "And you're sleeping with him?"

Wyatt held Van's lawyerly gaze with his own Wild West one. "Not that it's any of your business, but no."

"She's my sister."

"She's a grown woman who knows her own mind," Wyatt said. Nice one, I thought. Till he ruined it. "When we make love," Wyatt insisted, "it'll be between us. No third party involved."

When? Gee, Wyatt was taking a lot for granted. And he was forgetting Sofia.

Any second now he and Van were going to butt heads. I two-fingered a whistle. "Time out. Nobody's going to do anything without my okay."

Ignoring Wyatt, Van took another tack. "Where have you been?"

"I told you. I'm working a case."

He ran both his hands through his thinning hair. "How come I don't know anything about it? The least you could have done is keep Noelle up to date." He grabbed my wrists. "What if something happened to you?"

"I'm old enough to take care of myself."

He dropped one wrist and pressed a palm against my forehead. "Obviously not. You're running a fever." He turned to Wyatt, forehead lowered as if he would charge him. "Did she tell you about her heart? Do you know how dangerous a fever is for her?" He snapped back to me without giving Wyatt a chance to answer. "I can't believe you're being so cavalier with your health."

"Whoa, Van, now you're going too far. I'm tired but I'll be fine after some sleep. And just so you know, I chose to come home and rest instead of pursuing a lead, so back off."

Fortunately Wyatt didn't spoil the moment by adding that he'd all but forced me to come home.

"You can't take a fever casually," Van insisted.

"He's right, Sierra," Wyatt said. "Your health comes first."

"Stay out of this, Wyatt." At least I knew all that sweat had a biological reason and not a hormonal one.

"I want you to go for a checkup," Van continued.

"Couldn't hurt," Wyatt added.

I hated that they were both right.

I threw my hands up. "That's it. Gang up on me." No need to tell either of them that would put me exactly where I wanted to be—the hospital—with a built-in reason to visit Captain Lamphere's room. "I'll make an appointment with my cardiologist in the morning." I opened the door and swept an arm. "Now, go home to your wife and kids. They're the ones who need you to worry about them."

"You'll make sure she keeps her word?" Van asked Wyatt.

"I'll haul her there myself."

I shook my head. "Between the two of you, I feel like I've stepped into a really bad caveman movie."

Van dragged me outside, shutting Wyatt out. "Have you checked this guy out?"

Wyatt inched the door open ready to come to my rescue.

"Yes, Van, I have. He's a worrywart just like you."

"This isn't a joking matter."

"I know how to do my job, okay? I still have over two weeks on the month you promised me." I shrugged. "And I like him." The admission blindsided me for a second.

Van blinked once, as if seeing me for the first time since he'd knocked at my door. "Well, maybe there's hope for you yet."

I frowned. "What's that supposed to mean?"

He blew out a breath and shook his head. "Nothing. You're right. It's late. I should have waited till morning. Make sure you see your doctor tomorrow."

I gave him a quick peck on the cheek. "Go home, Van."

He left. Wyatt cornered me. "Level with me. The fever. How serious is it?"

"Could be the start of an infection. Could be nothing but fatigue."

"You're not going to pull one of your pretexts on me and try to get out of seeing the doctor tomorrow."

Not a question, I noticed. "Why would I do that? I like living as much as the next person."

Monday, April 24

The one-hour drive to Boston the next morning turned into two because of an accident on Route 3. Talk about flashbacks. The flecks of broken glass speckling the pavement popped Sofia's nightmare in full Technicolor, and I almost ran off the road.

You'd think that would have brought Sofia out again, but no, nothing. Why was I even bothering to worry about someone who didn't exist?

My low-grade fever was gone by the time I'd woken up from my short, restless night, but Dr. Durant squeezed me in, anyway, and I now sat in a lovely paper gown on his examining table. He poked and prodded and listened with his instruments but, as usual, not with his ears.

"My heart feels too heavy in my chest." And had since Sofia had started haunting me. I hated to admit how much that scared me.

"It's all in your mind. The heart is just a pump, nothing else. Everything checks out perfectly."

A sigh of relief. I wasn't rejecting. "I told Van the fever was nothing."

"I'll adjust your meds. Take it easy for the next few days. Call if the fever flares up again."

Because Dr. Durant expected compliance, I made all the right noises. There was one more thing I needed to do before I went home and wrapped up this case. "Sure, Doc."

"Otherwise, I'll see you in September for your biopsy." That delightful procedure where they snipped a piece of heart muscle to check for signs of rejection.

"I have you penciled in."

Instead of getting dressed in my own clothes, I put on the nurse's scrubs I'd brought from home—a souvenir from my previous stay here. The amount I could fit in my tote was amazing. I twisted my hair into a braid and grabbed a stethoscope from the exam room wall.

Making a pretext work was all in the attitude. I walked out of the examining room as if I belonged, took a detour to avoid Wyatt sitting patiently in the waiting room and stowed my tote in the hallway bathroom. He wouldn't be happy I'd gone solo again but that couldn't be helped. I didn't know what the situation was on the fifth floor, only that they'd moved Captain Lamphere to a private room. A nurse or a doctor would have sure access to the pilot; anyone else could be turned back. Wyatt would get in the way.

Using the elevator, I made my way up two floors. The hospital stench of sickness and disinfectant was getting to me, turning my stomach like sour milk.

Out of the elevator, I headed left and stopped at the first corridor. I leaned my head out and peered at the nurses' station. The half-moon desk was angled, but I had a clear enough view. I noted exits in case I needed to make a quick getaway.

I'd been in this hospital often enough in the past year to know the rhythm and flow of the nursing station. A look at my watch told me that in a few minutes all the nurses would be busy dispensing meds. I waited for the desk to clear and headed for the pilot's room.

His room was located at the intersection of two corridors. Not the best of places for an incognito heart-to-heart. Even with the nursing shortage, someone was bound to notice me.

My breath came too fast. It heightened my senses but would choke me if I wasn't careful. *Breathe.* I nodded at a doctor as I breezed by him.

I slipped into Lamphere's room and closed the door behind me. I didn't know where he was in the meds rotation, so I had to make this quick. "Hey, soldier."

Lamphere's head snapped in my direction, his eyes rounding as if the gentle click of the door had detonated an explosion.

I smiled to reassure him. "You're awake."

He nodded, head sinking back into the pillow. The sight of the man, skin as pale as the sheets tucked around him, of the tubes snaking out of him like some sort of experiment gone wrong, the muted beeps of machinery keeping time to his pulse flashed me back thirteen months. A moan of helplessness, pain and fear bubbled up in my throat. I shook my head. God, I hated hospitals.

Swallowing hard, I checked the captain's vitals and started a conversation. "I hear you're quite the hero."

His laugh was a rough gargle. "No hero. Just an ordinary guy."

"Anyone who steers a plane away from a crowd is a

hero in my book." Shoot, his pulse jumped up under my fingertips. Not good. But I needed the information. I had to push him. "So what happened?"

He shook his head, compulsively licking at his lips.

"It's good to talk about it," I said, gentling my voice.

He scrunched his eyes closed as if trying to shut out vivid images flaring on the screen of his lids.

"It's okay," I said. "I understand. I was in a massive car accident last year. It took me forever to get back behind the wheel. I still can't drive on a highway without having flashbacks."

"It's like I'm right back there," he croaked.

I exaggerated a shiver. "I know. I can hear every single twist of metal. Smell the gasoline. Taste the blood." Which wasn't that far from the truth, given how many times Sofia had made me relive her ordeal. "All I was trying to do was get to work, and I almost died."

The pain, Sofia moaned.

You're back. What did it say about the state of my mental health that I was relieved she was there?

Some places are harder to come through, Sofia said, her voice faint. *Emotions get in the way.*

Beads of sweat popped out on the pilot's forehead, and he blinked fast as if that could scrub away the unwanted memories.

"Something went wrong with the instruments." Captain Lamphere licked his dry lips. I offered him the straw from his water glass and he drank. "I'd rolled the airplane upside down and was completing the loop by diving and pulling up at the last moment when all of a sudden I realized I was roaring toward the ground." His voice hitched. "My speed was so high that I'd never pull up in time."

Using a cool washcloth, I wiped the sweat sliding down his brow. "But you ejected."

"I was thinking I'd have to eject. But there was the crowd. So I kept thinking, no, not yet. Got to steer away more."

Footsteps approached in the hallway, then retreated. I let out my caged breath.

"The runway was right below me." His pulse rocketed. I stroked his arm, keeping an eye on the instruments. I didn't want the readings to alarm a nurse. "I reached for the eject handle but then I could feel the sink rate was going to kill me. I had to get the sink rate under control first."

Sink rate—how fast the aircraft and ground are rushing toward each other. I remembered that from my skydiving days.

"The ground kept coming at me." His fast-beating heart shivered the johnny over his chest. "I thought if I wasn't going to survive, anyway, I might as well keep pulling and see if I can get farther around the loop, farther from the crowd."

If he'd bailed out too soon, he'd have died. If he'd waited too long, he'd have died. The most extraordinary part of his tale was that his window of decision was about half a second.

"My body just said now's the time," he said.

Instincts and the best training around.

"After I pulled the handle…" His mouth continued

to move but nothing came out. He swallowed hard. "I remember being yanked into position, the canopy popping off, then nothing. I didn't come to again until I got to the hospital."

With the G-force he'd experienced, passing out wasn't surprising at all. The plane was on the ground and in flames just 0.8 seconds after he ejected from the aircraft, according to a news report this morning. His courage had saved a lot of lives.

"Were you flying with the HART engaged?" I asked.

"How did you know about the HART?"

I shrugged. "My sister-in-law is Air Force. Flies the F-117. She's mentioned some trouble with the HART."

He frowned. "No trouble. At least not that I know of."

"Which instruments went wonkers on you?"

"The attitude indicator. It sort of went spinning, and then I couldn't tell if I was flying right side up or not."

Sofia's excitement stirred static along my arms. *A surge.*

"Did the spinning happen after you engaged the HART?" I asked.

His forehead crimped painfully. "After, yeah. I flipped it on for the third fly-by to show off for some bigwig in the tower."

A voice squawked over the PA. With all the advances in technology you'd think someone could invent a static-free system. Time to get out of here. I'd already stayed longer than prudent.

"I didn't mean to tire you out." I patted his shoulder. "You rest now. I'll check on you again later."

He grasped my arm. "No, stay. You're right. Talking helps."

"I'd love to, soldier, but if I don't make my rounds, I'll get in trouble."

"I don't want to be alone."

I'd put myself in a squeeze. I'd made him open up; I couldn't just leave him hanging so raw. "Okay, I'll see if someone else can come chat with you for a bit."

His grip tightened. "You get it. The flashback. I can tell from your eyes."

The door sprang open and a nurse with a face as crisp as her uniform stepped through. "What are you doing here?"

"Taking vitals," I stammered, gearing up for the new-girl excuse. "I was taking his blood pressure when he became agitated. I was coming to get the charge nurse."

Her frown deepened. "Who are you?"

"The temp." I pinched myself to work tears up into my eyes.

"I didn't order a temp."

"I...I just got here. They sent me up to the sixth floor and—"

"You're on the fifth floor." The "idiot" was silent but understood.

"She gets me," Captain Lamphere said. "I need her to stay."

Ignoring the patient, the nurse made a sour-pickle face at the sight of my tears. "For Pete's sake, get yourself together."

I swiped at my cheeks. "I'm sorry. It's my first day—"

"Get out of here."

With a silent apology to the pilot, I didn't wait for a second invitation. I put distance between me and Nurse Ratchet. I took the stairs two-by-two back down to the third floor, locked the bathroom and changed back into my street clothes, then went to collect Wyatt from the waiting room.

One more stop to confirm.

One more stop to expose.

Then I would be free.

As I stepped up to the waiting room area, Wyatt stopped midpace. I curled my upturned fingers in a Come-on gesture. He was at my side in three long steps.

"What took so long?" he asked.

I led him toward the stairs. I had too much nervous energy pulsing through me to wait for the elevator.

"I got sidetracked."

"Everything okay?"

"I checked out healthy as a horse." I headed down the stairs.

"Wrong direction," he said. "Visiting hours are starting soon. I checked. We can go up to see the pilot."

"I've already talked to him."

"You were supposed to wait for me."

His stormy eyes cemented with annoyance at my having ventured out alone.

"I saw an opportunity and took it." I punched through the parking garage doors. I unlocked Betsy and tossed Wyatt my cell phone. "Call your sister. Have her get us on the base at Pierce Island."

Chapter 11

Maybe in these times driving a white van with a few cosmetic flaws to the gates of a military base wasn't the smartest thing to do. The late-afternoon light, heavy with solar glare, must have turned Betsy into a threat, because the guard at the front gate of the Pierce Island Air Force Base pointed his weapon right at me as he motioned me to stop. Another guard shoved a long-handled mirror under Betsy's undercarriage, checking for bombs.

If only Van and Wyatt could see me as that fierce.

Wyatt's body tensed into ready mode. "I told you we should've rented something more sober."

"This adds excitement."

"As if we need any more."

I rolled down my window. "Wyatt James and Sierra Martindale. We're here to see Captain Tracy James."

The MP checked his list, signed us in and gave me and Wyatt each a visitor's pass while we waited for Tracy to escort us onto the base. The constant stir of activity around us with its underlying backbeat of muffled working machinery reminded me of an anthill. I had the sinking feeling that getting a look at the HART wasn't going to be easy.

Wearing a flight suit, sunglasses twirling loosely in one hand, Tracy met us at the gate. She held her questions until we were out of earshot from the guards.

"So," she said, long legs eating up the ground as she headed toward the mess hall, "what's all the hush and hurry about, Wyatt? And what are you doing in this part of the country? For your sake, you'd better not be checking up on me."

"I need a favor."

Her forehead scrunched. "Now there's a first. My big brother actually needs *my* help. Why would you need to fly all the way out here when I was home just a few days ago?"

"I need a look at the HART system."

Tracy stopped midstride and stared him down. "Why?"

"I might be able to figure out what's wrong with it," Wyatt said. Between him and Sofia checking out the system, we should be able to come up with some sort of answer. "But I have to get in the cockpit and turn it on."

Tracy shook her head. "No can do."

Maybe I could get to Tracy another way. "Any word on what caused the crash yesterday?"

"I can't discuss it."

"Even if you could stop future crashes from happening?"

Tracy's gaze compressed. "And just how would you be able to do that when the people who work with the planes can't figure out what's wrong?"

"The HART causes a surge of some sort that makes the attitude indicator go nuts."

"And you know that because…?"

Saying the information came from a ghost was only going to get me booted off base. "I talked to the pilot who survived the last crash—barely."

She spun away from us, then bounced back. "I can't believe you stuck your nose in business that isn't yours. You've really done it this time, Wyatt." She jabbed a finger at her brother's chest. "Look, I know you've never given a flying fig about what I do, but I love my job, and I'm not going to do anything to jeopardize it. Do you realize how hard it's been for me to get where I am? Letting a woman fly an F-117 is a *huge* deal. I'll turn you in before I let you mess up my career."

"He's not messing it up," I said. "He's trying to save it."

She lit into me. "Yeah? Then what did you do to Captain Lamphere?"

"Me? Nothing. Just asked a few questions."

"He's dead."

For an instant I forgot to breathe. "What? I just saw him a few hours ago."

"Sierra's trying to save lives," Wyatt said between

clenched teeth. "Yours included. She wouldn't have hurt him."

"Yeah, well, word came an hour ago that he died. Why do you think the flags are flying at half-mast?"

The detail only now registered. An hour ago. I took in a long breath. Not long after I left him. Coincidence? "How did he die?"

Stiff and straight, Tracy crossed her arms. "Complications from the injuries he sustained during the crash."

"The man I saw looked like he was just a day from walking out of that hospital room on his own steam." The death seemed a little too convenient. Had Glenda sent her ice-hearted assassin to make sure the pilot didn't talk about what had gone wrong on his flight? Had Rey followed us to Boston?

Tracy swiveled toward the gate. "You should both leave now."

Wyatt stepped in front of her. "Sofia was killed because she suspected a fault in the HART."

Tracy's eyes bugged. "But that was a year ago and the planes—"

I butted in. "The HART system was installed last month."

"Can you get us close enough to look at the installed system?" Wyatt's tone was gentler than mine.

She shook her head. "Even if I was stupid enough to want to risk my career, I can't get you within twenty feet of the hangar. See those guys?" She pointed to a couple of military police standing in front of a metal structure. They were armed. "No one gets past them."

"Not even to show your brother who's visiting from

out of town where you work?" I asked. There had to be a way around this.

"Not even. Especially not after yesterday's incident."

A crash made for bad publicity, especially when it happened during a goodwill air show. "We really need to take a look."

"Don't push, Sierra," Wyatt warned. "Tracy would help if she could."

"You're not going to break, are you, Tracy?" I asked, recognizing the warrior in her.

"I handle tougher guys than you every day." She crooked an eyebrow. "Did I mention that my brother has a hero complex?"

"I've noticed." And I was doing my best to resist— both belting him for it and falling for it.

"This is the abuse I get for trying to help," Wyatt muttered.

"We're doing fine on our own," Tracy insisted.

Wyatt's closed expression gave away none of the roil of emotions playing in his eyes. "This could mean your life, Tracy."

I pressed the point. "Captain Lamphere told me he didn't lose control of the airplane until he engaged the HART on display circuit."

She swiped a hand over her short hair and came to a decision. "Okay, tell you what. Tomorrow there's going to be some sort of media event. They'll have an F-117 on display. Best I can do is get you a press pass for it. I know someone in public relations."

Another damn delay when a few hours ago I thought I'd had this all but sewn up. "Why the circus?"

Tracy's chin cranked up. "To prove that there's nothing wrong with the stealth fleet."

"Until the HART's integration with the other avionics is checked out, every day you fly, you take a chance," I said, laying out the risk factor for her. "Airborne Russian roulette."

"The HART's gone through a rigorous testing program. They wouldn't have put it in the airplane if it wasn't safe."

"Unless someone had hidden the discrepancy on purpose. You're a smart woman, Tracy. Do the math. The HART was installed a month ago in a third of the stealth fleet. Now five airplanes are down. Wanna bet they all had a HART?"

She rammed sunglasses over her eyes. "Even if you're right, we're at war, and no military officer is going to discuss weapons failing. They're not going to say anything that might tarnish their victory. Plus there's the public image at stake and the fact that Congress is discussing adding to the budget to build more stealth fighters as we speak."

"So they'll let pilots die?"

She shook her head. "They're conducting an investigation. Just keeping it under the public's radar."

"Keeping up appearances could get more pilots dead."

"When are you scheduled to fly?" Wyatt asked.

"Thursday."

"Don't." His voice was a stone.

Tracy got in his face nose-to-nose. "It's my job, Wyatt. I'm not going to refuse to do it. I've worked too hard to give it all up now just to please you."

"You don't want Ma to start calling the head of the Air Force, or worse, the president of the United States asking for an explanation as to why her daughter is flying an unsafe aircraft."

Tracy wasn't falling for the guilt card. "Keep your big trap shut, and we won't have to go down that road."

"If you can," I said, understanding that sometimes a girl had to take risks, "avoid turning on the HART."

"If it's part of the mission, I'll have to."

She'd been warned. She knew the odds. She knew how to load the bullets to stack them in her favor. Taking action—or not—was up to her. "How do we get our hands on those media passes?"

"I'll leave your name on the press list." Tracy's gaze bounced between us. "I've got to get back to work."

Wyatt caught Tracy's elbow. "Be careful, okay?"

"Always."

Wyatt and Tracy's goodbyes were stiff. I was sorry for the tension I'd brought between brother and sister but sorrier still for the people who'd had to die unnecessarily. Wyatt and Tracy would patch their differences.

"There's no point going home just to drive right back in tomorrow," I said once we were back on the road. I had my computer and my notes. I could work anywhere. And a walk on the beach always helped clear my thinking. My sister-in-law's family owned a vacation home near York Beach. After checking with Dana, I got the secret combination to open the door.

Too bad solving my problem wasn't as easy.

Wyatt's line of thought must have run along the same

line. Temper scudding across his face, he scoped out the house as if it was a fortress full of holes.

Wyatt and I spent the evening working through possibilities, his rough-edged voice pushing for answers. All that got us was more questions. We finally gave up and climbed upstairs to separate bedrooms.

Sleep wouldn't come. Not even the lull of the ocean or the bracing salt air outside my window could calm my whirling mind. Had someone killed Captain Lamphere deliberately? What had I missed?

Bedsprings creaked. Having Wyatt tossing and turning on the other side of the wall didn't help with the relaxation factor. Not when it was all too easy to imagine the feel of his mouth on mine, how satisfying it would be to tangle the sheets with him. I rolled over, turning my back to him.

Sofia's fretting, filling the air with restless static wasn't helping, either.

Wyatt's virtue is safe with me, Sofia. Stop worrying your ectoplasmic head about it. Now leave me alone and let me get some sleep.

Something had to change. If chasing the truth wasn't working, maybe I could smoke it out.

Tuesday, April 25

The media circus was already in full swing by the time we arrived on base after lunch. I'd dug through the closet at the beach house and found a navy skirt that hit Dana at the knee and me midthigh and a light blue blouse that could pass as a reporter's uniform once I rolled the sleeves up. Dana's black pumps were a size too small and pinched my toes but I could endure the torture for a few hours. Wyatt, armed with one of my cameras, played my fictional small newspaper's staff photographer.

"I feel like a jackass decked out like this," he muttered, obviously not happy in his supporting role.

"The vest looks cute on you." I'd outfitted one of Van's fishing vests with some of my photography equipment.

"Cute?" he growled.

"Get used to it."

"I'd rather not."

"People won't see cute as a threat."

He shot me a withering look. "You stray too far and you'll see how cute I can get."

"Yeah, yeah, I'm scared," I said, leading him into the tangle of reporters.

"I'm serious, Sierra."

"Let's see if we can get close to one of the airplanes."

News outlets from Maine, New Hampshire and Massachusetts, as well as all the national networks, jockeyed for prime space from which to report. Reporters and TV crews were given extraordinary access to the stealth fighter in its high-tech hangar protected by armed military police. Each reporter crew had an airman escort and the one airplane on display had several more keeping an eye on the crowd.

"Guess they trust us about as far as they can throw us," I said to Wyatt.

"Make sure you don't do anything to get us thrown out bodily."

"Oh, you of little faith."

I conducted fake interviews and let a hunky airman dressed in his snappy Class-A uniform help me climb into the cockpit. Wyatt, with his camera, was told to wait outside the hangar doors. He glowered at me from his post.

I wedged into the pilot's seat and took in the intimidating array of instruments. *Okay, Sofia, you're on. What do you need to look at?*

Turn on the electrical system.

Of course there was nothing labeled "Press Here."

Static crisped around me as Sofia seemed to tear her hair out. Her utter silence as she studied the avionics display grated against the background buzz of the people milling around on the ground below the jet's wings.

"So what do all these things do?" I asked my escort.

He obliged by squeezing in closer and pointing at each display in turn. He didn't smell half as good as Wyatt. "This is the display control. Here's our mission board. The radar, the EW—"

"EW?"

"Electronic warfare." He continued his tour of the cockpit instruments. "Communications, navigations and identification. Infrared search and track. Diagnostics."

I laughed. "Do they feed you ginkgo biloba along with your breakfast so you can remember all that?"

His smile gleamed. "It comes naturally after a while, ma'am."

"So this radar thing is pretty important, huh?"

"Our whole mission is to go somewhere and not be seen."

"I don't see a place for a key. How do you start this thing?"

He chuckled. "No, ma'am. It's all done with switches."

My hand moved of its own accord toward the instrument board.

"Like this one?" I asked and toggled it. Nothing happened.

"Sorry, ma'am, no juice."

I exaggerated a pout. "You guys are no fun."

"Some aspects are classified."

I quirked an eyebrow. "Like the HART."

His politeness vanished like a UFO. "There are others waiting for a turn, ma'am. And the press conference is going to start in a minute."

I gave the airman my best smile and accepted his hand as I extricated myself from the cockpit. What now?

"Get anything?" Wyatt asked when I found him in the crowd. "Or were you too busy flirting with Mr. Crew Cut?"

"Ha, you're jea-lous." Warm pleasure steamed into my bones at seeing him rattled.

He scowled.

"The power was turned off," I said. "You get anything?"

His jaw tightened. "There's an industry trade show later this week in Fort Worth. Sounds like the HART's going to be on display."

"That'll be our fall-back plan." But damn, I wanted this to be over. Today. I didn't want to go back to Fort Worth. Now that the P.I. fire was racing through my veins again, I just wanted to get back to my life.

It wasn't so much the case that bugged me. It was not having a choice. It was her in my brain when I didn't even know if she was real. Of course, if she wasn't, I was in serious trouble.

Wyatt jerked his chin toward the television cameras set up at a safe distance from the runway. "The show's about to start."

We found a spot near the front of the circus ring. Brigadier General Green stood beneath one of the odd-shaped airplanes. I could see why he'd been picked to handle the public forum. Put Santa Claus in an Air Force uniform and you have a picture of the brigadier general. You could take someone like that on faith.

"I'm here to assure all of you that our stealth fleet is combat ready," Brigadier General Green said. "News media likes sensation and they've exaggerated the stealth fighter's problems. It's already had to fight off the image of being a fair-weather weapon and problems with its radar-absorbing materials."

The general droned on enumerating the aircraft's successes.

"Are the seal joints and seams still coming apart during flight?" one reporter asked when the Q & A session started.

"No, we've made some great improvements in that department. See for yourself." Brigadier General Green introduced the show-and-tell portion of the program. A stealth fighter did some touch-and-goes on the 12,000-foot runway.

When the question period resumed, I jumped in. "Is there a connection between all the recent crashes?"

"There's no apparent connection between the incidents," the brigadier general assured me. I got the feeling that if I'd been close enough, he would've patted me on the head. "They involved several different types of aircrafts."

Man, I hated being patronized. "What about the HART?" I pressed. "According to a source, it's the reason the airplanes are crashing."

The brigadier general reddened. "No, absolutely not. Your so-called source is misinformed."

"Isn't the installation of the system recent?"

His grip on the lectern turned white. "The HART has undergone considerable testing. We would never allow a faulty system to be installed on an aircraft. That would be stupid and costly."

With each stealth fighter topping one hundred million dollars a copy, that was an understatement. "I'm sure the dead pilots would agree their life wasn't worth risking over faulty equipment. If it's not the HART, what do you think is causing the crashes?"

"We're still investigating. It's unfortunate all four accidents happened so close together. Often we find pilot error is the cause. But I can't comment on the inquiries until the investigation is finished."

Yeah, that's it, blame it on the dead guys.

The brigadier general deliberately turned away from me and answered questions from journalists on the other side of the gathering. We stayed until the end but didn't learn anything new.

"That was a waste of time," Wyatt said as we hiked back to drop off our passes.

"At least now the possibility that the HART is at fault is in the air. They won't be able to ignore it."

"But it doesn't solve the problem. Tracy's still at risk. And I'll be damned if I let her become one of their statistics."

"We still got some public attention for the problem with the HART, and that's the last thing the military or Allied Defense wants. They'll have to prove the HART works."

"That's what I'm afraid of. Tracy could be the next pilot they're willing to sacrifice."

"Then we just keep digging for more information. Captain Lamphere's death is still in the news. If my hunch is right, he had a little help in crossing over—just like Sofia."

Wyatt shook his head. "A hunch isn't a fact, and it won't ground those planes."

"In my line of business there's no such thing as a coincidence." I dug out my keys and unlocked Betsy's doors.

"Then it's time to change business."

"Is that an offer?" Looking at him over Betsy's hood, I loosed the question to make him feel awkward, and he turned the tables on me.

"Could be."

I hated it when he looked at me like that. Made me want to do reckless things. I got in the driver's seat. "I'm not Sofia. I don't need rescuing."

He slammed his door. "Maybe I'm the one in need of rescue."

"Yeah? From what?"

He puffed air into his cheeks and let it out. "From myself."

My stomach jittered but I kept a fierce expression in place as I started Betsy. She purred on the first try.

I had Sofia's take on him, but he had nothing to go on but a psycho P.I. who claimed to channel his dead wife. Still, Sofia's feelings for Wyatt were soft and gushy. This was…primal.

Shaking my head, I pointed Betsy toward the highway and drove south, back to Nashua. A slice of moon hooked a glitter-studded sky. On a Tuesday night, I-95 was fast, and I gave Betsy her head.

"You said there was an industry trade show in Fort Worth." My mind-wheels were spinning, planning, but I didn't like the direction they were pointing. On the other hand, sticking with hard facts and data was easier than dealing with the messy emotional stuff. "If Allied Defense is smart, they'll have some sort of demo to prove that the millions invested in the HART program weren't wasted."

Wyatt studied me for a long time. "We're going back to Fort Worth."

"Yeah." I couldn't help the sigh. Leaving home again. Van would have a fit.

"Maybe you should stay here," Wyatt said. "I can keep digging on my own."

"And make yourself into a target? I don't think so. I take a case. I close that case." In that way we were alike. A matter of obligation for him; pride for me. The results were the same. The job got done.

"I figured." He smirked. "Admit it. You can't let me go, because you haven't slept with me yet."

"Dream on, cowboy."

Wednesday, April 26

As we rushed to catch our flight back to DFW, a news story flashing on the television screens suspended from the ceiling caught my attention. I grabbed Wyatt's arm and forced him to stop.

"Defense Secretary Walter Sturgis has ordered a militarywide halt to training flights this afternoon," the television reporter said, her voice grave with import. "Although officials have detected no common thread in the accidents, Secretary Sturgis ordered all the services to ground their training flights for twenty-four hours. The stand-downs will be staggered over the week, starting on Thursday.

"'Perfection is impossible but that is our goal for aviation safety,' Secretary Sturgis is quoted as saying in taking the action.

"Secretary Sturgis's grounding affects training but not operational flights. Special missions in the national security interests of our country will continue without interruptions."

Which put the pilots most likely to use the HART in the gravest danger.

Tracy had earned a reprieve. For now. But time was running out.

Hand in hand, we hurried to our gate.

I had the smoke. Now to trace it back to the fire.

Chapter 12

The Tarrant County Convention Center was shaped like a giant flying saucer and took up fourteen city blocks between Houston and Commerce in downtown Fort Worth. Noelle, my assistant, had secured me a couple of passes to the industry trade show being held there over the next three days.

While Wyatt had attended to neglected ranch duties, I'd spent most of yesterday learning the layout of the booths in the 150,000 square feet of convention space and memorizing every possible escape route.

Stealing government property made me claustrophobic. I had no desire to spend the rest of my life locked up in a cell with Sofia telling me, "I told you so."

As we crossed the street, I shot Wyatt a sideways glance. I didn't want him to know what I was up to until the last possible moment. Given our mutual goal and our ongoing differing ideas on how to get there, the less time I gave him to index the reasons why my plan was such a bad idea, the better chance of success for my mission.

Colorful flags flapped from lampposts in time to my ragged pulse. Our shoes clacked on the brick walkways that fit around the flying-saucer-like spokes. Those decorative bushes would definitely slow us down if we had to make a quick getaway.

Once Wyatt was cornered, I knew he'd do the right thing. I liked that about him. He could fight me each step of the way, but when it counted, he was there like a partner I could depend on.

Not that this was a permanent arrangement. I worked alone. And he already was Sofia's partner. Her husband. It didn't matter that she was dead, especially since she spent so much time in my head, reminding me how deep their bond was. Wyatt had a life here in Texas, and I couldn't imagine myself being a part of it.

As we neared the entrance, he fingered the knot of his tie as if it were a noose that was too tight, and his discomfort pinched at my conscience. I couldn't put off telling him my plan any longer. "We need to borrow one of the chips Sofia worked on."

Door in hand, Wyatt lurched but regained control as fast as he'd lost it. "You're talking about committing treason," he said between clenched teeth, eyes darting to make sure no one had overheard me.

"Look, I'm not asking. I'm only telling you what I need to do." Afraid of the answer as to why I even cared what he thought, I didn't look too deeply. My shrink would have a field day sorting through the mess I'd jumped into. "You can drive on home and leave everything to me."

He shook his head. "No way. No cotton-pickin' way are we stealing a chip. Are you insane?"

As a matter of fact, yes, I nearly bit out. *Your wife talks to me.* "No one asked you to take any risks." I could snag the chip myself if he wasn't willing to do it. I'd just have to nab the whole device—as long as it fit in my tote—and figure out which part was which later.

Wyatt bore down on me. "Excuse me? You're the one who showed up at my ranch. You got me involved in your investigation the second you told me Sofia was murdered. That's what you wanted from the get-go."

"Getting involved was your choice." I really hated that he was right. But I didn't have time to argue. "Don't sweat it. I know a good lawyer."

Muttering under his breath, he planted a hand on the small of my back and guided me through the door. I really wished he wouldn't do that. It wasn't professional, and I was supposed to be the boss—a businesswoman looking to procure some of the independent minority contracts available. Wyatt was posing as my token male employee.

I moved away to a respectable boss/employee distance. Sunshine spilled through the glass lobby. Voices echoed all around us. Following the signs, I strode toward the exhibit hall. "The only way we're going to prove Sofia's claim is by getting hold of one of the integration chips. I'm going to send it to a trusted source to reverse-engineer and tell us what Sofia saw during testing.

"Once we have hard evidence, Allied Defense and the military won't be able to sweep these crashes under the tarmac. They're going to have to do something about them. They may have grounded some of the fleet while they investigate but the pilots on duty in the Persian Gulf are still in danger."

I jerked open the exhibit hall door. An explosion of color and noise burst like a carnival in full swing.

Wyatt blocked my way with his arm. "And just how do you plan on getting this chip?"

I reached up and straightened his tie. "That's where you come in. Once we've located the Allied Defense booth, I'm going to distract whoever's manning it while you pull the chip. Easy." I cleared my throat. "If anything happens, run."

He glanced at the rent-a-cops with their guns and their walkie-talkies. "Run?"

"Fast," I suggested. My fingers lingered on the silk knot at his throat. He looked hot in his cowboy duds, but even hotter in charcoal superfine wool.

I drew close enough to him to catch the warm piney scent of his cologne. "This is phase one. We're just looking. Then we'll leave so the security cameras catch us going out. We'll come back with a different disguise."

He mumbled something I was sure wasn't thanks. He'd do what I'd asked of him—for Sofia. He couldn't help himself.

We showed our passes at the registration table and were given a neck holder for our passes and a map of the booths. Major players like Raytheon, Boeing and Lockheed Martin manned booths, as well as smaller companies looking to tap into the lucrative government contract pockets.

We hooked a left and started for the northwestern corner where Allied Defense had set up their booth. Before we reached the far aisle, my gaze snagged on a banner that looked oddly familiar. Then it hit me where I'd seen that logo before. The truck that night at the plant. White with a swash of blue. I slowed as I recognized the man in the dark suit.

I elbow-jabbed Wyatt and nudged my chin in Antonio's direction. "Why would a garbage man participate in a defense industry trade show?"

"All big companies recycle." Wyatt grabbed my waist and aimed me away from the Castille Disposition Services booth. I resisted his suggestion. A stream of people flowed around us, giving us cover.

"We should go say hello."

No! A bolt of ice lanced through my heart and Sofia's fear shivered through me.

"Bad idea," Wyatt said.

"They're family."

"Not anymore."

At the sight of the display, flashing behind Antonio, one and one collided loudly in my head and added up to a possibility I hadn't entertained. Antonio recycled for Allied Defense. Rey worked for Antonio, and Wyatt had found a toothpick in his office—the kind that dangled from Rey's lips. "So the data sheet that disappeared from your office could possibly mean something to Antonio."

"I doubt it," Wyatt said. "Not without context."

"What if he has context?"

"The recycling part of the business is where Antonio made his name. Antonio's younger brother now runs that. About five years ago, Antonio started an IT disposal division. They can't afford to steal."

"IT as in information technology? Computers?" This was worse than I thought. Computers would give Antonio access to a lot more sensitive information. Had he used his own daughter to gain access to that information?

Antonio gestured broadly at some sort of presentation while Inez sat, hands in her lap, back straight, eyes a thousand miles away. What was she even doing there? She looked so out of place in her depressing black dress—as if she were at a funeral instead of a business promotion. How could she help Antonio's business with her gloomy presence?

"Antonio's service disposes of any piece of technology—computers, PDAs, cell phones—safely." Wyatt's grip on my waist tightened as he tried to get me back on track toward the Allied Defense booth. "They sanitize the memory so that no one can recover any sensitive information. They refurbish the equipment and distribute it to charity organizations or resell it. That's important when companies upgrade their equipment and can't just dump old equipment away."

I faced Wyatt, my peripheral vision scoping out Inez who looked pale and much too subdued. She was a far cry from the screaming harpy I'd met. What was wrong with her? "So Antonio could steal information?"

Wyatt shook his head. "The disks are wiped before they leave Allied Defense. Then they're run through with disk sanitizers and declassifiers at Castille Disposition before the devices are repurposed."

Inez pressed two fingers against her sinuses as if something smelled bad. She searched through her purse, came out with a lace handkerchief and dabbed it at her dry eyes.

"But before the hard drives are erased," I said, "he could look at what's on the hard drive."

"Antonio runs the business. He doesn't do the dirty work."

"Right. He has somebody else do it. Like Rey."

Wyatt blew out a long breath, and exasperation laced his voice. "There are DOD standards involved in IT asset recycling. If he didn't follow the standards for disposal, he wouldn't last in the business. There's too much at stake."

"Yeah, well, there are laws but not everybody follows them." I'd certainly bent a few over the years.

"If you want to survive in this business, you do. Reputation is everything, and reputation drives Antonio."

Why was reputation so important to a man whose appearance pretty much shouted he didn't care what others thought?

Both hands crimped around her purse, Inez stood up in a robotic fashion, and while Antonio had his back turned to her, she sidled out of the booth and quick-stepped away.

Something wasn't right. I needed to lose Wyatt

and corner Inez. "How do you know so much about the business?"

"Yet another way I disappointed my in-laws." A somber intensity darkened his eyes. "Antonio wanted me to join the family business—just like he'd done when he'd married Inez and took her name."

What? Why hadn't my background check revealed this? "Why would a proud man like Antonio take a woman's name?"

"To show that the son of a garbageman was good enough for Inez."

"Funny that Inez would be so hard on you for being unacceptable if she also married beneath her station."

"I'm not Catholic." He shrugged. "I could've joined the firm. I could've written cryptographic code. But my dad had just died and the ranch needed me."

"If your heart wasn't in it…"

Palming both my elbows, he turned me away from the Castille booth. "Let's find the Allied Defense booth and get out of here."

I nodded, distracted. Something fired in my brain but I couldn't get the synapses to make the right connections. "I have to use the ladies' room. Scope out the location of the Allied Defense booth. I'll meet you there in five minutes."

His gaze narrowed with suspicion. "If you're not back in five minutes, I'm coming to get you."

"You're not big on trust, are you?"

"I'm huge on trust. There's just something about your thought process that gives me the willies."

I showed him some teeth. Did he really think so

little of me? "That's what gets people ahead, you know—thinking differently. It's how we're going to solve this case."

"Yeah, if we're alive to enjoy it." He hooked a hand around my nape and rubbed his thumb up and down my neck. "Stay out of trouble. We have unfinished business."

"I'm just going to the ladies' room," I told Wyatt. "How much trouble can I get into?"

He exaggerated a shudder. "I'm afraid to answer that."

I smiled at him and he smiled back, and the smile so changed his face that the sight of it broadsided me.

"Five minutes," he warned, serious again.

I nodded and headed toward the last place I'd seen Inez, my legs not quite as steady as I'd like. The macho stuff I could handle. The nice stuff unraveled me. What did that say about me?

The sight of Inez pushing through the bathroom door sobered me. I entered behind her and followed her to the sinks.

Inez's eyes rounded as our gazes collided in the mirror, then creased to acerbic slits. "What are *you* doing here?"

"Looks like I'm washing my hands." I squirted soap into my palms and rubbed away whatever germs I'd picked up on the entrance doors.

"What business do you have here?"

"I'm still looking for Sofia's murderer." I cocked my head in her direction. Something about her rubbed me the wrong way. Maybe that was Sofia's doing, too. I don't know why I'd wasted a second feeling sorry for Inez or worrying about her health. "Want to know how the investigation's coming?"

Her expression pinched and she refused to look in my direction. "I have nothing to say to you."

I rinsed my hands. "How about Sofia? Anything you want to tell her? She's right here. She can hear you."

Inez backed away from me, crossing herself with one hand and letting her handkerchief fall between us like a shield with the other. "You are a devil!"

A storm of fear erupted inside me, blowing through every one of my muscles like a winter blizzard.

What did she do to you? I asked Sofia.

Sofia was tomb silent with only the rumble of her terror thundering through me.

"What did you do to Sofia?" I asked Inez, curiosity aroused.

Inez bared her teeth at me. "I did nothing to her. I gave her everything."

My throat burned with the salt of Sofia's tears. Then something in me popped, and I was out of my body, watching myself with Inez as if I had a front-row seat just off the ceiling. Everything had an edge of gray, as if an inch of dust coated the TV screen. Water dripped from my fingers and plopped onto the floor, but I couldn't feel it. My limbs shook, but I couldn't feel their shiver. My heart? Was it failing? What was happening to me?

"Everything? Everything?" Sofia's voice spewed out of my mouth like venom.

Get out! You can't do that, Sofia! It's my body. My life. Get back to where you belong. You're dead. I'm alive.

It's my *heart.*

I fought to leave my ceiling perch but my body didn't

respond—as if someone had shot it full of Novocain. I panted, panicking, fighting the numbness of my being, the crushing of my chest. It was like that night when I'd died. My heart beating out of tune. My breath smoke-thin. The world blackening. There was nothing I could do, except watch. Helpless. I didn't want to disappear.

Sofia! Let me go!

She ignored me.

What if I couldn't get back? I wasn't done with my life. I had things left to do. *Sofia!*

Using my body, Sofia advanced on her mother, fists balled hard at her sides, trapping Inez against the tile wall. "You gave me nothing. You smothered me until I couldn't breathe. Why do you think I was so glad someone wanted to marry me? Take me away from my prison?"

"Sofia?" Then, as if she met up with the ghost of her daughter every day, Inez slapped me/Sofia across the face, leaving a red imprint of her palm on my cheek. "I raised you with every advantage. Gave you everything you needed to make you strong, to turn you into a proper lady."

"Except the freedom to figure out who I was and what I wanted."

"If you'd have listened to me, you could have had the world."

"I didn't want the world. I wanted your love."

"Love is an illusion." Fire burned bright in Inez's eyes. "It doesn't protect you from the harsh realities of the world."

"The world couldn't be harsher than what I experienced at home. Ask yourself this, Mama? Why do you think it is that I love Lorraine more than you?"

Inez gasped. "Sofia, no. Why do you wound me this way? I sacrificed my life for you."

"I love Lorraine because she always treats me as if what I want is important. She always asks for my opinion. Don't you see, Mama, if you'd only given me the chance to choose, I would have turned to you for help. But you never listened. I had to escape."

Inez crumpled against the sink, keening.

Get out, Sofia. You can't have my life.

Why not? You're so willing to take mine.

Sofia resisted my attempt to regain control of my body. But as Inez sobbed her heart out and the heat of Sofia's emotions cooled, Sofia could not sustain the intensity needed to stay in my body. Her spirit peeled away in a flurry of static that flickered the lights and hurt like a Band-Aid being yanked off raw skin. Never before had I so welcomed pain. I collapsed against the sink beside Sofia's mother. Inez reached out for me, and I was too weak to push her away.

"Sofia?" Fear and hope both warbled through her voice.

As I rubbed warmth along my arms, Inez's swollen, red-rimmed eyes peered up at me beseechingly. "Sofia..."

I found I could not leave Inez with Sofia's vitriol as the last words she would carry from her daughter.

"In spite of everything, she loved you," I said. And somehow I knew that was true. Just as I realized I would always love my own mother. She may not have been there for me, but the freedom she'd granted me had molded me into who I was. And frankly I liked that person—when Sofia wasn't sucking the life out of me—

even if I didn't meet Van's or anyone else's standards. And for all her faults my mother had never tried to change my nature.

Inez's mouth opened and her voice cracked on her sob. "I did not know Sofia felt so caged. I was trying to free her from the bonds that kept me a prisoner."

"How could you when she never said anything?"

Inez flinched. "I did to her what my own father had done to me." Her admission was barely a whisper.

"I'm so sorry."

She straightened and jammed her hands under cold water. She wet her handkerchief and dabbed at her smeared makeup, closing me out. "I don't need your pity. You never should have come here."

So much for trying to be the nice guy. I glanced at my watch and saw that Wyatt's five minutes had elapsed a minute ago. I gave Inez the last piece of advice that would set her free if she chose to hear it. "Let Sofia go, Inez. The shrine you have for her…it's not healthy. Live your own life. It's not too late."

Without giving her a chance to answer, I went back to finding her daughter's killer.

Chapter 13

I found Wyatt pacing near the Allied Defense booth, scanning the crowd as if he was ready to murder somebody. He stopped when he spotted me.

What surprised me most was that his first glance was one of pleasure—as if he was glad to see me. Then "Are you okay?" flashed through his eyes. Only next did anger flare. He looked pointedly at his watch.

I shrugged as much to toss aside the warm feeling as to show I didn't care. "What's the scoop?"

He plunked himself next to me, armor against the river of people trekking through the narrow aisles. I squeezed some space between us but didn't challenge his he-man tendencies. I was already asking him to put aside too much of his usual nature.

He jerked his chin in the direction of the booth. "The scoop is that you got lucky."

"Luck is nothing more than opportunity plus preparation."

"That and the fact Allied Defense brought a show-and-tell version of the HART. Which means all I have to do is pull the card from the test stand." His jaw flinched. "If I can get close enough to it."

"I'll make sure you do." Since he was going against all his principles for me—well, for Sofia—the least I could do is make sure he got out safe. I scoped out the booth. Only one man staffed it at the moment. "Come on."

Back at the truck, I changed into a shapeless dress, granny shoes, a blond wig and added a pregnancy belly. Absently I patted the roundness, and sadness stung me. All the drugs I took to stave off rejection made pregnancy a dangerous proposition. Another reason to get my life back on my own terms. If I couldn't have a family, what I did for a living had to make me happy.

I helped Wyatt with his disguise. Even the cheap brown suit couldn't quite hide his fine form. I had him put on a set of yellowed and crooked teeth. With the help of a makeup kit, I added a ragged scar that jagged along his cheek. The high school drama club experience had paid off in spades over the years. This close, the piney musk of his scent seemed to fill the cab of the truck and made me sweat.

He yanked on the rearview mirror to view my hand-iwork. "I feel like an ass."

"Even better, you look like one," I teased, combing his part to the wrong side. "It's all about impression.

People don't notice details. Later, if they remember us at all, what they'll recall is your scar and my big belly."

He grunted an answer.

I unfolded the trade-show map of the booths and went over the exit strategy with him. "The important thing is to not panic. All you have to do is pretend like you belong, like you don't have a care in the world and get to one of these two exits."

"The guards have guns," Wyatt reminded me.

"They aren't going to use them in a crowd. They can't afford the stampede. You take the card, pass it to me and go."

"I don't want to leave you back there alone. Not if you're holding the chip."

"If we're apart, it'll be easier for us to get away. And they won't be able to connect us. We'll meet back at the truck. If something goes wrong and it's safer to meet elsewhere, go to the Mustang Bar and Grill in Sundance Square." I pulled one of Van's business cards from my tote. "And if you get caught, call my brother."

"I don't like this."

"You wanted in. Deal with it." I stuffed everything back into the plastic bag and shoved it behind the seat, throwing a blanket over it. "You go first. I'll follow in a few minutes."

"In and out. No side trips," he warned, then strode toward the convention center with purposeful steps.

"Wait," I called. "Put a pebble in your shoe. Then take it out after you have the card."

"Why?"

"Your walk's too macho. It doesn't fit with the rest of your disguise."

He rolled his eyes skyward but did as I asked. The slight limp gave him a pathetic edge that would have people glancing away in pity.

Foot jiggling as I sat in the truck, I traded my faithful leather tote for a plain beige canvas one and counted the minutes until I could spring into action. Waiting was always the hardest part for me.

Sofia? I asked, but got no answer. How hard had taking over my body been on her? Had it zapped her ability to penetrate my mind? I shook my head. It didn't matter. Getting the card, the hard evidence was what I had to concentrate on. I'd asked a lot from Wyatt; I had to make sure this ploy succeeded.

I took on a harried demeanor as I made my way back to the convention floor. Notebook from my canvas bag poised, I stepped into the Allied Defense booth. The pass dangling at my neck was conveniently twisted as I approached the young man with the tightly coiled blond hair, a used-car-salesman smile and a stiff new suit. I clumsily juggled my notebook and bag and stuck out my hand, which he folded into both of his sweaty ones.

"Hi, I'm from *Defense Today*," I said, oozing warmth into my voice. "I'm doing a piece on the trade show and I'd like to include Allied Defense."

"Tad Ahearn," he boomed, then grinned as he pumped my hand. "You've come to the right place."

Tad nodded at Wyatt as he stepped into the booth, but he quickly turned back to me. "What would you like to know?"

My pulse hiked as I ignored Wyatt and concentrated on Tad's hawkish gray eyes. "What's new, what's in the works."

Wyatt took up a position along the far end of the booth, amazing me with his ability to pretend he was totally engrossed in one of the brochures spread along the display table.

Tad's voice spooled out in rapid-fire excitement. "I'm sure you've heard Senator Kenneth Tharp's announcement today that the Department of Defense Appropriations has allocated more than $50 million for Allied Defense. That includes $6.6 million to continue developing HART technology."

"They must have a high degree of confidence in the system," I said.

"Extreme." Pride resonated in Tad's voice. He jabbed a finger at the radar display. "Let me show you how this works."

"That's not necessary."

"I've sent a signal like so," Tad plowed on, ignoring me. "And here the F-117 is flying along. See how there's still a faint echo on the radar. It's not much but it's too much if we don't want to be seen." He toggled a switch. "Now look, nothing. Absolute invisibility."

"That is something." I kept Wyatt in my peripheral vision as he made his way closer to the black test stand holding the cards.

Tad kept showing off while I played interested reporter. Wyatt looked wired and restless. His energy was contained but dangerously so. Asking him to steal was bad enough. Making him stew in the possible consequences of his actions had to be killing him. But I couldn't move Tad from his toy. Time for desperate measures.

"Oh." I reached for my temple with a hand and back-pedaled a bit as if I was about to faint.

"What's wrong?" Tad rushed to my side and balanced me with his damp hands on both my arms. "Is it the baby?"

"I'm feeling a little woozy."

Tad helped me to the lone chair in the booth and offered me a bottle of water.

"Just give me a minute. I'll be okay." I gave him a weak smile. "This baby's got to be a boy with all the energy he saps from me."

"My wife was the same way when she was expecting our son." Tad reached into a messenger bag under the chair. "Here, have some crackers. You need to keep up your strength."

"Thanks, that's so sweet of you." The salt content on these things was probably a week's worth allowance for me but I made a show of accepting his offering and nibbling on a cheese-and-peanut-butter cracker and washing it down with the water.

Wyatt edged closer to the test stand that ran the sim-ulation. My heart knocked around in my chest and con-centrating on Tad's patter was getting harder by the second. Wyatt's hand reached out to the display and as he got ready to flick the HART switch off, I dropped the water bottle and bent over awkwardly to pick it up.

"I think I'm okay now." I rose as gracefully as a hippo, letting Tad help me up.

Wyatt reached inside the stand, hit the quick disconnect holding the card in place and pulled out the card. He slipped the nine-by-five card into his jacket. I let out a whoosh of relief.

"You've been really nice," I said to Tad. "Do you have a business card so I can write a thank-you note to your supervisor?"

Preening like a peacock, he whipped out his wallet. "It's been a pleasure. Call me if you need to verify anything."

I took his card and slipped it into my notebook. "Thanks."

I caught up to Wyatt as he turned at the end of the aisle. He ditched the card with the chip into my canvas bag as I went by him, heading in the opposite direction.

I slanted one last look at the Allied Defense booth. Tad gestured wildly at two security guards. Their radios hissed like rattlers looking for prey. Shoot, they'd already discovered the card feeding the HART simulation was missing.

I was nearly at the back exit when two guards converged my way. My stomach twisted as I spun through options. I didn't have many.

I stepped into the Electronic Data Systems booth and snaked through their back panels and into the Ball Corporation booth. Two more security guards popped at each end of the aisle, hurrying to some unknown destination. I fell in step with a group of burly guys. One security guard strode right by me, not even glancing my way.

I sucked in a breath. They were looking for someone else. Wyatt? Had my scheme put him in danger? That's what I got for involving someone else. I should've done this on my own.

When I reached the end of the aisle, the group of businessmen broke apart, leaving me exposed again. Heart pounding, I kept a cool demeanor as I studied the guards' hurried movements toward the front of the exhibit hall.

As I neared the entrance, a cordon of guards blocked it, letting people out only after searching their bags. Not good since mine held what they were looking for. At least it would give Wyatt a clean getaway. I'd have to find another way out.

I milled around the outside ring of booths until I spotted a technician unlocking a utility access. As the door started to close, I squeezed in before it automatically locked behind him. I plunged into a dim staging area littered with miles of electric wire and criss-crossed with vents. The dusty space throbbed to the sound of air-conditioning pumping out air and smelled of machine oil and dust.

I had bigger things to worry about than germs right now.

While my eyes adjusted to the dim light, I flattened against the wall. A minute later three guards poured in through another access door. Their radios crackled as they spread out, drawing their guns. I spotted a breaker box to my left. Using a pocket tool, I broke open the lock and flipped all the breakers. The place went dark. The air-conditioning groaned to a halt, throwing the space into an eerie quiet.

The guards shouted, their light beams flashing madly. Hugging the walls as best I could, I patted my way to the nearest outside door. I huddled there for a second, listening for the guards. A flashlight caught my face briefly in its beam. "Security! Stop!"

I slipped behind a duct before he got a good look at me. He called for backup as I made my way around him.

"Sorry," I said, and took the legs out from under him with an electric wire at his feet. He landed flat on his back, the wind knocked out of him and his flashlight under a duct, leaving us in the dark again. Before he could recover, I dragged him to a steel beam and handcuffed him to it. Then I gagged him with his own handkerchief so he couldn't call out for help once his breath returned.

Footsteps stomped my way and a voice called out. "Steve? Where are you?"

I broke through the emergency exit door. Sun blinded me, forcing me to slow down. Police cars, lights flashing, squealed in front of the convention center. I needed to follow the advice I'd given Wyatt: "Don't panic." The guard hadn't gotten a good look at me. I hadn't gone anywhere near the test stand, so I couldn't be Tad's prime suspect.

Going back to the truck was out of the question. I needed to lose the pregnancy disguise before I went anywhere near the convention center again. Scouting the surroundings, I matched them to the map of downtown Fort Worth I'd studied yesterday and merged into a group of tourists heading for the north entrance to the Water Gardens.

A cluster of guards appeared, searching the crowd. I let the group of tourists sweep me to the active pool, then bounded down the terraced stairs, water chuting down all around me. I hopped across the concrete pilings at the bottom of the pit and scampered back up the other flight of slab stairs and into the pedestrian traffic.

To be on the safe side, I took a roundabout way to Sundance Square. In a coffee shop, I took off the wig, dress and belly, washed off the makeup and changed into jeans and a Chocolate Is the Answer to Every Problem T-shirt. The outfit looked a bit funky with the granny shoes—not that many people would notice the shoes. I mixed with the tourist crowd strolling the sidewalks, going by the bar on the opposite side of the street before crossing over and going in.

The Mustang Bar and Grill was cool—cold, really, after my run—and my eyes took a moment to adjust to the dim light inside after the harsh sunshine outside. Wyatt was nowhere in sight. I picked a booth at the far end that hid me from passersby but gave me a clear look out the window.

Ten minutes ticked by. Where was he? What if he'd gotten caught? I took out my cell phone, ready to call Van for advice. Yeah, that'd go over real well. He already thought I couldn't take care of myself.

I downed a glass of water and bit the bullet. I wouldn't mention my tight spot right now, but I needed something else from Van, so I called him.

"I need an intro to your friend A.J. Turcotte," I said after Van's usual growled greeting.

Van's friend was your typical lab geek. Wild curly hair that was always in bad need of a cut and dressed like a slob. He and Van couldn't be more opposite but they'd become fast friends in college and still bowled together once a month. They said it relaxed them. Worse, they called it a sport. As if.

"Why?" Van asked, instantly suspicious.

"I need him to reverse-engineer a computer chip for me." I left out the part about stealing it.

"I'm not going to abet whatever foolish fantasy you're pursuing."

"Fantasy would imply I'm having fun." That the old P.I. juice was flowing again was beside the point. I just wished I hadn't involved Wyatt. I scanned the side-walks outside the bar. Where the hell was he? He'd gotten out before I had. He should be here by now. "This is more like being stuck in a horror movie set and the director never calls 'Cut.'" Which was also true. As long as Sofia was in my head, my life was on hold.

In his most lawyerly voice, Van presented point-by-point evidence of my stupidity. "You take off on some nameless case for days at a time without leaving word to anybody as to where you are. You don't give a care that I've been worrying my head off about you. What am I supposed to think? Stop whatever it is you're chasing, Sierra, and come home where you belong."

I bit my tongue to stop my usual shot from the hip. "I can understand how my behavior appears a tad crazy from where you're sitting. You're the one who wanted me to find my energy again, remember? I'm back, Van." Most of me, anyway. If I could just get Sofia out of my head, I could go back to full-time investigating.

"Do me a favor, will you?" I asked. "Keep your phone line open. If I can't get this chip analyzed, I might need legal representation. I know how bad things would be for you if my actions tainted the family name and affected the firm. And I'm really trying to protect you from bad publicity."

"Sierra," he growled, then sighed, giving in. "I'll call A.J. and give him a heads up. Hang on."

A.J. agreed to look at the chip but warned me that he wasn't promising anything.

"That's all I ask."

I ended the call and twirled the phone in my hand. Wyatt was still missing. Was he being hauled off to jail? At least he didn't have the chip on him, so he could yell and scream about false accusations and police brutality. If need be, Van would throw lawyerese at them and rescue him. Van was good at rescuing. Not so good at letting go.

I had to lose the chip. Then I had to find Wyatt.

Just as I was about to leave, Wyatt entered the bar—minus the teeth and scar. He carried the suit jacket over one arm and had the sleeves of his shirt rolled up, showing off tanned and taut skin. His step held a confident swagger that had the two big-haired, twentysomething women sitting at the front booth turning around for a second look.

I'd never been so glad to see anyone and couldn't help smiling like an idiot. He zeroed in on me as if there was no one else in the restaurant and smiled. Everything in me calmed. I'd never had that happen with anyone before. Then my well-honed survival instincts kicked in. Just relief, I told myself, not attachment. If Wyatt had gotten in trouble because of me, I'd have felt bad.

As he sat, Wyatt pointed at my T-shirt. A storm of emotions churned in his eyes. His pulse thumped at his throat. "How many of those do you have?"

I plucked at the shirt and chuckled, giving him time to reel himself back in. "About a dozen. I don't know where my assistant finds them all but she gives me one every Christmas and for every birthday."

"You're a chocolate freak?" he asked, as if he needed to stay away from the talk of treason for just a bit longer.

I played along. "Not as much as I used to be." I studied the flush of excitement coloring his cheeks. "Did you have to run to get away?"

"I stayed cool and got away with no problem. I waited for you in the truck, then thought maybe you'd run into trouble, so I came back here."

"Did anyone follow you?"

"I don't think so."

Wyatt ordered a hot chocolate for me and a beer for himself. I sidled over to the bar and bought him a black Mustang Bar and Grill T-shirt and got him to lose the tie and shirt. Just in case he'd made an impression on anyone.

"We can't go back to your truck," I whispered over the top of my hot chocolate. "The police will have the place swarming."

He chugged down half of his beer and sat back with a glow of aliveness I hadn't seen on him, except when he'd ridden his horse. "I've already called one of my ranch hands. He'll drop his truck off here and drive mine back to the ranch."

I resisted my impulse to reach forward and feel the rush of his pulse rioting at his throat. "You're getting good at this."

He shook his head. "Don't even go there."

"Admit it. You got a rush."

His hazel gaze blazed into me, stripping off clothes, leaving me exposed and naked. Oh, yeah, I knew that side effect of a rush. That's how I got involved with Leo in the first place.

Wyatt's voice dropped an octave and rumbled. "Only if you'll admit you want me."

My insides jolted in a primitive reaction and I swallowed hard.

"And if I did?" My voice was steadier than I expected. I could rationalize my attraction to Wyatt a dozen ways, blaming Sofia's messy emotions, the need to work with him on this case, the chase where we'd just barely escaped capture, but the one thing I couldn't do was deny it. I wanted him. Wanted to feel all the energy of the chase thrumming through his body flow into mine.

Worse, every line of his face said he knew it.

One side of his mouth quirked up. "You're not ready for me."

I was wet and willing. But he was right. I wasn't ready to make myself quite that vulnerable to someone else yet. Not when he still had so many emotions running through him for his dead wife.

"Wrong time," I said, regret spinning. "Wrong place." And because Sofia was bound to recharge her energy soon, I added, "Wrong person."

Wyatt grabbed my chin and forced me to look into his eyes. "I don't see Sofia when I look at you. You keep me off balance. I like that."

I liked it, too. Liked knowing I got to him. But I didn't believe he could look at me, at the scar on my chest, and not think of Sofia. "How can you not see her?"

"She was nothing like you."

"Then what do you see?"

He cocked his head, studying me. "I see freedom. A woman who knows what she wants and goes after it. A woman who knows who she is and makes no excuse for it."

Not so much in the past year but, yes, on the whole, he was right, I liked who I was and what I did. Worse, I liked that he saw me for who I was and wasn't afraid of it.

"But you're still carrying a load of guilt about Sofia," I said. "You're not ready, either."

A sad smile dimmed his previous thrill of the hunt. "I'd like to be."

"Me, too." But just because you wanted something, didn't mean you'd get it. Like me wanting my own heart back. It wasn't going to happen, so I had to adjust, learn to live with my new limitations.

I should have stuck to my guns and gone in alone. "I shouldn't have asked you to help me steal the chip."

"Proving Sofia's claim that there's something wrong with the HART is important, not just for you and me, but for all the people who depend on it to protect them." Wyatt finished his beer and his gaze went to the canvas tote. "The shit's going to hit the fan soon. Cops are going to be crawling all over the place. We've got to lose the chip. Fast."

"I've got it covered."

Wyatt nudged me. "There's John."

I emptied the contents of the canvas bag into the plastic bag that had come with Wyatt's T-shirt and followed Wyatt out of the bar. Once outside, I dumped my canvas bag in the trash. Wyatt switched places with his ranch hand and exchanged keys while I slid into the passenger's side.

Wyatt crammed John's cowboy hat on his head, then reached back for a horse blanket and threw it over me. "Stay down."

"Germs!" I squeaked.

"It's clean."

It did smell of detergent, so I relaxed and hunched down like a passenger in an airplane emergency drill. "If you see a post office, stop."

While I was bent over, I dug through the plastic bag for a padded envelope I'd packed, slipped in the card Wyatt had stolen and scribbled A.J.'s address on the front. "We'll stuff this in an overnight envelope. The sooner we get results, the sooner we can put all this behind us."

Chapter 14

Friday, April 28

I'd half expected the police or FBI or some sort of law enforcement to show up at the ranch and drag Wyatt and me off in handcuffs. But no one had knocked on the door, and the news had carried nothing on the theft at the convention center. I couldn't sit still, so I paced Wyatt's office, wearing a path into the nap of his carpet and glancing out the window to the ring.

After the rush of adrenaline had died down, reality had hit Wyatt hard and he'd become tense and anxious about what the test results would reveal. No doubt wondering if he'd risked his freedom for nothing. At least he was out riding his favorite stallion now. Maybe he'd get rid of some of his built-up stress. I needed to run and let out a little steam myself.

With a growl, I plunked into Wyatt's brown leather chair and stared at the screen saver on my open laptop on his desk as it flowed through a series of images of space taken from the Hubble telescope. I liked the photos because they reminded me of the vastness of the world and my own insignificant part in it. Van might believe I thought the world revolved around me but I'd known since I was a kid that it didn't. Today the photos of faraway nebulas brought another musing, one that went beyond this world.

If Sofia was real, then there was a certain comfort in knowing that even when the body died, part of one survived. "What's it like where you are, Sofia?"

Gray. Cold. Lonely.

Pretty much what I'd experienced when she'd taken over my body. Come to think of it, pretty much my life since the transplant. Fear had shackled me much more than I'd thought. I couldn't help feeling sorry for Sofia. "What about the light you always hear about? Angels? God?"

I haven't seen any of them yet.

"Maybe you will once you can let go of your ties to what you left behind." Strange as it sounded, I wanted her to find peace as much as I wanted it for myself.

I'm scared.

"New things are always scary." Like death. A year ago the thought that the transplant team was going to cut my heart out of me, that my chest was going to be empty, that I was going to die before they could bring me back to life with a stranger's heart beating inside me had scared me more than I'd admitted to anyone.

At least you got a second chance to live.

"Yes, I did, and I thank you for your generosity."

A mental shrug. *You're not so bad.*

"That's something, I suppose." As much of a pain as Sofia was, she was also starting to grow on me. Maybe it was her loyalty—a trait I'd always admired. Maybe it was the purity of her love for Wyatt—something I'd thought I'd had with Leo. Maybe it was her gentleness of spirit—something I could use a little of to smooth out the rough edges.

All this waiting was driving me nuts. With a swipe of my finger on the touchpad, I cleared the screen saver and checked on my neglected messages. Maybe A.J. had decided to e-mail me his results even though I'd asked for a phone call.

How long before you hear from your lab rat? Sofia asked.

"I don't know. Soon, I hope."

What if he finds nothing?

"Then maybe there's nothing wrong and you whipped yourself up into a lather for nothing."

I saw something.

"Then I'll keep looking."

Shoot. Nothing in my in-box from A.J. But among the usual deluge of spam, I found a message with the financials I'd ordered—and forgotten about—on Paul Farr and Glenda McCall. I opened the file and my stomach sank in a free fall. "They look clean."

But Glenda's final divorce decree was still pending, because of the custody dispute. Once the assets were split, things might not look so rosy. She'd made more than her husband. She'd most likely get stuck paying alimony and child support.

And Glenda had expensive tastes. Something clicked. "The guy that cornered Glenda at the cutting show. Remember him?"

Sofia's shiver reverberated down my spine.

"He threatened to take away what was most precious to her."

You can't think he'll hurt a child!

"He didn't strike me as the type who had a conscience."

But an innocent child?

"Makes for a powerful motivator. Maybe he's just toying with her. Maybe he's serious. Either way, she can't afford to call his bluff."

Glenda had probably gotten herself into this tight spot with no help, but sometimes people who found themselves cornered would take an out if they could find one. I'd give her a chance to redeem herself at the meeting Wyatt had set up with Paul. I reached for the phone.

"Glenda McCall," she answered.

"Hi, Glenda. This is Sierra Martindale, Wyatt's friend."

"What can I do for you?" Her voice was so tight it surely didn't require any lip movement.

I leaned back in Wyatt's comfortable chair, and for a second his arms seemed to wrap around me. "It's more what I can do for you. Meet me and Wyatt at The Watering Hole tonight at seven."

"I'd love to but I'm busy."

"I'd say it'd be to your advantage to stand up for yourself."

"I have no idea what you're talking about."

"The HART. I have proof that Allied Defense—meaning you—swept less-than-desirable test results under the carpet in order to meet your target dates."

"What kind of proof?" Glenda asked.

"Black-and-white. Paul's going to be there."

A printer whirred in the background. "You're bluffing."

"What if I'm not?" I asked. "Can you afford my exposing the data?"

"I have more important things to deal with than a private detective who's not licensed to work in Texas." Glenda slammed down the phone.

I smiled, pleased. She'd checked up on me. She knew I was effective. "She'll be there. She won't be able to stop herself."

At The Watering Hole, musicians were running through a sound check on the small stage. The lead singer's voice boomed on mics that shrieked feedback. A guitar, bass and piano pumped out mismatched notes. Paul and Glenda sat at a table as far from the noise as they could, but we still ended up having to lean in, huddled like good friends, to hear each other.

Paul cracked peanuts, discarding both shells and meats. Rings of sweat had formed on his black Allied Defense polo shirt. Glenda looked sharp, and much too crisp, in her navy Donna Karan suit. Attitude honed her cheekbones and pointy chin to a keen knife edge.

"You're late," Paul barked, his eyes invisible in the folds of his pasty face.

Wyatt eyed Paul and Glenda with flat suspicion. "Last minute information."

I nudged his knee, reminding him we'd agreed I'd lead the show. I'd get this last bit done for Sofia and free him from his final obligation to her.

"We put together something we knew you'd like." I pulled up a file labeled Proof. "A PowerPoint presentation."

Fortunately, A.J. had called half an hour before Wyatt and I were due to leave, and our little presentation wasn't a bluff. I set my laptop on the table and turned it around so both Paul and Glenda could have a good view. "Here we have the results of the analysis done on an integration chip from the HART. The reversed capacity tested fine on its own but failed at full power."

I let them follow the lines of data they would understand much better than I could. "Analysis points to mixed technologies causing random surges that in turn can cause false avionics readings. Something to do with a glitch due to asynchronous digital circuit design that nullifies something else in the COTS technology. The surge it emits causes the false reading. The randomness of the surge is what makes it look as if pilot error caused the planes to crash."

I moved on to the next slide. "This is one of the data sheets that disappeared from Sofia's briefcase thirteen months ago." The next slide showed a split screen. One side held Sofia's data sheet; the other one the data generated by A.J. "Allied Defense knew about the malfunction thirteen months ago."

"This doesn't prove anything." Glenda's shoulders were so square I could have set a level on them and had the bubble centered. "For all we know, you manufactured all this crap, because your dubious investigative skills have gotten you nowhere on your quixotic quest to find something wrong with the HART." She drilled a finger into the tabletop, emphasizing each of her words. *"There is nothing there."*

"I never received this information about a random surge from the Integration Lab." Paul tossed a handful of peanut shells to the floor.

Wyatt braced his mug of beer as if it took all his will to keep himself from throwing it in Paul's—or Glenda's—face. "Sofia was killed to keep it underground."

"Now you're reaching," Glenda said, her voice clipped and precise. The sweat, the eye tic, the ripple of tension vibrating through her whole body gave her lie away. "Sofia's accident was unfortunate, but it was an accident."

"The accident was deliberate." I encroached into Glenda's personal space. "That makes it murder. Now the question is—who is responsible for the delay in reporting the malfunction?" I cocked my head. "You?"

Glenda's mouth flattened to a thin bloodred line. She wasn't about to admit anything but she wasn't denying it, either.

Paul shot Glenda a look I couldn't interpret and drew the computer closer to him. "This data wasn't something we had at all. On the other hand, stealth is the hottest development in aerospace technology. Our firm's doing all it can to guard against industrial spies."

"Funny," I said, "I remember suggesting industrial spying, oh, a week ago."

Glenda glared at me. "This one piece of information isn't enough to hurt Allied Defense or to give anyone else enough to undermine the HART. And from what I can see, the numbers fall within the scope of acceptable norms."

Gaze glued to my computer, Paul shook his head. "If I'd seen this data, I'd never have let this project go forward unquestioned."

"What?" Glenda said. "You're not seriously considering this woman's claim at face value."

"Of course not. I'll need to review and analyze the data."

Glenda scrapped her chair back. "I don't have to sit here and have my ethics questioned."

"There's more at stake than hurt feelings," I said. "Who would most want this technology?"

"It could be anyone," Paul said. "The cold war's over, but industrial espionage has become an extension of research and development for foreign powers. California recently had two cases of engineers being convicted of stealth espionage." His mouth twisted as if he'd bitten into a bitter peanut and he grunted. "We're always reminding our folds not to sit in a bar and brag about what they do. We can't have people running their mouths off."

"Espionage paradise or not, that's really none of my concern," I said. "What concerns me is that the HART has a fault and that it's killing the pilots who are depending on it to protect them." I looked at Paul and Glenda in turn. "What are you going to do about it?"

Paul blustered. "If there's a mistake, I'm going to fix it."

Glenda pursed her lips. "You may have time to waste over this nonsense but I don't."

"Sierra's not asking for any secrets, Paul," Wyatt said. "Who else is working on stealth technology?"

"Could be the Russians," Paul finally admitted. "They're wanting to defeat this new technology. Then there's the French. They're working on something similar to the HART. They're nowhere near as advanced as we are. They're still in the prototype stage. We've got ours in service."

I sneered. "Right now that's really not a point in your favor."

Paul pinned me with his slitted eyes. "I would never knowingly let a defective piece of equipment go out the door. Nor would I risk other people's lives to advance my career."

Always the cool head, Wyatt said, "No one's accusing you or Glenda of anything. We're just trying to get to the truth. If Sofia was right, if there's a fault, we need to know that you'll stand up and make it right."

Paul's face reddened with his outrage. "I'd do no less. If you don't know that by now, then you're not the friend I thought you were."

Glenda reached for her designer purse. "This is a waste of time."

I took two sets of printouts from my tote and gave one each to Paul and Glenda. "Don't even think about getting rid of me the way you got rid of Sofia. The original report as well as a copy of the integration chip is in a safe place. Should something happen to me or Wyatt, it'll appear in every major newspaper and television network, not to mention on the FBI director's desk. Oh, and I should warn you that both your names also appear on that report."

"You." Glenda shot up from her seat. "You're the one who stole the card from the test stand at the trade show yesterday. I'm going to have you arrested."

"Yeah, we can share a cell."

Glenda's nostrils flared and fluttered. She turned on her heel and clipped away.

Paul's gaze ping-ponged from Wyatt to me. "You stole the chip?"

"Borrowed," I insisted.

More diplomatic than me, Wyatt said, "We had no choice. No one's listening to our concerns. We need to hold the chip hostage until steps are taken to fix the fault. My sister flies the F-117. I'm not going to have a damn glitch kill her."

Paul slapped the report with the back of his hand. "Who analyzed the chip?"

"A friend of my brother's who runs an independent lab." I pointed at the letterhead. "Call him. His number's there."

Paul rolled the report like a baton. "I can assure you that if these figures are true, I'll take steps to make the chip good, even if it costs us the contract."

Paul and Wyatt talked technical for a while, then

lingered outside the bar behind the bottle-green beater car between their vehicles, saying their goodbyes.

I leaned against the passenger's side of Wyatt's truck, waiting for him to unlock my door. The last flash of red sun sank into the horizon and disappeared. A scud of clouds, stirred by a breeze that cut the day's heat, brushed away the stars.

Out of habit my gaze roamed the area, taking in the people spilling out of the bar, the cars limping in and out of the parking lot, the buzz of traffic along the feeder road to the highway.

A blue Plymouth sitting near the edge of the parking lot caught my eye. I wouldn't have thought anything about it, except that the driver constantly scanned the street even though there wasn't much traffic going by and he could easily have left the parking lot a half a dozen times by now. In silhouette like that, he had the look of a vulture looking for road kill.

Behind him in the backseat, another black lump appeared in a vaguely human shape. It stared into the parking lot. When I followed its line of sight, my gaze fell on Paul and Wyatt. Paul lifted a hand and Wyatt turned toward me.

The hairs on the back of my neck bristled. Adrenaline swamped my veins.

My head whirled back toward the Plymouth. The car had started cruising out the exit, cutting off a red Honda. Yellow shine from a security light unmasked the man in the back. He lifted hands that were clutching something that looked like a transmitter for a radio-controlled car.

Thoughts looped too fast to catch. My body twisted, racing toward Wyatt. "Bomb!"

Chapter 15

I grabbed Wyatt, who was rounding the back end of his truck to unlock my door, and lunged us toward the grass strip separating the parking lot from the street. Moving Wyatt was like trying to displace a brick wall, but I had momentum working for me. As the ground rushed up at us, Wyatt hooked my waist and rolled me over, shielding me with his body.

Time stretched like a rubber band, slowing everything to frame-by-frame motion. Sounds bounced in pinball madness. And it seemed as if I was watching the whole scene unfold through a greasy window.

Tires screeched as the Plymouth made a getaway.

The bomb's detonation lifted the beater car off the ground and rocked it to one side. As the tires hit the ground once again, the car rumbled and exploded into a thousand pieces, sending up a red ball of fire into the air and blasting bits of explosive, metal and glass all over the parking lot.

The boom of the explosion sent Paul flying across the lot. Windows in the bar cracked, raining shards of glass onto the asphalt below. Black smoke billowed from the rooftop of the car, opened like a sardine can. Orange flames crackled and devoured the frame. The oppressive heat singed my skin. The caustic smoke smarted my eyes and stung my lungs. My head tolled in a full carillon of bells.

As soon as the ground stopped shaking, Wyatt lifted me up. "Are you okay?"

I couldn't really hear him with all the bells, but I understood what he was saying. I nodded and yelled back, "You?"

He pointed at my chest. "You're bleeding."

"You're one to talk." His shirt was cut from the pieces of falling debris.

He tenderly lifted the shreds of my blouse and swore. Hatch marks scored the front of my shoulder. I'd probably scratched it during my dive to the ground. I shrugged off his touch. "Paul. We need to help Paul."

"Stay here. Your chest is bruised. You need a doctor." With a press of my shoulders as if he was planting me in place, Wyatt took off to find his friend.

On shaky legs, I followed him. My first step shot pain up my ankle. I must have twisted it going down.

Paul's body lay like a grotesque mannequin in the middle of the parking lot. His black shirt and black pants were torn off. The blast had torn his back apart like raw meat by a wild beast. His left arm was gone and had landed somewhere on the other side of his truck. Incongruously, his black shoes were intact on his feet.

I couldn't look. I couldn't avert my gaze. Only a minute ago, Paul had been alive, determined to make things right. And now, all because of this damn HART chip—because I'd bluffed Glenda into coming to this meeting—he was dead.

I shouldn't have underestimated Glenda. I shouldn't have given her the chance to prepare to destroy the evidence of her treason. She might not have planted the bomb herself, but she'd let someone know there were some loose ends that needed taking care of tonight.

Shouts for help rang through the night. Patrons spilled out of the bar. The police arrived, their sirens piercing through the ringing in my ears. EMTs swarmed around what was left of Paul. Everything seemed unreal and far away.

I hobbled over to Wyatt who stood by Paul, his friend's voice now that he had none.

"Anyone else hurt?" I wished I could slip my arm around Wyatt.

He shook his head.

That was something at least. Only one victim when the crowded parking lot offered so many more. "Was he the target or were we?"

"Good question."

Pain swept through the veil of adrenaline, holding me upright, and pulsed from my head to my toes. I couldn't just stay here and watch all this destruction. I had to do *something*. "I'm going after her."

"What the hell are you thinking? You need to see a doctor."

No time for a doctor. Glenda could have left town by now for all I knew. I turned to the EMT and exposed the raw scrape. Who knew how many germs I'd picked up on this dirty asphalt. "Can you clean me up?" I pointed a thumb over my shoulder. "And him, too."

I guess the EMT had seen scars like mine before. He didn't even blink—just went to work on my cuts and ankle.

By the time the police took our statements and released us, it was past midnight. Most of my hearing had returned but my ears still buzzed.

With curt sentences, Wyatt directed the uniform driving us home past his mother's house to a much smaller building farther out on the property. It was late. He probably didn't want to wake up his mother or have her see us looking like war refugees with our torn shirts and bloodied jeans.

"Are you okay?" I asked him as the police cruiser disappeared down the lane.

He unlocked the front door and strode through the darkened house while I bumped my way behind him, my sprained ankle making me wince with each step. In the kitchen he turned the water on full blast and filled a glass. He swallowed it down in one shot and banged it on the counter, waves of hot anger steaming off him. Then he turned to me, eyes overly bright in the dim light eking through from the living room. "I'm not okay. I just saw a friend blown to bits. We could have died out there tonight."

Like Paul. Like Sofia. The words remained silent but vibrated between us.

"How can you do this?" He shook his head as if he was trying to understand. "How can you live like this?"

"I don't think about it. I just do what I have to do."

"Liar. You think about life and death all the time or you wouldn't be so hung up on germs."

Pupils wide and open, breath quick and shallow, body like a spring wound too tight, he moved closer, invading my space, until I was pressed against the counter. "Do you ever think about me, Sierra? Us?"

Sofia gasped. *No!*

But her fury faded to nothing more than white noise, covered by the hard hammer of my heart as he lowered his head, his mouth close enough to mine to feel the fast puff of his breath. "You're not Sofia, and I want you. Right here. Right now."

His hazel eyes pitched his pain at me like a dare. Did he expect shock from me? Denial? Outrage, so he could rein in his own raging impulse?

There was no us. This was a chemical reaction. A flood of dopamine. Normal after having witnessed a body blown apart. He'd just lost a friend. This meant nothing. He just needed to feel alive. So did I.

I moved in closer, my lips skimming Wyatt's. "Then take me."

Butt balanced up on the counter's edge, I opened my knees, allowing his tense thighs to thrust up against me. "You're not my type. You're too stiff, too meddling, too controlling."

"Stiff is good." He rubbed himself hard against me, scrambling my pulse.

"Control is good." The thorough exploration of his hands over my skin sent a heart-stopping shock ripping through me.

"Oh, yeah," I said, panting. "Definitely good." You could learn a lot more than reading, writing and arithmetic in high school. The fine art of kissing was one of them. "But try this."

I breathed him in as I threaded my fingers through his hair. Cradling his nape, I urged him to deepen the kiss, pushed him to let go of his iron control. When he did, I could taste the wildness of his hunger and it flooded me with a hot rush of need.

Hands splayed on either side of me on the counter, Wyatt tried to catch his breath, regain his fraying control. "Where did you learn to kiss like that?"

My mouth lingered on the mad beat pulsing at his throat. "Ryan Marks, behind the bleachers, high school, freshman year." Brother Gregory had caught us and called Van.

"No fourteen-year-old kisses like that."

"He was a senior." Van had threatened the poor guy with hauling him in for statutory rape, even though he'd never made it past first base. Ryan might have been a good kisser, but he had no intention of spending the prime of his life in jail. He never so much as said hello after his talk with my brother.

"You're crazy." Wyatt made it sound like a good

thing. His mouth trailed hot and hungry over my cheeks, throat, shoulders. His fingers worked the buttons of my blouse but something wicked in me needed to push the boundaries of his restraint.

"Let me." Filled with a powerful surge of energy, I pushed his hot hands away and slowly unbuttoned what was left of the silky material of my blouse.

"You're killing me," he groaned.

I laughed. "If you're hurting, you're alive."

"Not for long if you keep this up."

Never letting go of his gaze, I unhooked my bra, and let it fall to the floor.

"I want my breasts against your chest." My voice came out on a harsh whisper. The jump of his pulse at his throat jogged mine, and I practically purred with pleasure.

He ripped off his shirt and took one of my breasts into his mouth, palming the other in his hand and rubbing his thumb against the nipple. My knees went weak, and I clutched him so that I wouldn't fall off the counter.

He traced the scar bisecting my chest with his tongue, then pressed a delicate kiss along the pink line. He cradled his head there, cheek to my heart, listening to its frantic beat. I swallowed hard.

"Sofia's heart." My voice was scratchy. My eyes burned, angry that jealousy for a dead woman could rip me like claws. I should stop this before it got too far. But I didn't want to. I needed this heat to burn out the sight of Paul's blood.

"Your blood," Wyatt said, his voice night-dark. "Your mind. Your body."

Suddenly much too vulnerable, I listened for Sofia, but couldn't hear her.

Wyatt kissed me again. Possessively. Purposefully. A match flared in my chest. For tonight, all that mattered was that raw hunger, that need to forget, that need to feel alive.

My hand went to his zipper. He groaned as I tugged the denim and briefs over his hips and wrapped a hand around him, stroking him. The heat of his arousal throbbed in my palm.

"Shit," he ground out and wrangled my jeans free.

With a guttural roar, he slipped into me, hot and thick. I wrapped my legs around him, taking him in deeper and it felt so right. I drank in his appreciative moans as if I'd just found an oasis after a long desert trek. I was alive. Drunk with aliveness. Powerful with it. And I gave myself up to the moment.

Our shadow on the wall moved as one in the dark. A rough cry rasped out of him and he clutched me as if I was the only thing holding him up. And maybe I was.

The climax rolled through me, a gasp of pleasure so intense it made the world fall away—like pulling on a parachute cord and having the chute open, jerking you up and up before you floated down again. Loose and boneless, I had nowhere to go but deeper into his arms and they held me safe against his heart until our combined internal inferno cooled and our breaths evened.

"That was—" he started.

"What we needed."

"More than that." His mouth claimed mine again, gentler now, as if, possession complete, he could afford to take his time. He carried me to the living room and the yielding couch. We came together like old lovers, touching, tasting, lingering, smooth and easy until my senses were filled to overflowing. I came around him, calling his name as if he'd been gone a lifetime and I'd just found him after an unbearable separation.

"I've got you, Sierra," he growled into my ear, the sound too close to triumphant conqueror.

Sometime during the night we moved to his bedroom. After a shower we ended up in his bed. That's where I woke up at the first light of dawn poking through the open curtains. My arms and legs tangled with his in a way that should have been uncomfortable, but somehow wasn't. His hair was tousled. His jaw was slack in sleep. The lines of worry ironed out, as he lay relaxed and content.

In a few minutes I'd have to slide out of bed and hunt down Glenda. But I couldn't make myself move just yet. I'd missed waking up next to someone in my bed, missed the warmth, the closeness. I hadn't realized how alone I'd felt since Leo had left.

Fear—the kind that jolted through me when I woke up from a nightmare—drummed in my chest. I didn't want to fall for Wyatt. My hands went cold. My head went light. I used to think I was having a heart attack when that happened, but Dr. Katz, my shrink, said it was just anxiety. A battery of tests confirmed his diagnosis. Didn't make the symptoms easier to swallow.

Wyatt's eyes fluttered open. A smile tugged at his lips. "Hey there, sexy."

In the time Wyatt and I had made love, Sofia had been the furthest thing from my mind. I'd been able to shut her out completely. What did that say?

A pit formed in my stomach. I was feeling too much, too fast. Nothing that came that fast lasted.

Fingers closed around my heart. My eyes teared. This wasn't like me at all. I never cried. I rubbed at my chest and the scar throbbed.

"Hey, there," I finally managed. I reached across him and pulled up the alarm clock on his bedside table, showing him the glowing red numerals. "You should call your mother. If she sees your half-blown-up truck on the early news, she'll worry."

He ground the heels of his hands at his eyes and grumbled. As he reached for the phone, it rang. He answered and shot up on the side of the bed.

A wall fell over his features, hardening them, masking the intimate connection we'd shared all night long.

I drew the sheet high over my breasts and glanced around the bedroom. A picture of Sofia on the walnut nightstand next to his pillow was all the reminder I needed that this wasn't my life and never would be. I'd known that all along. I shouldn't be disappointed.

Wyatt's spine cranked up, stiff and straight, as if it had been rammed with iron bars. "I'll be right there."

"What is it?" I asked as he hung up.

He strode to the closet and started yanking out clothes. "Glenda. Sounds like she's been drinking all night. She says she wants to talk."

Saturday, April 29

Glenda's call had saved me the trouble of tracking down her address. We found her hunched over a card table in the nondescript apartment near the Allied Defense plant where she'd lived since her husband had asked her to leave their home. The place reeked of alcohol. The walls, carpets and furniture were all in shades of beige. The only spot of color was Glenda's disheveled auburn hair and the discarded green wine bottles on the carpet.

"Glenda?" Wyatt said.

Glenda moaned, not bothering to look up from the juice glass she held in both hands. Black smears of mascara pouched her eyes. "I never meant for any of this to happen."

Needing to rest my still-tender ankle, I took the chair opposite Glenda. "What happened?"

Tears gurgled in her throat. "I'm not sure. One day I was living my life. A perfect life. The next I was in a nightmare." She wiped the run of tears on cheeks red and puffy from crying. "Jack got everything. Justin. The house. He even got the fucking dog." She tunneled one hand through a pile of papers, sending it shooting up like a geyser. Papers fell all around her. "I got all the bills." She knocked back the inch of red wine in her glass and filled the glass again. "I thought that I could fix it. Everything. But I just fucked it up more."

How could she admit anything was wrong when she was so identified with living the perfect life?

Wyatt crouched and picked up the papers, making a neat pile once again. "You said you wanted to talk about Paul."

She burst into ugly, wet, openmouthed sobs. "I never thought they'd kill him."

"They, who?" I asked.

She shook her head. "I waited a long time to have Justin. Put it off to break through the glass ceiling. I thought I could have it all. I *had* it all. But the manipulative son of a bitch used my success against me. He lied to get what he wanted."

"Who?"

"Jack. He knew this would kill me. That's why he did it."

Love and betrayal. Why did they seem to walk hand in hand? Another reminder not to depend on anyone for anything.

"What does your divorce have to do with hiding the fault in the HART?" I asked Glenda.

"Everything." She choked on the word. "I did it for love."

"You hid the fault for your husband?" I asked, confused.

Glenda wiped the back of her hand under her nose. "For Jack. For Justin. For our life." She shook her head. "I made one mistake. And it kept getting bigger. I needed that bonus to erase it."

Why hadn't this mistake shown up on the financial? Maybe it wasn't financial. Maybe it was personal.

"There were rumors of an affair," Wyatt said. "Is that it?"

Glenda sobbed louder.

I swallowed my frustration and forced my voice to stay calm. "Who is behind Paul's death?"

"You," Glenda said, spittle flying. "It was supposed to be you. You were supposed to die. If you'd minded your own business, none of this would have happened."

"The jets would have still fallen out of the sky."

"I was on it," Glenda said. "It was getting fixed."

"Not fast enough," Wyatt said. "My sister flies the F-117."

"It wasn't personal." Glenda reached for the bottle. Wyatt took it away from her. "I'm going to lose everything I have left. My clearance. My job. It was all for nothing."

I wanted to slap her sober. Didn't she realize how many lives her selfishness had already cost? "Who do you work for?"

Her brown eyes were bloodshot and couldn't quite focus as she looked up at me. "If I tell you I'm dead."

"If you don't tell me—" I reached forward to strangle the truth out of her, but Wyatt stopped me with a hand on my shoulder.

"What makes you think whoever is holding this over you can afford to let you live?" I pushed Wyatt's hand away. "This isn't a game. Lives are at stake."

Glenda shook her head. "It doesn't matter. Nothing matters."

"The truth matters," I insisted. "There's still time to make it right."

"They have leverage." She lifted her glass at the ceiling and panned across the room, sloshing cheap burgundy over the lip and down her arm. "They're listening."

Wyatt and I shared a look over the table. Drunken paranoia?

"They who? What leverage?" Temper made my words hard and choppy.

"Who's listening?"

I envied Wyatt's evenness, given how she was jerking us around. She didn't want to help, and I suddenly sensed a trap. She'd called Wyatt to snare us in her web so her assassin could take care of the last pests who could expose her secret. She'd said I was the intended target, and alive I was still a threat to her. We had to get out of here before she added two more bodies to her count.

Glenda grabbed a napkin and scribbled what looked like an address. "I don't have anything left." She handed the napkin to Wyatt. "That's it."

"There's going to be an accounting," I said. "You still have a chance to redeem yourself by telling all you know."

"Please leave."

"Glenda—" Wyatt started.

She gave him a sad smile. "I'm sorry. I truly am. I never thought it would get this far."

She got up on shaky legs and disappeared into the bathroom. "Leave!"

Wyatt stared at the door Glenda slammed. "We can't leave her like this."

"Why not? She doesn't care about anyone but herself." Right or wrong, I didn't care if she choked on her own vomit. She had the ability to put a halt to this mess and was too weak to act. I moved to the window and peered through the miniblinds, scanning the parking lot for anything out of place. No way I was going to end up like Paul. "We have to get out of here. She's setting us up."

"She's upset."

"She's dangerous."

Our argument was cut short by the sound of a gun firing.

Chapter 16

Wyatt kicked in the flimsy bathroom door, holding me back with one hand as he looked inside. But he wasn't fast enough. I got an eyeful of blood and brain sliding down the white tile of the bathtub. Glenda's body was crumpled half in, half out of the tub, the Beretta still in her lax hand. She'd definitely meant business.

Minutes later we were once again swimming in cops. Suspicions ran high when the homicide detectives figured out we'd been at The Watering Hole last night. They separated Wyatt and me—no doubt so we couldn't coordinate our stories.

I flashed my P.I. badge at the detective and dropped the names of a couple of my contacts at the Nashua and Manchester P.D.s so he could check me out. That only cranked up the questions about Paul and Glenda and how Wyatt and I came to have the misfortune to witness both their deaths. That fact alone had moved us to the top of the suspect list.

"Paul was Glenda's boss," I repeated for what seemed like the hundredth time. "They were close."

"Close how? Like lovers?" the detective asked.

His eyes were slightly crossed and it hurt to look at him directly. "I don't know. I don't think so. She was going through a divorce."

He scratched his chin. "So she's pining away for her boss and she offs herself?"

"I don't think it's the one thing. It's the divorce, losing custody of her kid, troubles at work."

He stared at his notes, then screwed a confused look onto his face. "What's an out-of-state P.I. doing mixed up in investigating crashing jets again?"

Biting back my temper, I stayed as close to the truth as I could—leaving out Sofia and the fact that I'd taken part in stealing the chip at the convention center. And because I didn't have a choice, I told the detective about the HART and gave him the address Glenda had scribbled on the napkin—Castille Disposition Services.

Three hours later, like some one-star movie, the detective closed his notebook and said, "Don't leave town. We may need to follow up."

Not that I was planning to leave town until I nailed down the last few pieces of this puzzle.

"This is a mess," Wyatt said, half an hour later as he turned into the ranch driveway. "I've got to go see Jack. Try to explain what happened to Glenda."

"Just don't expect her ex-husband to be too welcoming. He might think you're trying to blame him."

Wyatt nodded, his mouth a straight line on the grim landscape of his face.

With a pang of guilt, I realized I'd already screwed up Wyatt's quiet life too much by allowing him into this investigation. Time to do what I did best and work the rest on my own.

"You're going to be okay while I'm gone?" he asked.

"No sweat." I didn't exactly deal with dead bodies on a daily basis, but I'd learned early how to compartmentalize my feelings and get on with what needed to be done. While Wyatt paid his condolences to Glenda's ex-husband, I planned to change and gather some information. I'd sweet-talk Lorraine into letting me use one of the ranch vehicles.

Wyatt idled my rental in front of his mother's house. "I'll see you later, then."

I forced a smile, giving him the smart-ass response he expected. "I'll count the minutes."

His gaze pinned me. "Stay put."

As I studied the layout of Castille Disposition Services, color completely drained from the sky. No moon. No stars. Just a thick layer of black clouds heavy with foreboding and rain, waiting to swallow me.

Castille Disposition Services—IT Division—consisted of a huge warehouselike building in Burleson off 35W. Like the company trucks, the building was painted white with a wide blue swash on the side. I lay flat on my stomach—too close to dirt for comfort—on the edge of the property, surveying the building through binoculars.

Sofia's father recycled Allied Defense's computers. Even if she didn't want to believe he could betray his country, what if he'd come across something by accident? What if he'd blackmailed Glenda because her mistake cost Sofia her life?

Sofia's energy spiked like frying bacon through my muscles, making them twitch.

Glenda had known she was going to take her life. She wouldn't have wasted her last effort on nothing. There was only one way to find out. I stood and traced my steps back to the ranch car.

I dumped the binoculars in the backseat, retrieved a black cap and added a jeans jacket over my navy T-shirt. Keeping a keen eye out for anything that moved, I made my way to the chainlink fence that surrounded the property and found the hole I'd spotted through the binoculars.

The guard in the gatehouse was busy reading the newspaper and didn't notice me slinking to the building. I reached the back of the building and the loading dock.

Getting in was a lot easier than it should be for a place that dealt with sensitive information. I hopped onto a loading dock and went through the open door, sidling by two workers shooting the breeze over sodas, cigarettes and a forklift.

The warehouse part looked, well, like a warehouse. Nothing pretty—bare floors, bare walls, bare ceilings. Shrink-wrapped piles of equipment waited on pallets to be processed. The fluorescent lighting was stark and left many nooks and crannies in shadows. Good for me as I hopscotched my way farther into the building.

The processing section was a bit cleaner with painted walls and assembly-line-type stations where the equipment was inventoried and sanitized.

In a janitorial closet, I appropriated a pair of coveralls and a cleaning cart. I stuffed my hair into the black cap and shuffled my way to the offices at the front end of the building as if I was bored out of my skull.

The offices were dark and empty. A small cube farm, housing secretaries' and salespeople's pods, took up the center of the space. The managerial offices lined the outside circumference.

Interestingly enough, Antonio's office—big and bold, smack in the corner with two windows—seemed unused. The leather on his chair hadn't molded to his shape. The blotter wasn't scuffed with marks. No piles of work filled the in- or out-baskets. Did Antonio not run his own company?

I remembered how well the recliner in his living room fit him. Would a man pretending to run a legitimate business risk tainting it with the proof of his spying? Not likely. He'd keep things close at hand.

I pawed through files that seemed rather thin on substance. Parked in Antonio's chair, I turned on his computer and took a tour of his desktop. Just as I'd expected, it was clean. Much too clean. I wouldn't find anything there.

The sudden stink of sandalwood filling the office registered a second too late.

"Didn't I warn you, *chica,* that the next time I saw you I couldn't protect you?"

"Rey. Fancy running into you here." He wore navy pants and white shirt with a gold shield-shaped patch that said Security. That would explain all his free daytime to harass me at the show. The gun at his belt looked real enough. Did he have the guts to actually use it?

"What is it you expect to find in a respectable businessman's files?" Rey's hand rested on the butt of his gun, finger twitching as if he was dying to squeeze the trigger.

I leaned back in Antonio's chair as if I didn't have a care in the world. With my bum ankle, I couldn't outrun him—or a bullet. "It's one of those I'll know it when I see it type things."

"Ah."

I cocked my head at Rey. He had a knack of showing up in the wrong places at the right time. "You know, there's something about you that bothers me."

He shot me a crooked grin. "My good looks? My winning smile?" He hiked up his gun belt and thrust his hips in my direction. "Or is it something else you would like to try? I have never had any complaints."

"It'd be kind of incestuous, don't you think, with Sofia's heart keeping my body alive? With you being her cousin and all."

He shrugged. "The heart is just a pump."

I lifted a brow. "And the body just a body? Do you have to get your dates drunk to get past first base?"

He rolled the toothpick in his mouth with a twist of his tongue. "You are not a trusting woman. It is too bad that Sofia's gentler qualities did not follow her heart."

"I'd say it's a good thing, considering she was murdered."

He tipped his head toward the computer. "You will not find your answers here."

"Then where will I find them?" Every bristling hair on the back of my neck said he had the answers I was looking for. Would he kill me to keep them quiet?

He snuffed the genial mood as easily as he'd turned it on. "I have already told you that it is better if you leave this business to those who are able to give the situation the attention it deserves. If you keep sniffing, you may find a fish, but what good is a fish if the shark is still in the sea."

"Okay, so what are you? FBI? DEA? Homeland Security?" I was getting a definite cop vibe from him. It wasn't just the uniform, either.

Rey turned his palms up. "I am just a poor worker trying to eke out a living."

"Right, and if I believe that, you've got some land east of Florida to sell me."

His dark eyes turned to flint. "I must insist you leave, or I will be forced to sound the alarm."

"Fine." I wasn't going to find what I needed here anyway.

Gun pointed at my back, he nudged me out of the office and toward the side door.

"So tell me," I asked as our footsteps echoed on the industrial tile, "how was Sofia involved in all of this?"

"Sofia? I don't know what you mean."

"How did Sofia's work come to be compromised by her father?"

"Sofia is just an innocent bystander."

If she wasn't, she was an even better actor than Rey. "But she was used."

"Her good nature, her desire to please unfortunately made her easy to exploit."

"By you?"

"By everyone."

"Antonio used his own daughter for industrial espionage?" I asked.

"You have quite an imagination."

At the side door—the employees' entrance, not the client's primped area—I turned and faced him. "Come on, Rey. Poor working shlub to poor working shlub. Give me a little if you want me to leave it alone. If you don't sate my curiosity a little, I won't be able to keep myself from looking. It's a disease with me."

"One that could kill you." The toothpick rolled from one side of his mouth to the other. "Weakness. That's where you start. You take people, put them in your debt, and they repay you with loyalty."

The piece of the puzzle that connected Allied Defense to Antonio fell into place. Under the guise of charity, Antonio had helped the poor, wretched people who'd arrived here with nothing. He'd found them homes. He'd offered them jobs. He'd given them hope. And with that he'd bought their loyalty. "The Open Hand and Heart Program at the church."

"Leave now before you endanger yourself," Rey said, his voice cold and commanding.

It all made sense. Janitors, maids, gardeners. The people nobody noticed. How clever of Antonio to place them with companies from which he could steal valuable information to resell. I remembered reading an article on disk sanitization in the last couple of days, how the theft of proprietary information caused the greatest financial loss in many sectors of business.

Some of the biggest companies around had fallen prey to such scavenging—Morgan Stanley, the state of Kentucky, the Bank of Montreal. And Antonio's companies gave him access to both electronic information and the often mismanaged discarding of paper. Defense industry. Lawyers. Banks. All the bits of data a man could amass from one company and sell to its competitor for a price. Dumpster diving took on a whole new meaning.

As Rey started to open the door, I blocked the opening with my body. "When?"

His dark gaze stared at me for a long time and this time he didn't bother pretending he didn't know what I was talking about. "Soon. All must be in its proper place."

"People are dying."

"Which is why it must be done right. Go home. Forget everything you know. Let the professionals handle it."

"Glenda McCall killed herself this morning."

His gaze remained steady. "I do not know who she is."

"She's the woman you were following at the cutting horse show."

He showed me a wide span of white teeth that reminded me of fangs. "I was there for you, *chica.*"

"And the warning from Inez the day I arrived, it wasn't really from her, was it?"

He cocked his head. "I was trying to protect you, just as I tried to protect Sofia. You must believe that if nothing else."

"Somehow, that's not very comforting."

"This is no game, *chica*. Your life is at stake. I have been kind to you because of Sofia. Now it must end." Before I could read his intention, he grasped one of my wrists and slapped handcuffs on, looping them through the door's handle. Watching me from a safe distance, he dialed his cell phone. "Wyatt? This is Reynaldo. Your girlfriend is about to be arrested for breaking and entering. Come and get her before I am forced to call the authorities."

Chapter 17

Wyatt picked me up from Castille Disposition Services and drove me back to the ranch in silence. He bypassed his mother's house.

I wasn't ready for more one-on-one time with him in his small house with pictures of his dead wife to remind me I didn't belong. "Where are you going?"

"Where I can keep an eye on you and keep you out of trouble."

The way we'd spent last night flashed before my eyes, and a roll of fear somersaulted in my stomach. Caring about him was a problem for me. "You can't lock me up."

He narrowed his gaze at me, all business. "Try me."

"You can help me or you can hinder me, but either way, you can't stop me."

"You almost got blown up yesterday. You almost got shot at tonight. Enough is enough. We gave the cops all the information. Let them handle it."

I could see it all now—the bureaucracy, the paperwork, the legal shackles. "They're not going to put it together in time. Think of your sister. What if Tracy's flying the next jet to go down? Could you forgive yourself for not doing everything you could to stop her useless death?"

His jaw flinched. "What exactly are you planning to do?"

"Keep looking for evidence. Someone was blackmailing Glenda. She pointed the finger at Antonio. He had the means and opportunity to find something incriminating on her. If he's not hiding his trail at work, then it has to be somewhere."

"Just where are you planning to break and enter this time?"

"The church where Sofia ran her volunteer program."

He shook his head, hands gripped hard against the steering wheel. "That's crossing the line."

"With or without you, Wyatt. I'm going."

St. Alban's Church slumbered, dark and quiet. The leaves and blossoms of azaleas were muted to the color of dried blood in the dearth of light. This preternatural quiet left my senses alert and bare.

"This is a bad idea," Wyatt whispered even though we were still inside the car on a side street and nobody could possibly hear us.

"That's what makes it such a good cover," I whispered back. "Who would suspect a church?"

"Let Rey handle it."

"I thought you didn't like Rey."

"I don't, but I'd rather see his hide behind bars than mine—or even yours."

"That's so sweet. But I'm not sure exactly which side of the fence Rey is playing. If he's one of the bad guys, then Sofia's problem doesn't get fixed. If he's one of the good guys, then we're just helping him out."

He joined me on the sidewalk, mirroring my scan of the area. "Somehow I doubt Rey will see it that way."

"That's his problem." I picked out the darkest path to the front of the church, whose doors, according to Sofia, were left open until eleven each night. "Sofia is mine."

Breath shallow, I pushed in the heavy door. No creaks—just a whisper like a warning as the thick wood glided over the cold marble floor of the vestibule. The only light came from the tiers of votive candles, emitting an eerie red glow that made me think of a carnival haunted house. I half expected something or someone to pop out from behind a column, yelling, "Boo!"

I probed the nave for desperate worshipers, a genuflecting priest or a custodian seeking to lock up early.

Churches all smelled the same. I didn't know if it was the years of incense, wine and candles that accumulated and tainted the air with that unique odor or if it was one of those sense memories brought back by so many Sunday mornings spent polishing a pew with my restlessness as a child.

"Where's the Open Hand and Heart Program held?" I asked.

"In the school. They have a classroom." Wyatt jerked

his chin toward the transept at the far end of the church, and we made our way up the side aisle. Darkened stained-glass windows depicting the Stations of the Cross marked our progress and made me feel as if a crowd of eyes were following me.

Wyatt reached for the brass knob on the door linking the church with the school, through a corridor on the right hand side of the cross-shaped building. "The door's locked."

"No problem." I handed him the maglite from my pocket. "Hold the light steady." I took out a set of lock picks and had the dead bolt open in less than a minute.

"I don't even want to know how you learned that."

I shrugged. "Get locked out of the house often enough and it becomes a survival mechanism."

The corridor was dark and reeled with gyrating shadows from the oaks stirring in the moaning wind outside. The old building, feeling its age, creaked and cracked. Azalea branches scratched against the windows lining the path. The other end met us with another locked door, which I picked open.

"Next to the library." Wyatt stood guard while I let us into the room.

A small conference table took up most of the center of the room. A dozen cubicle desks and half a dozen computers lined the outside of the room, separated by a bookshelf here and there and a bigger "teacher's" desk near the windows.

"Not too many hiding spots," Wyatt said. "If Antonio is mixed up in this, he'd have to have a ton of files to make the con work."

"Files get smaller and smaller all the time."

"But concrete proof doesn't, and he'd have to keep some around in case someone turned against him."

Sitting to rest my ankle, I started with the desk, keeping my search methodical. "If I were a piece of blackmail material, where would I hide?"

"A bank vault."

"No, I'd have to depend on other people to get access to it. Not good. Criminals tend to be paranoid."

"Then he'd keep it closer," Wyatt said. "At home. He's always there."

"The second place the cops would look if he ever came under suspicion." I turned to the small filing cabinet behind the desk. "It's here somewhere." Had to be.

While I searched the bookcases, Wyatt turned on the computer on the main desk.

I came to a glass-fronted case filled with CDs, videotapes, a VCR and a couple of Walkman CD players. The lock wasn't even a challenge. Not that the glass fronts would have made it impossible to steal the contents. Interactive English-as-a-second-language lessons on tape for the VCR and on CDs for the computer and Walkmans.

"It's going to take time to hack into the system," Wyatt said.

"You can hack?" Curiosity piqued that an honest man like him could be so devious, I stood beside him. His fingers blurred over the keyboard, spewing out a series of letters and numbers I couldn't keep up with.

"If you want to protect a system from hackers," he said, "you have to be able to do what they do—only better."

"What are you doing?"

"Footprinting—gathering target information. It's like when you went into Allied Defense. You didn't just walk in, you gathered information about the plant, the security and the best route to get in. I'm harvesting information about the system."

"What's it telling you?"

"All the users who have access to this machine. Most people use easily guessed passwords and this little program I'm typing lets me get inside quickly." He stared at the gobbledygook on the screen. "Looks like most of the users are underprivileged."

"What does that mean?"

"They don't have access to the administration. Okay, let me read some more. There're a couple of strange files, but I'm not seeing anything interesting. I'm going to try and get superuser control."

"I've always liked superheroes."

"Super Geek at your service." The keenness of his eyes and the flush of his cheeks told me he was way more into this than he'd admit. Like a hound on a scent, he wasn't going to stop until he had his prey treed. "There are a couple of added security measures here. It's going to take time."

"We have less than an hour until someone comes to lock up the church."

"I'm not exactly comfortable here. In case you'd forgotten, we're breaking and entering. Again."

"We could take the whole computer with us."

"I think we've done enough borrowing as it is."

Thinking one of the language CDs might have something more interesting than lessons, I stuck a CD into another computer and watched a staged scene unfold. Vocabulary words flashed on the screen at regular intervals.

Forty-five minutes went by before Wyatt blew out a frustrated breath. "Something's missing."

"What?"

He ran both hands through his hair and pinched the back of his neck. "I don't know. There are files I can get to, but they don't make sense—as if they need something to interface with."

I glanced at the CD playing on the computer. "Like a CD?"

"Only if it had a program with some sort of key."

"Look at this." I showed him the strange blip that came and went almost before the brain could register what it was.

"Let me see." He stuffed the CD in the reader of his machine, let his fingers do some magic. "Unbelievable."

I looked at the screen. Wyatt clicked the icon on the CD. It flashed away the language lesson and left behind a password inquiry. Wyatt found a way in and decrypted the files there with a master key he'd unearthed.

"And you call what I do scary," I said, amazed at his skill.

"Actually, this system wasn't very hard to hack into." Wyatt jerked a shoulder in an aw-shucks gesture and scrolled almost faster than I could read. "Someone called El Patron shopped trade secrets to a French competitor."

"Antonio?"

Wyatt shrugged. "He sold them the information

found on Sofia's BlackBerry and on other computers that were supposed to be sanitized for Allied Defense."

Wyatt pointed at the screen. "According to this, the French—a company called Systèmes Electroniques Agnant—will be coming out with similar product to the HART. They were sold details of the HART, costs and strategies. The French used this to understand what happened and fixed the HART's fault. It's slated to come out next month."

"Smart. Gives them just enough time to have the government put together that HART plus plane equals crash. Then, voilà, they're the heroes with the solution."

A change overcame the stillness of the room as headlights slashed the mist outside the window in blurry ribbons.

"Someone's coming," Wyatt growled. "We have to get out of here."

He started to turn off the machine but I stopped him. "We can't leave without the evidence. I'm not going to let Antonio get away with murder. For that, I need proof."

Fingers of one hand drumming on the desk, Wyatt copied files while I stuffed a whole stack of the pseudo-learning CDs in my tote. Footsteps echoed on the wet pavement.

"Ready?" he asked as he pulled the CD out.

I nodded and headed for the door. Wyatt followed. Clinking keys rattled from the direction of the church. I moved toward the exit at the opposite end of the school. Just as we were about to exit the building, the door opened and a light flashed into my eyes, blinding me. I stepped wrong on my sore ankle and stumbled back, right into Wyatt's arms.

"You!" Inez's voice ground like worn gears. "I should've known you'd be mixed up in this. You were the first person I thought of when I noticed the break-in."

"You didn't call the police?" I went over the layout of the place in my mind for an escape route.

Inez's smile spread like a stain. "Who says I didn't?"

"We've been here for over an hour. Their response time is slow but not that slow."

The smile blinked off. "The signal comes to me, not the police."

"Why would *you* answer the alarm?"

"I took over running the program after Sofia died. Continuing her work is my tribute to her good soul."

But an alarm that went straight to Inez? That made no sense—unless there was something here to protect and that meant...

"El Patron," I said. "You're El Patron."

"El Patron is a protector of our people," Inez said, voice wire-taut, yet mocking. "A figurehead who helps immigrants find homes, good jobs and learn the language of their adopted land."

Antonio walked in through the door that linked the school with the church. "What's going on?"

"This is not your business, Antonio." Impatience snaked out of Inez. "I told you to wait in the car."

"Who are these people?" He squinted. "Wyatt?"

"They are the ones who would destroy all that gives meaning to my life."

Not taking my eyes off Inez, I said, "She gets the

people your program helps to steal information for her, then she resells it to your clients' competitors. The really neat part is that, if things go sour on her, she's got it all set up to make it look as if the whole thing was your idea."

Antonio blinked at his wife. "Inez? Is that true?"

"Where do you think the money for our lifestyle is coming from? Your salary? That's a joke. You pump it all back into your damned garbage business. And my dear father left everything to his son."

Tendons jutted at Wyatt's neck. "You killed Sofia."

"She cast those dice herself when she caught me downloading the contents of her BlackBerry."

"*Madre de Dios,* Inez. You murdered your own daughter. How in God's name could you do that? Your only child!"

"Not my child." She spit the words out as if they tasted bad. "Your child. You forced yourself on me. I never wanted her. Or you. Because of her, I had to marry you so that my family would not turn their backs on me. Do you think I *wanted* to be a garbage man's wife? My family was respected. We had money, status, prestige. I lost it all the day I married you."

Antonio reached a hand out to Inez. "I loved you from the first day I saw you, *querida.*"

"You loved that I was a Castille. Isn't that why you didn't fight me when I asked you to take my name?"

"I loved your spirit." Antonio moaned as if someone was ripping out his heart. "Sofia was your flesh and blood."

"I never loved either of you." Rime coated Inez's

voice. "I tried to make the best of a bad situation. I tried to mold her, to show her the way to freedom. But like you, she made all the wrong choices. She repudiated me. She chose you." Inez turned her angry mouth and viper eyes on Wyatt. "She chose *him*."

"You took all her things," Wyatt said. "You made a shrine out of them."

"I had to make sure there was nothing to implicate me. The added bonus was that doing so hurt you."

"Inez…" Antonio started toward his wife.

Growling like a monster coming to life after a long sleep, she lifted a gun from the folds of her black dress. "Take another step and you will join your daughter."

"You killed my child."

"You killed her spirit with your iron rules long before I killed her body. Her death was necessary. She was about to bring down the whole operation. She didn't care that I'd sacrificed my life for her. If you want to be angry at someone, be angry at her." Inez jerked her chin in my direction. "And her, for forcing me to kill her twice."

Antonio's dark eyes flashed hot with temper. "You would kill my heart again?" His hand shot out, grasping Inez's wrist. "I won't let you."

Mean fingers wrapped around the grip of the revolver, Inez squeezed the trigger. The bullet exited with a muffled swoosh, thanks to the silencer.

Papa! Sofia shouted.

Antonio, mouth wide open, stood still, holding his bleeding arm. "Inez? I gave you all you asked. How can you do this to me?"

With an eerie calm, she shot him in the head.

His body folded into itself and dropped to the ground.

Making a shield with his body, Wyatt launched me toward the door.

"Stop or I will shoot." Inez turned the gun on us. "I hate taking the garbage out, but this time I'll have to do it myself." She aimed the muzzle at Wyatt's face. "Tell me where the chip you stole is or your lover will die."

"Antonio needs help," Wyatt said.

"He is nothing. He knew his place. He overstepped his position and paid the price. Where is the chip?"

"We don't have it," I said.

Her finger squeezed the trigger.

Stop her! Sofia screamed.

"Wyatt! No!" I whirled instinctively. His body slid into my arms but I couldn't hold him and caved to the ground. "Inez, what have you done?"

"The chip," Inez said. "I want it. Now."

"I don't have it." I tore the sleeve off Wyatt's shirt and pressed the cotton against the spreading stain at his head. Cold heat needled my chest. He couldn't die. I wouldn't let him. *Wyatt, don't go. Hang on.* "The chip's at a testing lab in Massachusetts."

My senses hyped to the max. I had to live. I had to get out of here. I had to save Wyatt. A whole map drew itself with a big you-are-here X right in the middle. A rush of fear, then anger, then an almost trancelike calm barreled through me as fast as an SST.

There was no getting past the gun unless I was already dead.

Okay, Sofia, I said, letting down my defenses. *She's yours.*

My skin sizzled, then trembled at the loss of self, at the storm happening inside as Sofia banished me from my body. The prickling feeling, like just before lightning strikes. A rip of energy, like being struck by lightning.

My head tingled, standing my hair on ends. Pressure crushed my skin, my muscles, my bones. Pain sliced. Cells ripped. A nuclear blast and then…nothing.

Numb and helpless, I floated somewhere along the ceiling.

Inez's index finger stroked the trigger. A stone showed more emotion than she did standing there pointing a gun at my body. If any conflict played inside her, it was buried deep.

Sofia's cry shivered the air as she took over my body, moved through its heaviness.

A smile crawled over Inez's lips as she aimed the gun once more.

"I tried to love you, Mama," Sofia said. "I did everything you wanted me to do so you would love me. Except for Wyatt, I did everything just as you wanted. I got an education. I got a job. I spent all my spare time running the Open Hand and Heart Program. And without knowing it, I gave more. I gave you names. I gave you weaknesses to exploit. How could you use me like that?"

"Survival."

Anger exploded out of Sofia. In a move Leo had showed me, she spun my body off the gun's line of sight and hit Inez's arm from the outside in, shoving the gun away from me. Simultaneously she struck Inez in the face in a downward motion.

They grappled for the gun. The barrel turned toward my body.

No, Sofia, don't grapple. Don't tense. Snake your hand, strike like a jackhammer. Stomp step. Take up her space. Occupy her line.

With a warrior's cry, Sofia battered her mother with frenzied chaos.

Inez dropped the gun. It skittered across the polished floor. They both dove for it. Inez grabbed it. Before she could wrap her hand around the grip, Sofia let out a primitive scream and struck her mother's face with her left hand, coming up with the gun in her right hand. Crabbing backward on her behind, she leveled the gun at Inez in a two-handed grip.

As focused as a laser, Sofia's aim was true.

Tap, tap, tap.

Two to the heart.

One to the head.

"Survival," Sofia whispered, panting. Not giving her mother a second look as she fell.

Sofia turned to Wyatt and stroked his blood-matted hair. She kissed him deeply, tenderly. "Wyatt, my love."

Wyatt groaned and blinked open his eyes. "Sofia?"

Tears streamed down her cheeks. "Oh, my love, how I've missed you!"

"Forgive me."

She shook her head. "There is nothing to forgive, my love. And you must stop this useless guilt. None of this was your fault. The only happiness I ever felt in my life was with you. I love you, Wyatt. More than I can say. I will carry that love with me always."

"Sofia…" He reached a hand toward her.

She pressed a kiss in his palm, then flattened it against her heart. "Goodbye, my love. I release you. Be happy."

Sirens blared as police cars surrounded the church. The blue-and-white lights whirled through the deluge pouring outside, giving the tableau below me the look of a gruesome watercolor painting.

A fork of lightning stabbed the sky. Thunder growled and shook the windows.

Sofia's spirit separated from my earthbound form. For a moment we met, spirit to spirit.

"Thank you," Sofia said. Her smile was radiant. "The light, I see it, and it is beautiful."

I could see it, too, haloed around her translucent form so purely it filled my heart to overflowing. "Go in peace, Sofia."

Pain pierced every atom of my body, collapsing me on top of Wyatt as the world went black.

Chapter 18

I sat hunched over my desk, making sure every detail was included in my report so I could close this last case. Only two weeks had gone by, but Texas seemed a lifetime away.

The police had questioned Wyatt and me for hours after the church incident. The whole HART glitch had exploded on the news, and the blame game was still going on. The military had yanked the system out of all its aircrafts and had no plans to reinstall it in the near future. Tracy was safe—well, as safe as a pilot could be jockeying heavy metal objects into the stratosphere.

It turned out that Rey was ICE—Immigration and Customs Enforcement—working undercover. Immigration had recruited him a few years back when the flood of immigrants sponsored by Antonio and his company had raised eyebrows. They'd never expected to uncover an international industrial espionage operation. He was playing Inez's lapdog to gain her trust and to gather the proof he needed to bring her down when I interfered with his operation. I still didn't like Rey, but he had tried to make Sofia's death count for something, and he had tried to protect me from Inez.

After the dust settled, Wyatt had asked me to stay, and leaving him had been the hardest thing I'd done since the transplant.

"What do you mean you're leaving?" he'd asked, blustering like a blue-norther.

"I have to go home. I have to take care of some things."

"So that's it? You're just going to leave things like this? What about us?"

"Caring about you is a problem for me. I have to think."

Something I'd been doing for the past two weeks nonstop. And even without realizing it, I'd been settling things all along.

I'd cleaned up all of my open cases, training Noelle as I went. I'd paid up my back rent with the pay I'd earned since coming home, and let Mrs. Cartier know I wouldn't be renewing my lease. I'd even stayed with Mom this past week while I tried to figure out what I was going to do next. And we'd talked. We weren't going to bridge our differences in a few days, but the lines were open.

In a month I would get my share of my father's inheritance. Van had said he'd sign it over without a fight. That freed a whole new world of possibilities for me.

The thought of opening my own agency charged me with energy.

A knock at my office door startled me out of my concentration. Van strode in, wearing an emerald-green polo shirt and khakis. I couldn't remember the last time I'd seen him without a suit or wearing such a bright color.

"Van?" I said, squinting at him. "Okay, where is my brother, and what have you done with him?"

"Very funny, har, har." He plucked at the shirt and sat in one of the two chairs in front of my desk. "Dana's idea. We're taking the kids minigolfing after lunch."

I smiled. "Still couldn't resist coming to the office on a Saturday, huh?"

"I tried to call you, but you weren't home."

I pointed at the pile of folders in my out basket. "Tying up loose ends. Everything will be neat and tidy on your desk by Monday morning. All those billable hours should make your partners happy."

He tented his hands over his lap. "Who am I going to get to replace you?"

"Yeah, I know, it's going to be tough to find someone you can harass and control as easily as me."

"I'm trying to be serious, Sierra."

"I know." Forearms on the desk, I leaned forward and did an imitation of his scowl. "And I love you for it."

I went around the desk and hugged him. "I'm going to miss you, too. But Noelle can do my job every bit as well as I can. With the internship she's put in the past year, she'll be able to get her P.I. license soon."

Suddenly what I was going to do became crystal clear. "We both need to cut the cord, Van. You've been worrying about me for too long, and I've been depending on you to save me from myself for too long. You need to spend time with your family. And I need a purpose of my own."

Van studied me for a long time. "I hope he makes you happy."

Van had always been good at reading people—well, at least me.

Wyatt's face popped into my mind, and I smiled. "I shake him up. He grounds me. It's gotta mean something." I rocked back on my heels and looked up at my brother. "It's not like this is a permanent goodbye, you know. We'll talk. We'll visit."

"I know." He rose, taking me with him, and hugged me back bear tight. "It's good to see you happy."

I didn't know what was waiting for me in Texas but I knew I had to try. "It's good to be myself again."

Monday, May 15

Ten Oaks. The thought whispered through my brain as the ranch appeared on the flat horizon. Not Sofia's voice but my own. I could no longer hear her in my head, see her float above my bed or feel the static of her presence prickling my skin, but I liked to believe she'd found the peace she'd wanted when she first started to haunt me.

I turned into the driveway, and an unexpected rush of homecoming set my heart thumping hard. I parked by the main house. Lorraine, decked out in overalls and a floppy hat, looked up from tending her rosebushes and waved at me. She met me as I got out of the rental.

"It's so good to see you again, Sierra."

"It's good to be back. Is Wyatt home?"

"He's in the ring." She tried to swallow her knowing smile but couldn't quite manage the feat as she went back to her roses.

The soft sound of hoofbeats scrambled the arena dirt. Sinewy muscles on man and beast flexed and extended with power and grace. My heart raced as if it wanted to fly right out of my chest and into his arms. To hell with propriety. I climbed through the fence and into the ring.

Wyatt's smile packed a wallop of sex appeal as he brought Ten to a halt right in front of me and dismounted, handing the horse to a ranch hand. "What are you doing here?"

"Thought I'd try my hand at running my own investigation agency." I reached out and stroked the healing scar decorating the temple skimmed by Inez's bullet. "I thought I'd see if there was anything more than Sofia between us."

His eyes burned with intense heat. "Yeah?"

Needing to feel him, I threw my arms around his neck and let my mouth find his, drinking in the piney scent of his cologne. "I wanted to do that the first day I saw you."

He circled his arms around my waist and grinned. "Don't let me stop you."

I leaned back and looked up at him. "Are you sure that this is what you want? That I'm what you want?"

"I wouldn't break the law for just anyone."

"For Sofia."

He shook his head. "It's your smart mouth and your sweet ass I was trying to keep out of trouble."

"Thing is, Wyatt, you come from a long line of tradition." I looked around me at the vast expanse of his ranch. "Five generations. Always passed on to the oldest son. I can't have children. With all the antirejection drugs I have to take to survive, the odds aren't good."

He gave an easy shrug. "We can work on new traditions." His grin turned wicked. "We can start right now."

My body hummed in anticipation—like that moment right before jumping out of a plane—high about the jump, secure in knowing the parachute was properly packed. "Sex doesn't solve every problem."

Half his mouth quirked up. "But it's sure a great place to start."

Walking away into the noon sun wasn't quite as poetic as walking away into the sunset, but heck, we were going to be breaking new ground every day.

There were no guarantees. The parachute could fail. I'd always known that. That didn't mean I had to dive alone.

The heart was mine. So was my future. And I was going to make the most of it. Taking a chance with Wyatt was just the first step.

* * * * *

"OH, NO!"

The reaction slipped out before Emma Valentine could stop it, for there stood the very man she most wanted to avoid seeing again.

He didn't look any happier to see her.

"Well, come on, get on board," he said gruffly. "I won't bite." One eyebrow rose. "Though I might nibble a little," he added, mostly to amuse himself.

But she wasn't paying any attention to what he was saying. She was staring at him, taking in the royal blue uniform he was wearing, with gold braid and glistening badges decorating the sleeves, epaulettes and an upright collar. Ribbons and medals covered the breast of the short, fitted jacket. A gold-encrusted sabre hung at his side. And suddenly it was clear to her who this man really was.

She gulped wordlessly. Reaching out, he took her elbow and pulled her aboard. The doors slid closed. And finally she found her tongue.

"You…you're the prince."

He nodded, barely glancing at her. "Yes. Of course."

She raised a hand and covered her mouth for a moment. "I should have known."

"Of course you should have. I don't know why you didn't." He punched the ground-floor button to get the elevator moving again, then turned to look down at her. "A relatively bright five-year-old child would have tumbled to the truth right away."

Her shock faded as her indignation at his tone asserted itself. He might be the prince, but he was still just as annoying as he had been earlier that day.

"A relatively bright five-year-old child without a bump on the head from a badly thrown water polo ball, maybe," she said defensively. She wasn't feeling woozy any longer and she wasn't about to let him bully her, no matter how royal he was. "I was unconscious half the time."

"And just clueless the other half, I guess," he said, looking bemused.

The arrogance of the man was really galling.

"I suppose you think your 'royalness' is so obvious it sort of shimmers around you for all to see?" she challenged. "Or better yet, oozes from your pores like… like sweat on a hot day?"

"Something like that," he acknowledged calmly. "Most people tumble to it pretty quickly. In fact, it's hard to hide even when I want to avoid dealing with it."

"Poor baby," she said, still resenting his manner. "I guess that works better with injured people who are half asleep." Looking at him, she felt a strange emotion she couldn't identify. It was as though she wanted to prove something to him, but she wasn't sure what. "And anyway, you know you did your best to fool me," she added.

His brows knit together as though he really didn't know what she was talking about. "I didn't do a thing."

"You told me your name was Monty."

"It is." He shrugged. "I have a lot of names. Some of them are too rude to be spoken to my face, I'm sure." He glanced at her sideways, his hand on the hilt of his sabre. "Perhaps you're contemplating one of those right now."

You bet I am.

That was what she would like to say. But it suddenly occurred to her that she was supposed to be working for this man. If she wanted to keep the job of coronation chef, maybe she'd better keep her opinions to herself. So she clamped her mouth shut, took a deep breath and looked away, trying hard to calm down.

The elevator ground to a halt and the doors slid open laboriously. She moved to step forward, hoping to make her escape, but his hand shot out again and caught her elbow.

"Wait a minute. *You're* a woman," he said, as though that thought had just presented itself to him.

"That's a rare ability for insight you have there, Your Highness," she snapped before she could stop herself. And then she winced. She was going to have to do better than that if she was going to keep this relationship on an even keel.

But he was ignoring her dig. Nodding, he stared at her with a speculative gleam in his golden eyes. "I've been looking for a woman, but you'll do."

She blanched, stiffening. "I'll do for what?"

He made a head gesture in a direction she knew was opposite of where she was going and his grip tightened on her elbow.

"Come with me," he said abruptly, making it an order.

She dug in her heels, thinking fast. She didn't much like orders. "Wait! I can't. I have to get to the kitchen."

"Not yet. I need you."

"You what?" Her breathless gasp of surprise was soft, but she knew he'd heard it.

"I need you," he said firmly. "Oh, don't look so shocked. I'm not planning to throw you into the hay and have my way with you. I need you for something a bit more mundane than that."

She felt color rushing into her cheeks and she silently begged it to stop. Here she was, formless and stodgy in her chef's whites. No makeup, no stiletto heels. Hardly the picture of the femmes fatales he was undoubtedly used to. The likelihood that he would have any carnal interest in her was remote at best. To have him think she was hysterically defending her virtue was humiliating.

"Well, what if I don't want to go with you?" she said in hopes of deflecting his attention from her blush.

"Too bad."

"What?"

Amusement sparkled in his eyes. He was certainly enjoying this. And that only made her more determined to resist him.

"I'm the prince, remember? And we're in the castle. My orders take precedence. It's that old pesky divine rights thing."

Her jaw jutted out. Despite her embarrassment, she couldn't let that pass.

"Over my free will? Never!"

Exasperation filled his face.

"Hey, call out the historians. Someone will write a book about you and your courageous principles." His eyes glittered sardonically. "But in the meantime, Emma Valentine, you're coming with me."

Silhouette

Desire

**Introducing an exciting appearance
by legendary
New York Times bestselling author**

DIANA PALMER

HEARTBREAKER

He's the ultimate bachelor...
but he may have just met
the one woman to change his ways!

Join the drama in the story of a confirmed
bachelor, an amnesiac beauty and their
unexpected passionate romance.

**"Diana Palmer is a mesmerizing storyteller
who captures the essence of what
a romance should be."** —*Affaire de Coeur*

Heartbreaker *is available from Silhouette Desire*
in September 2006.

If you enjoyed what you just read,
then we've got an offer you can't resist!

Take 2 bestselling love stories FREE!

Plus get a FREE surprise gift!

Clip this page and mail it to Silhouette Reader Service®

IN U.S.A.
3010 Walden Ave.
P.O. Box 1867
Buffalo, N.Y. 14240-1867

IN CANADA
P.O. Box 609
Fort Erie, Ontario
L2A 5X3

YES! Please send me 2 free Silhouette Bombshell™ novels and my free surprise gift. After receiving them, if I don't wish to receive any more, I can return the shipping statement marked cancel. If I don't cancel, I will receive 4 brand-new novels every month, before they're available in stores! In the U.S.A., bill me at the bargain price of $4.69 plus 25¢ shipping & handling per book and applicable sales tax, if any*. In Canada, bill me at the bargain price of $5.24 plus 25¢ shipping & handling per book and applicable taxes**. That's the complete price and a savings of 10% off the cover prices—what a great deal! I understand that accepting the 2 free books and gift places me under no obligation ever to buy any books. I can always return a shipment and cancel at any time. Even if I never buy another book from Silhouettte, the 2 free books and gift are mine to keep forever.

200 HDN D34H
300 HDN D34J

Name	(PLEASE PRINT)	
Address	Apt.#	
City	State/Prov.	Zip/Postal Code

Not valid to current Silhouette Bombshell™ subscribers.

Want to try another series?
Call 1-800-873-8635 or visit www.morefreebooks.com.

COMING NEXT MONTH

#105 SPIN CONTROL by Kate Donovan
Defending FBI agent Justin Russo against a murder rap would
take every skill in attorney Suzannah Ryder's arsenal. His top
secret activities, his suspicious confession and disappearance
before the trial—nothing added up. With Justin refusing to
be straight with her—for her protection, he claimed—could
Suzannah prove him innocent as the evidence mounted against
him?

#106 DARK REVELATIONS by Lorna Tedder
The Madonna Key
Trapped into becoming an antiquities thief for the powerful Adriano
family, Aubrey De Lune had given up her daughter, her career,
everything. But when she stole a sacred 600-year-old manuscript
attributed to Joan of Arc, Aubrey discovered the Adrianos' dirty little
secret...as well as the key to *her* heritage, *her* power...and getting
her life back.

#107 GETAWAY GIRL by Michele Hauf
Getaway car driver Jamie MacAlister had finally "gotten away"
from her dubious past working for a clandestine rescue force at
odds with Paris law enforcement. Or had she? When clues to
her former mentor's murder lured her back to the fast lane, the
chase was on...but could Jamie put the brakes on her attraction
to the prime suspect?

#108 TOO CLOSE TO HOME by Maureen Tan
By day she policed a small Illinois town. By night, she worked for
the Underground, rescuing runaway women and children from
abusive men. But Brooke Tyler's two worlds collided when she
discovered the remains of a woman who'd died a decade ago,
exposing secrets and unleashing a killer who would test her like
never before....

SBCNM0806